Big Wheat

Books by Richard A. Thompson

Fiddle Game
Frag Box
Big Wheat

Big Wheat

A Tale of Bindlestiffs and Blood

Richard A. Thompson

Poisoned Pen Press

Poisoned Pen Press

Copyright © 2011 by Richard A. Thompson

First Edition 2011

10 9 8 7 6 5 4 3 2 1

Library of Congress Catalog Card Number: 2010932088

ISBN: 9781590588208 Hardcover
9781590588222 Trade Paperback

Poisoned Pen Press
6962 E. First Ave., Ste. 103
Scottsdale, AZ 85251
www.poisonedpenpress.com
info@poisonedpenpress.com

Printed in the United States of America

For Caroline
…a true daughter of the prairie

Acknowledgments

Once again, I am enormously indebted to my astute and trusted beta reader, Margaret Yang, without whose input and encouragement, this project would have died more than once. A million thanks, precious friend. Keep the faith.

Many thanks also go to Professor John Fraser Hart of the University of Minnesota, for his very helpful insights into the history and evolution of the American farm.

Author's Notes

The threshing era was a unique period, perhaps the only time in modern history when the application of industrial technology to a traditional way of life actually brought people closer together, rather than isolating and estranging them. A threshing operation needed the labor of the entire rural community, in addition to that of several outsiders and a lot of machinery that few individual farmers could afford to buy on their own. Hard work notwithstanding, the event took on the air of a carnival, a family reunion, and an interdenominational faith rally, all rolled into one. It was the social event of the year. I believe it is for this reason that the practice of the threshing bee persisted until the end of World War II in some areas, decades after newer technology had rendered it unnecessary.

As a very young child, I lived on a farm in southeastern Minnesota, which is neither Corn Belt nor Wheat Belt but a close cousin to both. I vividly remember the last threshing season there. Though I wasn't allowed very close to the action, I could feel the energy and excitement of it. And as I got older, I instinctively collected harvest stories, some of which are included in this book.

In order to better transport myself back to that time and farther, I have freely borrowed the names of many of my childhood relatives and neighbors. But only the names. All characters in this book are entirely products of my imagination and bear no resemblance to anyone I have ever known, seen, or heard of.

The town of Ithaca, the not-quite town of Hale's Corners, and the Unitarian church in the middle of the prairie are fictitious. All other settings in this book are real and as accurate as I could make them, as they would have appeared in 1919. The machines are also real, as are the background news events and the topical opinions of the day. As thoroughly as I could, I wanted to recapture that world.

Welcome, then, to the world of the steam traction engine, the threshing machine, the bindlestiff, and ultimately the high road to the Dust Bowl. Welcome to the world of Big Wheat.

Chapter One
Graveyard Shift

Late August, 1919
Somewhere on the North Dakota prairie

The harvest moon was down to its last sliver, feebly backlighting the wrinkled gray crepe that hid the stars. But for the man with the pick and shovel, it cast light enough. He had dug many graves in the hard soil of the high plains, most of them in the dark. He was an old hand at it. He occasionally used a hooded lantern to check his progress or reorient himself, but he really didn't need it. He could do the job with his eyes closed.

It didn't have to be as deep as a real grave, only deep enough so that the coyotes or stray dogs couldn't dig the body up, and the spring plows would glide harmlessly over it. Waist high was good enough, two or three hour's work. He threw the dirt all to one side of the hole, away from the mountain of straw from the day's threshing operation. The straw pile screened him from the farm buildings a quarter mile away and gave him a sense of security and privacy.

He looked down at the dead girl and decided the hole was big enough. She was so pale that even in the dim light, he could clearly make out her naked body. The eyes that had so recently shed tears of despair were now frozen in perpetual horror. The mouth that had tried to scream was slack and shapeless, just another dark gash to match the many others, where he had bled her to purify the earth.

And the earth needed so very much purifying.

He rested for a moment, leaning on the shovel handle, and looked across the field of stubble, just starting to be covered by a thin layer of ground fog. For hundreds of miles in every direction, he knew, it was the same: the land of the buffalo, the land of the cowboy, the land of the billowing prairie grasses, all torn up, leveled, plowed, planted and plucked. God's prairie had been beaten into a money factory. It was more than just wrong; it was obscene. Sooner or later, he was absolutely certain, both God and the earth would have their revenge. But until that day, he preserved some semblance of balance in the universe. He watered the ground with blood. He atoned for all the folks who were too self-satisfied or stupid to do it for themselves. He was the last virtuous man on the high plains, and he was virtuous enough for everybody.

"You must have broken a lot of hearts with those big doe's eyes," he said to the corpse, "and that pouting mouth that just begged to be kissed." And that, of course, is what had made her such a good sacrifice; many people would mourn her loss. He felt a slight lump in his pocket from the locket he had taken from her, and he snorted at the thought of it.

"What kind of a person has her own picture in her locket?" And also her name, professionally engraved. He didn't usually know the names of his offerings.

He mentally chided himself for speaking out loud, but he was feeling expansive. He had done such a fine job, after all.

The fog was beginning to drift down into the open grave. He threw the body in and shoveled the dirt on top of it. He took his time, tamping down all the loose corners, leaving no soft spots to settle and call attention to themselves. When he was done and the whole area was stamped down thoroughly, it was just slightly higher than the surrounding ground. It was also noticeably cleared of mown wheat stubble, but that would not be a problem.

He put the shovel and pickaxe off to one side and picked up his other tool, a pitchfork. From the huge pile next to the grave, he pitched straw on top of the dirt until it was covered to the depth of his knees. In the morning, the nearby threshing machine would be cranked up once again, the job of harvesting the field would be finished, and the pile of discarded straw would be even bigger. Then the machine would be moved away and the pile would be set on fire. And when there was nothing left of it but smoldering ashes, nobody would notice or care if there was a break in the stubble pattern. It had worked before, many times. It would work again. He had been purifying the land since 1914, when the people of Europe had started purifying their own overworked fields with lakes of blood. Their work was finished now. He didn't think his would ever be. It was good, having a vocation.

He admired his handiwork one last time, then put out the lantern, picked up his tools, and had a last look around the flat landscape. And froze.

Ten yards away, a man stood looking at him, saying nothing. He was tall and solidly built, but lean, with the easy erect posture that only comes with youth. He had light-colored, possibly even white hair that hung down on his forehead and a heavy pack on one shoulder. He did not move. There was no way to guess how long he had been there.

"Do I know you?" said the young man. He sounded confused, quiet, mumbling.

"No."

"I think I—"

"No."

The gravedigger began to back away slowly, moving into the black shadow of the straw pile. He had no qualms about killing the stranger, but he had no advantage of surprise and no edge of any other kind, either. And he made it a point never to attack anyone unless he had an edge. He took several more cautious steps backward, and when the stranger didn't follow, he bundled his tools on his shoulder, turned, and walked into the welcoming vastness of the dark prairie.

He walked with a slight limp, the memento of his father's older brother. When he was eleven, the uncle had grabbed his foot as he was sitting on the family couch and had twisted it, saying, "Who's the best uncle in the world?" When the boy said nothing but "Ouch!" he had twisted harder. Finally, the boy called him the worst name he knew, and the man twisted until something snapped, bathing him in excruciating pain. Nobody took him to a doctor. He wasn't important enough to be worth the money.

Three months later, he had limped across the newly plowed Kansas fields by the light of a gibbous moon and had set fire to the uncle's farmhouse. He waited by the front door with a hickory axe handle cocked on his small shoulder, ready to bludgeon anybody who tried to run out. But nobody did. Years later, when a sharp winter wind or a severe storm front sent sudden pangs of pain shooting up his bad leg, he would remember the screams that had come from the second-story bedroom window of the burning house, and smile. It had been his first experience with righteous killing. The memory was good.

Chapter Two
Wandering Son

The way Charlie Krueger's life was going, the strange man pitching worthless straw in the moonlight barely rated a second glance. Four days earlier, the only woman he had ever loved had taken his heart in her soft white hands and broken it like a twig.

Her name was Mabel Boysen, who pronounced her first name as if it were spelled Mae Belle and who had a thousand other little quirks and vanities that made her the most desirable young woman who had ever walked the earth. She grew up three farms over from the Krueger place, a mile and a half of country lane away. They met in the fields as small children, sent to pick wild mustard plants out of the growing oceans of oats or barley. They saw each other on the main street of Hazen on Saturday nights when their parents came to town for supplies, and in the Lutheran church on Sundays. They winked over the pews at each other and made hand-signal jokes about the day's sermon. And eventually, they met secretly as lovers. In the hay loft of Hans Buck's barn, which was midway between their own farms, she taught him something she called a "French kiss," which he found strangely wonderful. "And it doesn't leave a hickey," she had said.

A few days later, they had met in the waist-high wheat fields, in broad daylight. As she approached him, she locked her eyes on his, smiled her loveliest smile, and pulled off her dress and underclothes and threw them aside. Then she wrapped her arms around his neck. He was too astonished to know how to react.

"Have you ever seen a naked woman before, Charlie?"

"Um, ah, sure."

"Really?"

"Well, no, to be honest. I just—"

"You can look as much as you want. I don't mind." She stepped back half a pace and spread her arms out. "But you have to take your own clothes off, too."

He hesitated, and she stepped up to him and began to undo his shirt buttons. "Don't be shy, Charlie. I know what an aroused man looks like. And there's something I need you to do for me."

He was amazed that he didn't lose his erection from sheer embarrassment. But Mabel was not embarrassed at all. With calm self-assurance, she taught him how to caress her body, where to put his hands, how to tell when she was ready for him. And how to enter her, of course, make her wet with his seed, giving her a solemn promise that mere words could never convey. Had she made any promises? Had she even said she loved him? Surely she must have, but he couldn't remember. What he did remember was her saying, "We shouldn't meet at the same place more than once. I'll pass you a note in church, tell you where to go next time."

And there had been many next times, each one more wonderful than the last. The other things, the questions of her love and her promises, he put out of his mind. Sometimes he was very good at putting things out of his mind.

What he did put in his mind was that they were Romeo and Juliet, Tristan and Isolde, Cinderella and Prince Charming, but without the castle or the kingdom. They were the most wonderful love story in all of history, and they were surely destined to be married and live happily ever after. His father had said he intended to give the family farm to Charlie's sister, but what of it? He said a lot of mean things to Charlie, especially since Charlie's brother had died. Charlie was sure if he took a fine wife, the old man would change his mind. In some dim corner of his mind, he felt that the farm shouldn't matter, anyway. He and

Mabel should have many adventures all over the world before they settled down to raise beautiful children in some city. He didn't know what city, but he thought it should be a big one. Big cities had big opportunities.

But Mabel got very distant when he talked like that. She thought cities were evil, impersonal places. He dared not displease her, so he dropped the topic. Even more than he feared the erratic and often irrational wrath of his father, he feared her tiniest displeasure. So for an entire, blissful spring and high summer, he settled for dreaming of being married to the most beautiful woman in the world. If that also meant he had to be a farmer, well, that would somehow work out.

Then Mabel got pregnant. She told him with a huge smile, in the shade of a small walnut grove where they sometimes met. He took it calmly. It was a simple piece of information, natural enough, without any real emotional impact. He had always intended to have children with her. Now, the sequence of their lives would be different than he had expected, but nothing else would change. After all, they were in love. Didn't love make everything work out?

Mabel Boysen, woman in charge, woman who knew exactly what she was doing and exactly what she wanted, was delighted with her own news, but not at all for the reasons he might have imagined.

"Now I can make Harold Bow marry me," she said.

"Why on earth would you want to marry Harold Bow?" *When I'm the one who loves you more than life itself.* The thought was so obvious as not to need stating, not that it would have mattered.

"Because he's the oldest Bow son, of course, and his family has a whole section of land and their name on a brick in the church. You're a good time, Charlie, but you can't give me any of that."

"But he's an idiot! He has buckteeth and bad manners, and he couldn't pour piss out of a boot with instructions written on the heel! I can't believe you'd give him the time of day."

"He's also probably sterile, but he doesn't know that. You've been a lot of help, Charlie, and really, really sweet. I can't thank you enough for giving me your child."

"Giving you a child? But I mean to give you a whole life! I love you, Mabel. How can you not know that?"

"That's a silly word."

"Love is a silly word? But you—"

"No, Charlie, you never heard me use that word. You men get all confused when you're in heat. All I ever said was there was something I needed you to do for me. And now you have, and I'm very grateful. But if you ever say a word about it to anybody, I'll have to accuse you of rape, and then you'll get run out of the county on a rail or lynched or who knows what. Just be happy that we had some good times and that there will be a beautiful little girl who will be just like you."

"How do you know it will be a girl?"

"Silly Charlie. Because that's what I want. And I always get what I want, don't I? But don't be sad. Maybe in a year or so I'll need your help again."

He turned and walked away from the grove without another word. If he had stayed, he might have wound up hitting a woman, or worse yet, crying in her presence. He felt as if he had been shot in the gut with a cannonball made of ice.

That night he decided to leave home, though he didn't yet know where he would go or how he would live. His present life was intolerable, but any other he could think of was terrifying. At some level, he felt as if he had been holding his breath for years, waiting for an opportunity such as this. The only thing tying him to this piece of land and to the father who constantly insulted and abused him had been his love for Mabel. Now that he had lost that, he could do whatever any adventurous young man would do. He tried to see that as a good thing. He couldn't.

He assembled a traveling pack, including all the military gear his brother had sent him that he had never expected to need. He had a folding field compass and a fine, canvas-covered quart canteen and a real bayonet in a belt sheath and a new kind of mechanical cigar lighter, for which he had not yet been able to buy fuel. Kerosene, he had found, did not work well at all. He also packed a seven-millimeter Luger pistol. He didn't know if his brother had taken it off a dead German officer whom he had personally killed, or merely picked it up on the field of battle. If the stories he had heard about the carnage were true, it might have been hard to tell the difference. In any case, soldiers were allowed to ship packages back home free of charge, and a small tidal wave of war souvenirs was the result.

Lugers were highly prized. There were sevens and nines, his brother had written him, and they had opposite magazine sizes. The seven millimeters held nine bullets and the nine millimeters only held seven. Plus one in the chamber, of course. But he didn't have an extra bullet, only a single loaded magazine. It would have to be enough. How dangerous could the high prairie be, anyway?

All this and more, Charlie assembled into the makeshift backpack, including a shovel with a broken handle. The next day, he rose even earlier than usual to feed the livestock and milk the family's four cows. After the milking, he put out a battered pie pan full of milk and stale bread crusts for the pack of semi-feral cats who lived somewhere in the barn and kept it free of rodents. He always smiled as he put down the pan, because his father had sternly forbidden the practice. He put the rest of the milk in a galvanized steel can and put the can in a tank of cool water in the well house, where a windmill kept it full. Then he harnessed the horses. It was the start of threshing, and the day would be a long one.

He did his part to bring in the annual Krueger harvest, driving a team of horses pulling a reaper/binder, and the next day sacking the clean grain that was coming out of the Yellow Fever separator and hauling it away with a different team. It was a duty he felt he owed, even though he knew he would not share in the bounty. You weren't much of a son if you didn't help with the harvest.

"Was it a good harvest, Robert?" said Charlie's mother at supper that night.

"Pot liquor," said his father, with sneering venom. "Can't make no money off a piddling hundred acres. If Bob, Junior, hadn't a got his self killed in that damn war, I could buy some more land and raise enough wheat to make some real money. But with just Charlie? Ptah! Now if Charlie'd been the one to die—"

"Then you still couldn't get rich," said Charlie, "because you'd still be out in the barn getting drunk half the time."

His mother and sister gasped. No one ever dared raise that topic.

"What did you say to me?" He rose from his chair, slowly, seething with rage and radiating menace. "You don't talk to me like that, you young snot. Not now and not ever. I'll take my belt and whip you into next month, is what. First, though, you gotta know you ain't having no supper in this house."

They had played this exact scene before, many times, sometimes for some trivial reason and sometimes for no reason at all. Charlie remembered the beatings out in the barn, starting in early childhood, and how he had felt belittled and somehow cheated as much as physically hurt. And suddenly he realized that all of the beatings, whatever their stated excuses, had a single purpose: to make his father feel important by making Charlie permanently afraid of him. But this time, he felt no fear.

His father reached across the table and wrapped his fingers around the rim of Charlie's plate, dragging it toward him. Time stood still, and Charlie stepped outside himself. As if from a vantage point somewhere at ceiling height, he saw himself pick up the carving knife from the meat platter and stab it viciously down on the fleeting plate of food. Meat and potatoes flew in every direction, the heavy plate snapped in two, and the knife pinned his father's hand solidly to the wooden table. He let out a cry that was not quite a word and looked at his son in astonishment. He trembled as he tried to pull the knife out. It didn't budge.

Nobody was more shocked than Charlie. But fate and reflex and a whole ocean of pent up anger had taken charge, and he didn't see any way he could retreat. *Might as well be hanged for a goat as a lamb.*

"You're all done taking things away from me, Pa. And you're all done beating me, too." He came around the end of the table and wrapped his own belt around his knuckles.

"I'll kill you, you worthless piece of—"

"Just as soon as you get your hand free? Then I'd be stupid to wait, wouldn't I?" He stepped behind his father and hit him on the ear, so hard it snapped his head down onto his shoulder. Charlie drew back his arm to do it again.

"No! Please, Charlie! No more! I didn't mean none of that stuff, I swear."

"Swear to somebody else. I'm leaving." He was amazed at how easy it was to say that. For years, he thought he'd never be able to stand up to his father's bullying. But now that he had done so, he couldn't imagine what had taken him so long. He put his belt back in his trouser loops. To his mother, he said, "I don't suppose you could go to the trouble to make me some sandwiches?" She fled to the kitchen with obvious relief.

He collected his pack from his room, then came back to the dining room to say goodbye to his sister.

"I'm afraid, Charlie."

"You'll be all right, Ruthie. I put a slide bolt on the outside of the barn door last night. Next time pa goes out there and starts drinking, lock him in. In the morning, if he comes out screaming bloody murder, hit him in the head with a number ten skillet, right off."

"I don't know if I can—"

"Don't think about it, just do it. Bullies are all cowards when you stand up to them. You just saw that. Anyway, you need to do it for ma, if not for yourself. If the old man starts getting after either of you anyway, send me a letter to general delivery in Minot. I don't know where I'll wind up spending the winter, but I'll check there before I head farther north. If he's not treating you decent, I'll come back and kill him, I promise." He said it loud enough that his father could not have failed to hear, and he punctuated it with a hard look in that direction.

"Oh, Charlie, do you really have to go? You said it yourself; now that you stood up to Pa, things will be different."

"I have to go, Ruthie. There's a big hole in my heart that I can't talk about, and I have to go see if I can find a way to heal it."

"Then be careful out there." She gave him a tight hug.

"For you, I'll try."

His father had freed his bleeding hand by then and wrapped it in a kerchief, but he was still sitting at the table, whimpering quietly.

"You ain't ever been out of this county, Charlie boy. You think life is easy out there? You think people are just dying to help out a worthless sum bitch, hits his own father? You'll see. You'll wind up eating out of somebody's hog trough and sleeping in a ditch."

His own thoughts were not so very different, but he gave them no voice. There was no backing out now, and no return.

He collected a pile of sandwiches wrapped in waxed paper from his mother, kissed her and his sister on the cheeks, and left. He decided he would walk a while before he looked for a convenient haymow to sleep in. His mind was a jumble of worry and hurt and anger, but under it all, also a sort of quiet exhilaration. Something very important was about to happen.

He didn't know how far he had gone when he encountered the strange, scarecrow figure in loose clothes and slouch hat, pitching straw in the moonlight.

The man's movements were jerky and even in the dim light he could see that his eyes were wild, set wide apart from a beaked nose that looked as if it had been broken more than once. Charlie wondered if the whole world was full of crazy people on that night, himself included. But then the fellow just sort of melted into the darkness, limping, and soon Charlie had forgotten all about him. He had enough on his mind.

◇◇◇

The next day, Mabel Boysen's parents missed her when she didn't come in the house from her morning chores of feeding the chickens and picking the eggs. They finished breakfast first, then looked in the farm buildings for her. Then her father, Djelmar, hitched his draft team to a buggy and began searching the fields. Finally becoming alarmed, he drove to all the nearby farms to ask about her. At the Krueger farm, he was met by a hung over Bob, Senior, with his hand wrapped in a blood soaked rag.

"My boy Charlie run off last night, too," he said. "Maybe they went together. He always was sweet on her."

"If she eloped with him, I'll whip them both with a knotted plow line."

"Amen to that. I'll help hold them."

"You'll mind your own beeswax, is what you'll do." Djelmar had never liked old man Krueger. He got back on the buggy, clucked to the horses, and drove all the way to the town of Beulah, where he told everything to Sheriff Amos Hollander. Hazen, which was ten miles closer to his farm, didn't have a sheriff. The Sheriff told his deputy to get the official Model T pickup gassed up, greased, and ready to travel. He apologized to the panic-stricken father for not having any budget to send out telegrams to notify other lawmen around the state. For his part, Djelmar Boysen apologized for not having a picture of his daughter to give to him. But he provided some cash for the sheriff to give to Western Union.

Hollander said he didn't need a picture of Mabel Boysen. He knew her well. And although he did not know Charlie Krueger, he could damn sure find him, all the same. He sounded mad. Boysen wasn't sure what to make of his little rant, but he said nothing. He was glad for all the help he could get.

Two hours later, the sheriff and his deputy set off, swearing to stop at every farmstead to enquire about the path of the threshing crews and the possible appearance of a beautiful young woman. The sheriff did a lot of swearing of other kinds, as well.

The moving harvest, at least in the mind of Djelmar Boysen, was a bit like the circus: sometimes people ran away to join it. Especially young people. A lot of them were not seriously missed for quite a long time, and some of them never at all. Wayward daughters, the ones who "always had a bit of a wild streak," were assumed to have become cooks for custom threshers. If they had less savory reputations, they were assumed to have become camp followers, "soiled doves," his wife would say, servicing the needs of the small army of men moving across the continent. But he didn't believe Mabel belonged in any of those categories. And he didn't believe she would have run off with that Krueger kid without telling him, either. He believed she must have come to harm.

Young men who went missing, on the other hand, like the Krueger kid, didn't require much explanation. They were supposed to be daring, footloose, pining for adventure, and eager to see the world. And they were expected to be more than a bit foolish. The story was of the prodigal son, after all, not the prodigal daughter.

But besides being prodigal, was young Krueger in trouble? The sheriff seemed to think so, even though he had said he didn't know the kid. And he also seemed to be mad at him. It was all very bewildering. And he had the sinking feeling that it was also about to become tragic.

Chapter Three
Bringing in the Sheaves

More and more, Charlie felt like a fool for hitting his father and walking out, but he would rather die than go back and apologize. He had walked all night, finding that he couldn't even think about sleep. At dawn, he hired on with a custom threshing operation that was getting ready to harvest a four-hundred-acre field. The crew was already set by the time he got there, but the separator operator, the man who stood on top of the threshing machine and controlled the flow of wheat through it, was badly hung over. The steam engineer didn't want him near any machinery, so he asked Charlie if he could do the job.

"Well, to be honest, I never ran a Case before." Which was true. It was also true that he had never run any other kind of threshing machine, either, but he didn't feel obliged to tell the engineer that. He knew everything about how they worked; he just didn't know how they *felt* yet. But he had never met a machine he couldn't run or repair.

"You'll find that the concaves won't clear themselves as fast as on a Nichols, so you want to watch you don't overload them. Other than that, it's about like any of the others. You keep her running smooth, I'll pay you eight dollars for the day."

"Let's go to work," said Charlie.

They shook hands and he climbed up on the machine, using the angle-iron frames on its side for steps. It had always struck him as odd that nobody built a machine with an attached ladder, even though operators always ran them from up top. He looked over his control levers, frantically reviewing what he knew about them. There was one for the belt feed, one for both the concaves and shaker trays, and one for the auger that unloaded clean grain from the machine's internal bin. They all took their power from a central shaft with a huge pulley on the end that connected to the steam engine by a fat rubber belt. The Windstacker, which blew the cleaned straw as much as eighty feet away from them, was started and stopped with a chain that had a spade handle on the end.

Charlie made sure all the levers were disengaged and then waved at the engineer, who was back on his own machine. He took a deep breath. *Lordy, lordy, can I really pull this off?* The engineer engaged the power takeoff, the belt pulled, and his own flywheel cranked up to speed.

The machine shook a little at first and then settled into a smooth machinery hum. He let the main shaft get up to what he hoped was its proper speed and engaged the concaves, then the Windstacker, and finally the belts that fed the raw wheat into the gaping mechanical mouth. On the machine's metal top, he found a small panel, which he could remove to look into the inner works. He didn't know what the concaves should look like when they were working right, but he assumed that he shouldn't let the space above them get totally jammed up with stalks. He stopped the feed belt now and then to keep that from happening. After ten minutes of cleaning wheat, he heard a bell behind him. It was attached to the discharge pipe of the grain auger, and drivers rang it to get his attention when they pulled up with a wagon to be loaded. He pulled the lever for the auger and watched with pure joy as a solid stream of golden treasure poured into the empty wagon. *My God, this is really going to work!*

After an hour or so, he found that he didn't need the panel anymore. He could tell by the vibrations coming through his feet if the feed was working right. Soon the sheaf pickers couldn't bring him the raw wheat fast enough, and while he waited for them, he jumped down and oiled the bearing journals or hauled water or wood to the steam engine. At the morning lunch break, around 9:00, two of the muleskinners talked about him as if he weren't there.

"What the hell's the matter with the new separator man?"

Charlie's heart fell into his boots.

"I don't know, but the way he's going, we're probably going to get our wages cut, on account of we didn't have to put in a full day."

"Yeah," said the first one, "what is he, anti-labor? I never seen a separator put out that fast."

The tone was deadpan, but when Charlie looked at the man, he saw that he was grinning. His pulse went back to normal.

"You leave my new man alone," said the engineer, "or I'll find plenty of work for you, trying to pull my one-inch wrench out of your ass."

"Ah, we didn't mean nothing."

"I did."

After hot corn fritters, apple pie and coffee, the farmer had all the wagon drivers line up their rigs in a single row with the steam engine and the threshing machine in the center, to pose for a picture. Fifty yards to the east, with the midmorning sun behind him, a man with a three-piece suit and a straw hat with a huge, floppy brim was fussing with a wooden box on a tripod.

"When I hold up my hand like this," he said, reaching as high as he could, "nobody move until I put it down again. You got it?"

Everybody nodded eagerly. Wagon drivers stood up on their rigs, reins in hand, Charlie and the steam engineer stood on top of their machines, and the farmer proudly stood in front of everybody, fists on hips. The photographer took a last look under a black cloth on the back of his box. Then he grabbed a black rubber bulb attached to the camera by a small tube and looked up and down the row.

"Aaaand…" He held up his hand again and squeezed the bulb. The box made a mechanical whirring sound for a while, then a clunk. "Got it!"

He changed the plate in the camera and took one more shot "just to be sure," then quickly went around the crew, showing them a print of an earlier threshing bee and taking orders. The print was about three feet wide and eight inches high, and it showed the entire operation in great detail, strangely transported to a brown and white world that he called sepia.

"Give me three dollars now and your mailing address, and I'll send you a print of the picture I just took."

"How long will that take?"

"I've got a lot more threshing crews to shoot, and then I have to take the film back to my studio in Sioux Falls. It'll be a few months."

"Will it be as good as that one?"

"It'll be better. This one has been out in the sun, and it's faded some. I guarantee you will be able to see everybody's faces, or your money back. It'll be something to hand down to your grandchildren."

"It will be," said the farmer. "I buy one from him every year." People reached into their pockets. Charlie would have loved a picture of himself standing proudly atop the Case, but he had no idea where to tell the man to send it. And he didn't have three dollars, anyway. He went back to his machine.

The rest of the day flew by in a blur of dust, heat and noise, sweat and food. Besides the morning and afternoon snacks, the job included the traditional threshermen's noon lunch, a huge bounty of meats, potatoes, gravy, fresh breads, pickles, deviled eggs, assorted vegetables, and fruit pies, all washed down with gallons of steaming coffee. It was served on a makeshift table of long planks laid over sawhorses, and the planks groaned and sagged under the weight. But as was the custom, there was no evening meal for anyone but the farmer and his family. Those who were neighbors or relatives simply made their way back home, frequently laughing and walking with arms over each other's shoulders, proud of the day's work. Most of the crew of hired day-laborers carried sandwiches and cakes that they had saved from the noon lunch. They ate them while they made their way to the next day's job. But Charlie knew that he would have no place on the crew the following day, if the regular separator man sobered up, so he offered fifty cents of his newly earned money to the farmer for an evening meal and a place to sleep in the hayloft.

"Hell, son, anybody works as hard as you do can sleep in my barn for free any time. And we'd be happy to have you to supper, too."

"Much obliged, sir."

"Name's Walter Christian, Walt to you." He offered his hand and Charlie shook it, telling him his own name.

"Mr. Cody, our photographer, is also staying to supper. He's not so good at camping out, and there aren't a whole lot of hotels around here."

"None, I would say."

"That's what you'd say, all right. You can wash up over by the pump house. It's okay to get some dirt in the cattle tank, but mind you don't get any soap in it. Makes the horses real sick. Supper in half an hour."

Supper was mostly leftovers from the big noon meal—baked ham, mashed potatoes shaped into patties and fried in butter, baked beans with brown sugar and bacon, peas, and cut corn. And of course, fresh bread. During the harvest, Mrs. Christian, whose name was Violet, baked three times a day. The whole house smelled like a bakery.

"These peas are really special," said Charlie. "Best I ever had."

Farmer Christian smiled with obvious satisfaction. "Lots of folks nowadays don't keep a vegetable garden, but I like my greens fresh."

"What do your neighbors do instead?" said the photographer.

"They put every square foot of land they have into wheat, and then they buy their food in town, in them new-fangled tin cans. Ed Henkie has already got a pile of empty cans behind his granary, so high that you can't see over it. He don't keep chickens or milk cows or hogs anymore, either."

"And neither should you," said his wife. "You could make eight hundred dollars a season on that field you keep in pasture."

"We've been over this before, Violet."

"And we'll go over it again. Ed Henkie's wife says they made over ten thousand dollars last year, and they only have half a section of land. Cash farming is the new way. Ordinary folks just like us are getting rich."

"Right. That's until the government quits guaranteeing the market price or the European wheat blight finally makes it across the Mississippi River or the rains don't come any more. Then you'll be damn glad for those chickens and cows and a few porkers."

"Rain follows the plow," she said, stubbornly jutting out her chin.

"I've heard that before," said the photographer. "What does it mean?"

"It means some people are damn fools."

"I'll thank you not to swear at the table, Walter."

"Some people," said Charlie, "believe that just the act of clearing more land somehow affects the weather, brings more rain." He shrugged.

"You believe it?"

"I don't know. No offense, Mrs. Christian, but it seems to me the place I most often see it is in advertisements for farm machinery or seed."

Walter Christian guffawed. His wife glowered.

"You're a smart young man, Charlie. I don't suppose you'd be looking for a regular job? We lost a son and a daughter to the influenza, and things been real pushed around here since then."

Mrs. Christian started to say something, but then bowed her head a bit and crossed herself.

"That's really kind of you, sir, but I think this is a little too close to home."

"You think your folks would have some problem with it? Hell, I can go talk to them, tell them—"

"It's not that."

"Well, what the hell is it, then? You don't like my woman's cooking?"

"This is the last time I'm going to tell you about swearing, Walter."

"Oh, relax, Mother. Charlie's heard it all before, and the pastor isn't here. What do you say, Charlie?"

"Your wife is a fine cook, sir." He looked over and saw her smile slightly. "It's just that it took me twenty-three years to get up the nerve to leave home. Now that I finally did it, I feel like I ought to go farther, somehow. I guess that doesn't make much sense, does it?" *And worse yet*, he thought, *if I don't go any farther than this, I might be tempted to go back.*

"Makes sense to me, anyhow. My old man was a no-good, worthless son of a bitch."

"Walter!"

"Well, he was. Stole from his own kids. Not worth the cost of the powder to blow him to hell or the match to touch it off with. I spat in his eye and came out here from Ohio when I was nineteen. You could still get decent homestead land back then, and I lied about my age to file a claim. It was a whole new life. Looks to me like you're a man looking for a new life, too. I hope you find it."

"What do you want to be?" said the photographer.

"I'm not sure. Something with machinery, I think."

"Up in Saskatchewan last year, I saw a machine called a 'combine.' It was like a reaper and a threshing machine, all put together. It took twelve horses to pull it, and a gasoline engine to run all the inside works, but it could move through a field mowing a twelve-foot wide swath and threshing it, all at the same time."

"What do they have for a crew?"

"Four men can bring in the whole harvest."

"Good heavens," said Mrs. Christian.

"That doesn't seem right, somehow," said Charlie.

"It would be the death of the threshing bee, that's for sure," said Walter.

"Well, it was definitely the end of my business," said the photographer. "If everybody farmed like that, I'd be back to shooting nothing but weddings and portraits."

"Why would anyone want to do that?" said Mrs. Christian. "The harvest is the best time of the year. There are neighbors we never see any other time. It's better than Christmas or Easter, even. It's the time when we're, um… Well, I would just cry if it all came to an end."

"Violet, my dear, I think we have finally found something we can agree on."

It had never occurred to Charlie that he might live long enough to see the passing of an entire era. He wasn't sure how he felt about it. He turned to the photographer.

"Can you promise delivery of one of your pictures by Christmas?"

"Sure. Everybody always wants that."

"Then I would like you to send one to my sister. Could you also put in a note saying, 'Merry Christmas from your loving brother?'"

"Easiest thing in the world." He produced a notebook from inside his coat and flipped to a clear page. "You don't figure you'll be making it home for Christmas?"

"Maybe not for a lot of them." He paid the man his three dollars, gave him the name and address, and got up to go to the barn to make his bed.

"Breakfast at dawn," said Walter.

"I'll make you some lunch to carry, too," said his wife.

Charlie hoped Walter was right about the best way to farm. He really wanted him and his wife to prosper.

Chapter Four
Bringing in the Bacon

Charlie's next job didn't go so well. After a day and a half of walking, he caught up with the same Nichols and Shepard Yellow Fever machine that had done his own family's threshing, and he hired on for the following day. He agreed to work as a spike pitcher, feeding forkfuls of grain from the constant line of hayrack wagons into the vee-shaped conveyor belts of the separator apron. It was the hardest job on the crew, the job that nobody else wanted, and the only job where there was never a moment's letup. The farmer agreed to pay him five and a half dollars plus his meals. The pay was to come directly from the farmer, since the custom thresher operator, who owned the machines, had only a fireman, steam engineer, and separator man for a crew. It was a common enough arrangement.

For Charlie, the worst part of any heavy labor was the anticipation of it. He had never been afraid of hard work, but he always wondered if this would be the day when his body betrayed him with muscle spasms or cramps or heat exhaustion. He didn't worry about pain or even injury, but he would rather die than look as if he wasn't holding up his end of the work. He never had, even in that autumn of his thirteenth year, when he had wielded a scythe for twelve hours. But he always thought it was possible.

He ate breakfast with the other hired help at 5:00 and then filed out into the dim predawn light. The sky was mercilessly clear and there was no wind. He walked over to the well pump and filled his canteen, plus a two-quart Mason jar the farmer's wife had loaned him, with cool water. He made sure the jar had a tight-fitting lid, to keep out the dust. Then he put on three bandanas, one on his head, one rolled tightly under the collar of his shirt, and one tied more loosely around his neck, from where it could be pulled up to cover his nose and mouth. He buttoned all the buttons on his chambray shirt and kept the sleeves rolled down, protecting as much of his flesh as possible from the irritating chaff and dust. It would be hot, but he would be working in the dirtiest area of the whole site, and he knew from hard experience that nobody but a complete fool took his shirt off there.

Finally, he put on a pair of soft leather gloves. That was a tradeoff. His grip on the pitchfork wouldn't be as good as with bare hands, so his arm muscles were more likely to cramp up, but he would also be less prone to single or multi-layer blisters. He had worked with blisters so deep they bled, both on his hands and on his feet, and he never wanted to do it again.

He walked over to the apron of the threshing machine, passing another stiff, who looked up at the sky and said, "She's going to be a bitch." There was nothing to be said to that.

As the sun was still barely edging above the horizon, the steam engineer set the big belt in motion, and the work of the day began.

The fields in that county were uneven and rocky, so the sheaf-binding attachments on the McCormick reapers didn't work reliably. Instead, the farmers used the "headering" method. Huge wagons with high frames on one side only were heaped as high as possible with the new mown wheat, straight from the reaper. When the threshing machine arrived, two men on each wagon pitched the load into a pile next to it, called a header. The spike pitcher, Charlie, would fork it up from there and throw into the feed belts. He made it a point of pride never to let the belts get empty.

After half an hour, his shirt was plastered to his back, and his own sweat would have poured in his eyes and blinded him, but for the bandana on his head. But then he slipped into the peculiar mental and physical state that he expected and welcomed but could not have easily described. Sometimes he thought of it simply as "getting oiled up." It was a form of intense concentration and indifference to discomfort. He saw the piles of wheat, and his hands and arms found exactly the best way to pick them up and move them, but nothing passed through his conscious mind at all. Everything was reflex and instinct, blind speed and easy power. He became a machine, an automated spike pitcher that never tired or slowed down. Now and then he would pause to pour some water on the bandana around his neck and to take a carefully measured drink from his canteen, but most of the time, he was locked in an unbroken rhythm. His mind, not being needed for the task at hand, drifted.

He thought about that first, endless field that he had scythed. The handle of the scythe was cleverly curved so the blade balanced from side to side. But it was still very heavy for his young muscles to hold up. So after the first day, he thought he would try putting a counterbalance on the end of the handle away from the blade. He rummaged around in his father's tool shed and found a big monkey wrench that seemed about the right weight, and he fastened it to the scythe handle with wrappings of heavy twine.

It did exactly what he wanted it to. He finished mowing the rest of the field with far less effort than the first half. But when his father saw what he had done, he accused him of stealing tools he didn't need. He broke the scythe handle, saying it was ruined, stuck the blade in a tree trunk, and beat Charlie within an inch of his life. The following year, he bought a McCormick reaper, so a scythe was never needed again. As far as Charley knew, the blade was still stuck in the tree trunk.

"What a horse's ass," he said aloud. Then he laughed, out of pure joy at being able to say it. In the roar of the machines, nobody heard him. His body continued to pitch wheat while his mind floated. He pondered over what his mother had ever seen in that man. Had they once been a loving couple? It was hard to imagine.

The popular story was that his mother, Hanna Clayton, had gone on a date with young Bob Krueger to the Mercer County Fair, one Saturday night in September. Knowing that when it came to demon rum, he could resist anything but temptation, she had taken a pint of whiskey along, hidden in her purse. As the night wore on, she freely plied him with the liquor. Late in the evening, when he was so drunk he couldn't find his head with both hands, she pulled him up onto the stage of a carnival sideshow, where the barker offered a ten dollar gold piece to any couple who would get married as part of the show. It was a common stunt, and a guaranteed crowd pleaser. A minister, by prior arrangement, was recruited from the crowd, the notary public who traveled with the carnival produced a license, and after three or four prompts, Bob Krueger said, "I do." And Hanna Clayton Krueger was a married woman with a mortgage-free quarter-section farm. The only problem was that her new husband never sobered up. And even that would not have been so much of a problem, but about twelve years later, he turned into a mean drunk. Charlie couldn't remember if he had been a decent human being before that.

The day wore on. At the morning coffee break, Charlie was too tired to eat, so he stretched out on a feed belt and grabbed a short nap. He had found, many times, that he didn't have the endurance of the older men, but a short rest let him almost completely regain his energy. An old man, he knew, could work much, much longer, but when he finally got tired, there was no quick or easy recovery. He wondered if there was a crossover age, when he would have the best of both abilities. Or the worst. He was sure he would find out.

Finally, after fourteen hours of gleaning the wheat berries, the threshing machine emptied its storage bin for the last time. The steam engineer blew a long blast on his whistle to signal the end of the day, and people all around began laying down their tools. Horses and mules still had to be watered and fed and put away, and the threshing machine made ready to travel, but that wasn't Charlie's problem. He pulled his filthy bandana down from his nose, stuck his gloves in his back pocket, and went back over to the pump where he had started the day. He bent down and ran water over his head and hands for a long time, then rinsed out his bandanas, blew his nose, and went to look for the farmer, to get paid.

But instead of paying him, the fat, moonfaced farmer got a funny smirk on his face, stuffed his hands in the pockets of his new bib overalls, and stared off into space. Charlie knew that look. As poor as he was at reading people, he knew all the looks that led up to some kind of meanness. That was the look his father used to wear when he was thinking up some excuse to beat him or take something away from him.

"I said, 'sir, you owe me five-fifty.' Now would be a good time to settle up, I think."

"How was that lunch, boy? That roast beef was straight from heaven, wasn't it?"

"The lunch was fine, but it doesn't spend at the general store, sir."

"And that cherry pie? You have more than one piece of that pie? Somebody did, because we run all out of it."

"Are you going to pay me what I honestly earned, or not?"

The farmer drew himself up to his full height and hooked his thumbs in the straps of his overalls, as if he were about to deliver a sermon. He jutted his several chins out aggressively and scowled.

"What the hell are you accusing me of, boy? You better watch your tongue, you know what's good for you. I'm a respected member of the community here. And you're nobody but a drifter, if you get *my* drift. Show a little respect. I always pay my bills."

"That's good, sir. When?"

"Now there you go again. You are aggravating me something terrible, you are. I ought to just cut you off, send you packing. But because I'm a fair man, I'll tell you what: you get your money the same as all the folks here, after I get my money for selling the crop. But first, of course, we got to get it to the railroad at Willow City and then off to the market in Minneapolis or Fargo. That'll take about a month." He grinned again, pulled a tooth-pick out of his pocket and stuck it in his mouth. "Maybe you'd like to do another job, meantimes, helping with the hauling."

Charlie could see there was no point arguing, even less point calling the man a horse's ass and a crook, which he obviously was. Instead, he turned away and walked to the curing shed, which was attached to the granary, which in turn was next to the hog run. He went inside and picked out a nice-looking side of bacon that was hanging from a hook on a rafter. Then he went to the chicken coop and helped himself to a dozen eggs, making a point of taking all the time he needed to pack them away carefully.

"You listen to me, you damn snot-nosed kid. You steal from me, you'll answer to the sheriff, and that's after I get done giving you a good whipping. You better just—"

"I'm not stealing, mister. I'm just taking a little security deposit. I'll bring it back when I come to collect my five and a half dollars. A month, you say? But if you want, we can go see this sheriff you talk about, and tell him the whole story, just so's he doesn't get the wrong impression. Like of exactly who the thief is around here. Should we do that?"

Charlie didn't say anything about the threatened whipping, but he let his coat fall open so the farmer could see the bayonet sheathed at his belt. If it came to a fight, though, what he actually planned to do was get up from gathering the eggs and knee the man in the groin. If that wasn't enough to take the wind out of his sails, he would also hit him on the side of the head with his broken shovel. He was not fond of fighting, as a rule. He even hated people who beat their livestock. But when he had to fight, he followed his brother's advice. "Don't mess around trying to look like a gentleman exhibition boxer or following any stupid rules. Hit the other guy first with the worst, because that's what he'll try to do to you. Go for the throat or the balls or the kidneys, whatever target he gives you. And if you can't stand the idea of hurting him, you had better not get in the fight in the first place."

As it happened, he didn't have to do any of that, or draw his weapon. The man sputtered a bit about thieves and tramps and threatened to go get his shotgun. But when he stormed into the farmhouse, slamming the door behind him, Charlie knew he wasn't coming back out.

Bullies and crooks are always cowards, said the voice of Charlie's brother in the back of his mind. *He won't come back.* The man had already lost one battle, without injuries or witnesses. If he started it up again, he might not be so lucky.

Charlie finished wrapping up his eggs in a flannel shirt and then realized he needed something to sling the bundle on without crushing it. So he went back over to where the Yellow Fever was sitting quietly in the twilight now, the dust of the day slowly settling on it, and he took the pitchfork that he had used all day. It made a good staff.

As he was walking away, the farmer yelled at him from behind the closed screen door.

"What's your name, boy?"

"Charlie Krueger. You need me to spell it for you?"

"I'm gonna remember you. I'm an important man hereabouts. You ain't never gonna find work in this county again, nor not even a place to lay down your head for the night."

"Break my heart, why don't you?" He did not turn around, and he did not hurry.

To the west, the sky had clouded up and exploded in a riot of color. Layered clouds from horizon to horizon lit up in golds and subtle pink-purples and rich oranges, backlit by the setting sun. Still farther west, maybe as far as Montana, towering cumulus clouds massed like a dark mountain range. *We might not have much in the way of scenery around here*, he thought, *but we sure as hell have sky.*

To the north lay the foothills of the Turtle Mountains. He thought they would have trees and creeks and rugged landscape, as different from the flat prairie of the Red River Valley as it could be. He suddenly felt a powerful need to see those things.

Chapter Five
High Prairie

He woke at 4:00, dreaming of his brother. Rob was standing on a small knoll, looking manly and smart in his uniform, carrying the Winchester thirty-ought-six that Charlie had bought and sent to him, because the French-made rifles the troops were issued were no good. Rob wore his familiar easy smile, and he was waving to Charlie to go with him. But the landscape behind him was thick with muzzle flashes and billowing, orange explosions. Nothing could survive there. Charlie tried to shout, even scream to him not to go, but when he opened his mouth, no sound came out. He waved his arms and tried harder, but still he couldn't speak, and he wept in frustration. His brother just smiled and beckoned one last time, then turned and walked into the inferno.

Charlie sat up and breathed in the cold air. It was still only August, but in the foothills of the mountains, the brief, blazing summer was clearly over. He was just as glad. It seemed to fit with his dream, somehow.

Back home, the standing joke was that Charlie got up and fed the rooster that would later crow to wake everybody else. But by now, the joke was on his hate-filled father. And if he had to feed the rooster and the rest of the livestock and do the morning milking with a hangover from hell, well, he had earned it. Charlie wasn't that happy about having stabbed and hit him, if only because he was ashamed of losing his self-control. But he no longer had either pity or love for the man who already seemed more like a distant, unwelcome uncle than a father.

He threw back the rough blanket and the canvas barn coat that he had slept under, crawled out from under the battered tarp that served as a crude tent, and looked out at the still black predawn.

Overhead, the moon was down, but the night sky was luminous with stars. The Milky Way was so thick that it was almost like a single light, and he half expected to see it swirl and flow, like white scum on the top of a meandering black river. To the southwest, he could see Betelgeuse outshining the rest of Orion's shoulder and indeed most of the rest of the sky, even Venus to the west. It was low in the sky now. And to the north, both the big and little dippers were laughably simple to spot. *Follow the drinkin' gourd* flashed into his head, the instructional song of the Underground Railroad, shepherding runaway slaves north, back before the Civil War. The only schoolteacher he had ever known, Miss DeKuyper, had told his class about it. She was the daughter of a Pennsylvania farmer who had been part of the secret organization, and was clearly proud of it.

Was Charlie a runaway slave? Should he follow the North Star, too? Yes to both questions, he thought. But at some point, he would veer to the west, toward the North Dakota Badlands, to the city of Minot, to keep his promise to his sister. Then, if all was well with her, he would move on north, over the 49th parallel to Winnipeg and Moose Jaw and into upper Saskatchewan, as much because he had never been to any of those strange places as because that's where the harvest was.

To the east and south, where the predawn light had still not appeared, the black landscape was suddenly defined and given depth by first dozens, then hundreds of flickering orange points of light. At first, Charlie didn't recognize them as boiler fires. There were so many, and they stretched to the horizon, as far as he could see. The steam engineers of the plains were lighting off their fireboxes for the day, warming up the big boilers to make steam for a day of hard and unstopping work.

It took a good half hour of steady fire to get a main boiler up to temperature, with enough actual steam in the top of the barrel-shaped tank to make the machine able to move itself. By the time the rest of the threshing crews rose and breakfasted, there had to be more, much more steam, all ready to go at the touch of a brass valve. The fires twinkled like a mirror image of the starry sky above.

In other spots on the darkened plain, larger but less intense fires still smoldered and sparked, where monumental piles of straw had been burned off the previous day. A few farmers, like Walt Christian and Charlie's own father, still practiced balanced systems of farming, with livestock and crops complimenting each other. These people had a lot of uses for straw. But most of the Dakota farmers had converted to pure cash-crop farming. With no livestock to need the straw, it was simply blown or pitched into the biggest piles possible and then torched. A few gloomy souls said the farms had lost their souls in the blind pursuit of money, and the huge straw fires were beacons on the road to perdition. Others said that there was never a boom that wasn't followed by a bust. Charlie knew all the arguments, but they, too, were questions for another day. For now, he needed the boom economy, for better or worse.

A hundred miles north and fifty miles south of him, and two hundred miles east and west, the scene was the same. Still farther south, the harvest was over. On the plains of northern Nebraska, the fieldwork was done for the year, and people left the stubble as it had been cut and prayed for early snow cover and late winds. Farther south yet, beyond the Nebraska Sand Hills, through Oklahoma and all the way to the Texas Panhandle, where people raised winter wheat, the earth had already been plowed again and replanted with the seeds of next year's crops. Now millions of acres had nothing to anchor the soil except frost and snow and some seedlings that wouldn't emerge for months. In a dry year, they wouldn't emerge at all. And more people prayed for early snow cover and late winds, and just a bit more moisture than the Farmers Almanac said they ought to have.

Charlie didn't pray for anything. His mother, who constantly prayed for a sober husband, was proof enough that it didn't work. Sometimes he thought that God, if he existed at all, had a lot to answer for.

He pulled on a pair of cotton socks that he had pointedly not slept in, added wool socks over them, and then pulled on his heavy work boots and laced them up. Then he put on the leather jacket that had been his brother's, beat his arms to get his circulation going, and started to make his own fire.

He had hauled a few bundles of dry straw with him to get things started, but straw was a poor fuel for a cook fire or one that had to last any length of time. It flared up hot and then blew away so suddenly it would break your heart. He had chosen his campsite partly because the little grove was one of the few places around that was not under cultivation, even in the foothills of the mountains, and also because it had mature trees that had dropped some dead branches. He had laid a cone-style fire with these the previous night, with crossed bundles of straw on the inside. Now he opened his precious box of Diamond safety matches, struck one on the emery strip, and touched it to the tinder. After a slight fluttering in the wind, it caught nicely, and the chill of the night on the ground retreated to a more tolerable distance. Charlie's nose quit running and he didn't have to suppress any more shivers.

He took a drink of icy water from his canteen and felt the chill return. It damn sure wasn't hot coffee. But unfortunately, he did not have a full mess kit or anything to heat water in, even had he had any coffee grounds.

"That's probably why they call it, 'living rough,'" he said out loud.

His brother would have laughed at that, he thought, and it was good that he thought it. Since Rob would never laugh again in the real world, it was important that Charlie carry the image inside himself, give it a tiny life there. That was one of the many things his father would seek to deny him, and he was damned if he was going to let that happen.

He lowered his crude pack from the tree branch where it had spent the night, secure from raccoons and bears. Charlie had never seen a bear and wouldn't know what to do if he did, but he had seen too many coons for his taste and had on occasion shot a few. He unrolled the pack carefully, since it still contained a half dozen fresh eggs, lovingly packed in soft cloth. He laid them out on the grass for the time being and cut several thick slices of bacon from the slab he carried in waxed paper left over from the sandwiches his mother had given him. These he spread on the inside face of the square-nosed shovel with the broken handle, the one item he had with him that he could be accused of stealing from his father. That, too, might have made his brother laugh. He tossed a few rocks into the fire that was now nicely roaring, for later cooking supports, then held the shovel over the fire and waited for the bacon to start sizzling. When it puckered and curled and smelled almost irresistible, he used his bayonet to turn it over. Then he settled back to let the rashers crisp up, sitting down on a large round rock and taking another swig of the cold water.

"You need some coffee with that."

He almost dropped his shovel into the fire.

"Relax, white boy. We quit making war on you people a long time ago." A large man drifted into the firelight, dressed in dark leather and canvas and a crumpled hat that might have started its life as a Stetson. He had coal black pigtails and a necklace made of bones and beads. Charlie had no idea if the fact that he was an Indian should alarm him or not. His father despised Indians, but what didn't he despise? That was almost a recommendation.

"Hello, there. I didn't hear you come up."

"Of course you didn't. You're not supposed to hear Indians come up. That's unless they're bent out of shape, of course. They're bent out of shape a lot these days."

Charlie hadn't heard that term before, but he assumed it meant drunk. He couldn't think of anything to say about it, so he changed the subject. "I got plenty of bacon, if you want some, and some fresh eggs, too."

"You need coffee."

"You said that already."

"That's because it's true."

"It's also just too damn bad. I don't have any coffee, and if I did have, I don't have anything to brew it in."

"You want some?"

"Are you serious? I'd kill for a cup of coffee. You got some?"

"You got any tobacco to trade?"

"No."

"Dogshit. You need a lot of help, you know that? But you offered to share what you have, so I guess I can afford to spot you some good will." He raised one finger in a gesture that said, "Wait here." As if Charlie were going to go anywhere while the bacon was cooking. The Indian disappeared outside the circle of the firelight. A short time later, still without making a sound, he returned with a blue-enameled coffee pot, two matching cups, and a cloth bag, presumably containing coffee grounds. He put the pot, which apparently already had water in it, onto some of the rocks Charlie had laid in the fire.

"I'm Injun Joe," he said, solemnly extending his hand.

"Now I think you're trying to shit me up a pound," said Charlie. "Nobody has a name like that."

"Except in the mind of Mark Twain," he said. "Damn good writer, for a white boy."

"I'll take your word for it. We don't have a library back home."

"We don't have them in the Nations, either, but once I hopped freight trains all the way to Chicago and worked in the stockyards for a while, herding cows into a slaughterhouse. Not a place you want to be, Chicago, but you could get books there. Would you believe I am Ten Bears?" He was grinning now.

"No."

"Why not?"

"Because I seem to remember that Ten Bears was some kind of warrior chief who died out in Arizona or New Mexico in the Plains Indian Wars."

"You're pretty smart."

"I went to school."

"It was New Mexico," the man said, nodding. "He was a Comanche."

"I'm afraid I can't tell one from another."

"Comanches look mad all the time. Always did. I am Lakota." He held out his hand again. "George," he said. "You couldn't pronounce my other name, but it means raven wing."

"I'm glad to meet you, George Ravenwing." He shifted the shovel handle into his left hand and offered his right one to shake. "I'm Charlie Krueger."

"We have boiling water, Charlie Krueger. Now you will see how an Indian makes coffee."

"If it's coffee, I'll like it, no matter how you do it. I'll fix us some eggs."

Charlie used his knife to slide the bacon rashers off the shovel and onto a piece of waxed paper, being careful not to spill the grease. Then he carefully propped the hot shovel level on a patch of bare ground and began breaking eggs into the grease. He couldn't see the rest of the eggs surviving another day in his pack, so he cooked them all. "I haven't got any bread left," he said. "Sorry."

"I have some. It's Indian bread, though. You ever have any?"

"No, but it's got to be better than grass or straw."

"And they say white folks are stupid."

"Who says?"

"All the real people."

He couldn't think of anything to say to that, so he concentrated on the eggs. When the whites had turned completely opaque, he did a quick flipping motion with the shovel, tossing them neatly into the air like birds in formation and catching all but one in the properly inverted position. One was crumpled on its own edge, the yolk broken and running into the hot grease. "I'll eat that one," he said.

"Not unless you want to fight me for it." George Ravenwing laid out roughly sliced rounds of coarse white bread on the grass and motioned Charlie to slide the eggs onto them. Then he poured coffee for both of them. Charlie hadn't realized how

badly he wanted some until the smell hit him from the rim of his
cup. He made a small gesture of salute and thanks, and George
nodded approvingly. The bacon was cool enough to handle with
their fingers now, and they ate it that way. If he had been on his
own, Charlie would have had a bit of trouble figuring out how
to eat the eggs, with neither bread to make a sandwich nor a
plate to put them on.

"Seems to me if you're planning to camp out for a long time,
Charlie Krueger, you need a lot better bunch of gear. Or maybe
you're on a vision quest?"

"I don't know what that is."

"Young Cheyenne braves, sometimes Lakota, too, go out to
starve a little and to hear the voices of the wilderness and learn
the truth of their souls. They don't take any gear with them,
except a knife and maybe a water bag."

"I don't want to hear the truth of my soul, and I damn sure
don't want to starve. I'm just looking for a job."

"Well, there's plenty of them around these days, unless you're
an Indian."

"Yeah, right. And unless you're bent out of shape, I bet."

"I can say such things about my own people," said George,
"but you should not. No matter how you mean it, it comes out
sounding full of hate."

"You're probably right," said Charlie. After a moment of
thought and a flickering memory of his spite-filled parents, he
added, "I apologize."

"Accepted. Are you a farmer, Charlie?"

"That's what I mostly know how to do, but I don't seem to
have much of a future there. I'm good with machines. I'm thinking maybe I can make some kind of life out of that."

"So you want to be a mechanical man?"

"I guess you could put it that way, all right."

"Most young men who know farming find a good woman
and settle down to screw up the land. Aren't there any good
women where you are from?"

Charlie sighed, said nothing. He looked at the ground.

"That bad?"

"I don't have a woman back home. I also don't have any land of my own, which means that I can't get a woman."

"Ah."

"What's that mean, that 'ah?'"

"That means white people are stupid, is what it means. The woman you want will only go with you if you own some land? Then you don't want her. You people worry too much about owning things. I have had two fine women in my time, and we lived off the land without ever owning any, except that all the people owned all the land. It was a good life."

"Yeah, maybe. But it's gone now for you and never was there for me. There are a lot of kinds of life possible, but not every kind. You can't hunt buffalo any more and I can't ask a woman to go with me if I don't have any land, and that's just the way things are."

"I guess that's true. Because the white man is in charge and that's the way he thinks. And that's the kind of thinking that took away our land and gave us some hardscrabble dogshit place to live that no sane person would want."

"It was good sharing breakfast with you, sir. I hope we aren't going to argue now." And he really did hope it. He was finding himself liking this man.

"No, we will not argue. This is not a place for arguing"

"It isn't?" What on earth was he talking about now? "Tell me why that is."

"You didn't know?" He raised both eyebrows and dropped his jaw a notch. "Then why did you pick this spot to camp?"

"It has trees," said Charlie. "Big, old ones. I brought some straw with me for the fire, but straw is no good unless you have a ton of the stuff. If you have old trees, there will be dead branches around for a fire, and you don't have to hurt the trees to get it."

"That's good," said George Ravenwing, nodding with his whole torso. "Good enough that I will tell you some things. This is a place of great power. Besides the small stuff, there are five great trees, of much age, and each one is a different race, do you see? Cottonwood, oak, hackberry, maple, and elm. Five is an important number, the biggest number that can be remembered for what it is, without putting a name on it. It is a sacred number. This might have been a holy place once. When you are done with your quest, you should come back here, to restore your soul and make yourself ready to reenter the real world. You could ask Wakan Tanka for some guidance. He would hear you, in a place like this."

"I was sure I told you I'm not on a quest. And I am damn sure not going anywhere that isn't in the real world."

"You told me that. You told yourself that, too, I think, but it is not exactly true. There are a lot of kinds of quests and a lot of worlds. Yours just doesn't have a name yet. But I'll let that pass for now. Tell me then, you who have no land and can't get the woman you want without any, what do you think to find out there that will speak to your soul and change who you are?" He made a broad gesture to encompass the whole of the plains that were finally beginning to emerge in the light of the first false dawn.

Charlie shrugged. "Steam."

"Steam," he repeated, but not as a question. "You answer very quickly when I ask you that. The big steam engines, you mean?"

"They're a start," said Charlie. "Big machines of other kinds, too. I get *The Farmer* and *Popular Mechanics* in the mail, and I look at the ads for machines and memorize the features and figure out what's what from the drawings. I understand them, is the thing. Not just what lever makes what happen. I mean I really *understand* them. Like they were people."

"Who you don't understand?"

"Well, I'll sure admit I don't understand women, anyway. Not my old man, either. He's scared to death, seems like, that I might become better at something than he is. In fact, he's scared that I might even be as good. And for some reason I can't figure out, he blames me for my brother's death. Rob died in the big war. He was set in his mind to go, and it's not even like I could have gone in his place. But my father blames me and hates me for it. Sometimes I think he hates me just because he can, but that's just plain crazy."

It suddenly occurred to him that he was telling an awful lot of details about his personal life to a total stranger, and one of a different race and maybe attitudes, at that. He shut his mouth and busied himself with cleaning up the campsite and getting ready to move out.

"Never mind about the people," said George Ravenwing. "When your heart is ready, the understanding will come. Tell me about the steam."

"Steam is power, of course," Charlie said, pausing in the middle of making up his pack, eager to tell somebody about his secret passion. "It's a lot of power. Hardly anybody realizes how much. It takes the huge energy of fire and stores it up and uses it to make things move. Big things. I don't know if there's any limit to how big a steam engine you could make, as long as you get the jewelry right."

"The jewelry? You mean like beads?"

"No. Jewelry is what steam engineers call the fine parts, the valves and regulators and such that control the big, heavy stuff. They're like the clockwork, you see? But they're better than that, even. They're the only parts that can't be made or fixed without a machine shop, and nothing will work without them. They're the brains. They're almost like the...well, I mean..."

"The soul?"

"Are you making fun of me, sir?"

The Indian shook his head gently. "I could believe that steam could have a soul. Maybe it could even be a god, who knows? And the machines that use it, too. Why not?'

"It doesn't make a lot of sense to most folks, but I believe it. Sometimes I believe that a steam engine is a living thing. And it's a thing full of mystery and magic, too. Someday I mean to understand the magic." He blushed, realizing that once again, he had gotten carried away, talking to a total stranger, though the man seemed less and less strange. "But I guess I don't really know how to do that."

"Sure you do. You just told me. Every chance you get, you learn more about it. You drink it in as if it were life itself. Didn't you just tell me that?"

"Well, I might have hinted at something like that." Charlie grinned.

The Indian drained his coffee cup, wrapped his arms around himself and stared into the dying fire, rocking back and forth.

"Can I give you some advice, Charlie Krueger?"

"Nothing has stopped you from doing that, up 'til now."

"Take a new name."

"Huh?"

"You say you're not on a vision quest, so I believe you. But you're on a quest of some kind, anyhow. You said so. You need to leave your old self behind, learn a new world, be a new person. A new name is a good way to start. I will give you one, since you will not know how to choose."

"Did I ask you to?"

"No."

"I sort of like being Charlie."

"Then just change your last name."

"I don't want to be named after some part of an animal. No offense."

"Who said you would?" He looked over at the remains of their breakfast. "From now on, you will be named Charles Bacon. It is a good name, and it will remind you of how you started your journey, here in the place of the five trees. You should also have a secret name, which you tell to nobody."

He tried Charles Bacon out a few times, repeating it in his mind, and he found to his surprise that he liked it. Charlie Bacon was okay, too. He decided his secret name would be C. B. "I feel like I should thank you," he said.

"Thank me by completing your journey, Charles Bacon. But for now, tell me something. When you have followed the wheat berries all the way up to the frozen lands in the north and the iron wheels freeze solid to the ground as you work the last crop, where will you go then?"

"You mean for the winter?"

"I mean for any time, winter or later."

"I guess I'll know that when the time comes."

"Well, if you don't know when the time comes, come back here."

"Here? You mean right here, this very campsite? Why would I do that?"

"This exact spot. Bring tobacco next time, as a gift to the land and to me. I told you, this is a place of great power. You can summon me from here, just as you did today."

"Hey, wait a minute, I didn't—"

"Be quiet and listen. I have a cabin not far away. It's not in the Indian Nations, of course, but what are they going to do to me for leaving? Take my land? They already did that. You can stay in the cabin if you want. Or you can camp in one of the deep ravines close to there. You will find your way there, if you have lost it. The earth will make you whole. That won't happen on those 'owned acres' you want so bad."

"That's a mighty fine sounding offer, but I don't know if I—"

"Trust me. When the time comes, you will know. Carry the offer with you in your heart, along with your new name, and you will know."

The sun was now pushing above the horizon, huge, molten and fiery red-orange. In the downslope fields the rosy light showed smoke rising from cook shacks and dust clouds billowing around the threshermen who were doing the first trial runs of the day on their Advance-Rumley or Case Junior Red River Special separators. The horses that would spend a long day pulling the sheaf wagons or the grain gondolas were also getting their breakfast and water, and in a thousand other large and small ways, the high plains were coming to life.

The Indian turned and walked back up the gentle slopes, toward some rocky scrub forest riddled with small ravines. He did not say goodbye. He was gone rather quickly. If Charlie had been watching, he might have seen him disappear.

Charlie, or C. B., or now Charles Bacon, packed up all his gear, making it into a backpack with a bedroll, which his brother had taught him to do when he was home on boot leave. He also packed a smaller bag that the migrant workers called a "bindle." He tied that to the center tine of a pitchfork, to be carried on one shoulder. He was a bindlestiff now, and for the first time since he had hit his father and walked out, he began to feel good about it.

He picked out the biggest steam and smoke flume that he could see, selected an appropriate road, and headed that way. As he walked along on his brisk three mile per hour pace, he found himself singing a half remembered song from his brother's war.

Over there, over there. Dum de dum, dum de dum, over there. The Yanks are coming, the Yanks are coming. And we won't come back 'til it's over, over there. He guessed it must still not be over, since he didn't know anybody who had come back.

◇◇◇

Some thirty miles south and east of Charles Bacon's campsite, Sheriff Amos Hollander and his deputy, Tom, looked out over the same ocean, more or less, of animated wheat fields. They stood in the bell tower of a Lutheran church in the tiny town of Ruso, not far from Cottonwood Lake, which had never seen a cottonwood tree gracing its muddy banks and probably never would. They had steaming mugs of strong coffee in front of them on the unglazed sill of the tower arch, courtesy of the pastor's hospitable wife. The sheriff had a large pair of binoculars with which he swept the scene below. He was a day and a half out of his jurisdiction, which was Mercer County. His office was in the town of Beulah, on the Knife River. He could justify one more day and then, unless he uncovered a major crime that had something to do with Beulah, he would have to go back.

"How you going to pick which one to go after?" The young deputy slurped his coffee noisily and looked as if he really didn't care.

"When they crank up the threshers to full bore, we should be able to see them. The farm that the girl disappeared from was custom threshed by an outfit with the new, bigger version of the Windstacker. Makes a pile of straw fifty feet high. You ought to be able to spot that kind of spewing from twenty miles away."

"And if we do see it, then what? You ain't thinking she's going to be there, are you?"

"Probably not, but most of the same crew will be. We go talk to them, find out what they saw, that's all. What's the matter, you starting to miss your mama?"

"You got no call to say things like that, Sheriff." In point of fact, the sheriff could plainly see him getting very homesick indeed. Tom had never been outside his home county before. "You need me, I'm here; you know that. It just seems like we're gettin' awful far out of our jurisdiction, for just a missing person case. I mean, how's the County Board going to feel about all this expense over what's probably just a runaway girl?"

"What makes you so sure she's just a runaway? Her pa thinks she wouldn't leave of her own free will, and so does her girlfriend."

What the sheriff thought, though he didn't bother to tell his deputy, was that Mabel Boysen, whom Hollander himself had fully intended to marry, had either gone off with or been abducted by that kid from the Krueger farm, just down from the Boysen spread. It was just too much of a coincidence for both of them to have disappeared at the same time. If they had eloped, well there was nothing he could do about that. He would grind his teeth and quietly drop the matter. But if that Krueger boy had taken her off to have his way with her and then abandoned her or hurt her, then he would hunt the son of a bitch down if it took the rest of his life.

"If she was abducted," Hollander went on, " she was most likely murdered, too, or she would have run back by now. And nobody, I mean *nobody*, murders somebody from my county and gets away with it. Are you understanding me okay here?"

"Yeah, I understand you, sir. But we got no body and no witnesses to any foul play, and you got chow wagons and whore-houses, even traveling gospel shows that she could have run off and joined. And that book I sent away for on modern crime detection methods says—"

"Son, you try to tell me my job just once more, and I promise you're going to regret it for a long time."

"I was just thinking—"

"That's the last warning you get."

"Yes, sir."

On the plains below, the smoke flumes got thicker and closer together, and soon a hundred roaring, shaking machines were spewing straw, chaff, and dust into the crisp morning air. Sheriff Hollander scanned it all with great care, missing nothing. When he looked straight east, into the rising sun, he used his hat to shade the lenses. He stared in that direction for a long time, then turned his eyes north again. Finally he put the glasses down and sighed.

"Finish your coffee, boy. You get your way, after all. Time to go back. They all look the same."

◇◇◇

Elsewhere, another man looked over the prairie, from the top of a Sears Roebuck deluxe seventy-five-foot steel windmill tower. He looked at the land that used to be covered with prairie grasses so tough, their roots so deep, that no storm God ever made could wash them away, no drought kill them off. He looked at the plains that were once dark with the moving seas of buffalo herds. He looked at the plains where once a man could wander free, breathe in the pristine air, be at peace. He looked at the plains and shook his head.

They raped this land, they did. Raped it bad, all the way from the middle of Texas to the middle of Canada, ripped it open and messed it up something awful. And for that, there has to be blood. Folks tear open every tiny patch of land in sight, just to make money they can't use, and the universe can't ever be right until somebody pays in blood.

It was the government's fault, of course, as much as anyone's. At the start of the war in Europe it had decided America should be the bread basket of the western allies, or some such rubbish, and had guaranteed a market price of two dollars a bushel for wheat. The number was preposterous, and he fumed with rage every time he thought about it. At that price, a farmer could make thirty dollars an acre growing wheat, while any other crop wouldn't earn more than a tenth that much. He had done the math many times, and it still got him mad. Farmers with a whole section of land could make a profit of eighteen thousand dollars for a single crop, at a time when an ordinary laborer didn't see a thousand dollars a year. It was obscene. But he couldn't make the government pay in blood, so he had to settle for somebody else.

Young women are the best, since they will also be missed. Maybe they will even make people study on the error of their ways. And of course, pretty young women are evil from the ground up, anyway, so hurting them is a moral duty all its own. The hurt they can cause without even thinking about it is worse than anything that happens in a war. But if no young women are handy, others will do. Lots of kinds of others. Yes. It's a sacred calling.

Fortunately for the good of an orderly universe and the great, cosmic reckoning of things, he was able to take care of that calling all by himself. He scanned the horizon to the north and east, deciding which direction needed his attention the most.

He had another agenda, as well. He had decided that he had to find the young man who had seen him covering Mabel Boysen's grave, though he didn't know the man's name or which way he was headed. He would never again be sure of his own safety until he had found him. The more he thought about that fact, the more he began to be afraid. And he did not like, would not tolerate, anybody making him afraid. Sooner or later, the man had to die.

Perhaps fifteen or twenty miles to the northeast, he could barely make out the spire of a church. That, he decided, would be his next viewing perch, though he always thought of himself as a windmill man. Harnessing the dark winds of the injured prairie; that was his role.

Far below him, some dumb hayseed of a farmer was hollering at him about what the gosh darned hell was he doing up in *his* windmill tower and he better get his ass down while it was still in one piece.

Blasphemy. Vulgarity. And worst of all, pride. He hated those things.

Unfortunately, the farmer also had a double-barreled shotgun that he looked ready to use. Pity.

As he climbed down, he began to rehearse his story. He would say he was looking for some sign of the crew that had left him two days earlier, when he had taken sick. He would talk about how worried he was about getting his job back, even though he didn't really feel well enough to work yet. He would be pleasant and humble and self-effacing and would say not a single word of truth. And it would work like a charm. It always did. If he told the right lie, he could call the birds down from the sky. In the end, he would not only get invited to breakfast, he would also find something to steal from the farmer's house.

Chapter Six
In the Land of the Bindlestiffs

Charlie headed south, away from the mountains and back toward the harvest. He didn't hear the truck come up behind him. In fact, he usually didn't hear much of anything when he walked. He had been on the road for a week now, though three days of that had been spent in one spot, working for day wages. He found that he could easily walk twenty or twenty-five miles a day and still have time enough to set up an orderly campsite for the night and find some fresh water. He could do thirty if he pushed it, but he seldom had a reason to push it.

Whatever it was he was after, all he knew for sure was that he hadn't seen it yet. He slipped into his long-legged, loping stride and drifted into a world of his own, almost a trance state. Sometimes he would suddenly snap out of it, wondering where he was, and he would chide himself for missing out on seeing new sights, new parts of the country, though in truth, most of what he had seen so far had looked the same. Rolling prairie, oceans of grain or stubble patterned with header stacks or standing shocks of cut wheat, waiting for the threshers.

The truck approaching from behind blew its horn, shaking him out of his reverie. He looked over his shoulder and recognized a Reo single-axle flatbed, apparently running unloaded, and he moved farther over on the left shoulder to let it pass. But instead, the driver stopped as he came alongside.

"Need a lift?"

"I wouldn't mind," he said, looking the man and the rig over. On the battered green door of the truck was a professionally painted sign that read:

James Avery
Wheelwright Machinist Blacksmith

Suddenly he found the prospect of a ride with this man a lot more interesting.

He threw his gear on the truck bed, and climbed around to the passenger seat. The driver was not a big man, but he had something of a presence, not least because of his heavy, brooding brows and a thick mustache of the sort Charlie had always thought was only worn by Mexican bandits. Well, maybe them and Theodore Roosevelt. He wore a blue striped shirt and a black necktie, common enough among artisan workers but not farmers, and a black leather vest that was shiny with wear. He released the hand brake and shifted into super low, and the truck chugged down the road again, slow but probably very hard to stop. The Reo was a hell of a truck, and Charlie looked over the instrument panel and the interior finish, which wasn't much, with great interest.

"You wouldn't mind a ride, huh? I'd hate to think you were doing me a big favor. I don't like having debts."

"I wasn't looking to be rude, sir."

"You call everybody 'sir?'"

"Everybody older than me." Which was a lot of people. "I was raised to respect my elders."

"Well, keep it up and sooner or later you're bound to meet one who deserves it. I'm Jim Avery." He took one hand off the wheel and extended it. "And I'm not a 'sir,' just Jim."

"Charlie Bacon," said Charlie. The words came out of his mouth so quickly, he didn't even have time to think about them. *So I guess my new identity starts now.*

"Pleased to meet you sir. I mean Jim. Are you really all those things that it says on the door?"

"Pretty much. I'm not sure there's a name for what I am, but that string of words was about as close as I could come."

"What's a wheelwright?"

"An anachronism is what it is."

"Excuse me? I had all the education I could get back home, but I'm afraid that wasn't much. I don't know that word."

"The word means it belongs to another time, not our own. Used to be, people could make a living just building wheels, so they were called wheelwrights. Then there were wainwrights, who built nothing but wagons. Hell, there were probably buggy wrights, for all I know. People who built stuff out of metals were mostly smiths of some kind, though, instead of wrights. Blacksmiths, coppersmiths, silversmiths, and so on. Anyway, all that's just about gone. Anymore, people still need their horses shod, but wheels are made in factories, and people buy factory hardware and make their own wagons, too. You work on a farm, you've probably made a wagon or two."

"A binder wagon, yes sir."

"There you go with the sir again. Relax, kid. You from around here?"

"Not exactly."

"Not exactly from around here and wouldn't mind a ride. You're kind of a foggy character, Charlie Bacon."

"Maybe I got confused, being taught all that respect."

He laughed. It was an easy, likeable laugh, with no trace of sarcasm in it. "I like that. Anyway, factories make all the tricky stuff now, and folks stick it together themselves, is the thing, except for the really complicated machines. But when the tricky stuff breaks, that's when they need somebody like me. If it's got gears or wheels or chains or belts, I can fix it. You give me the right materials, I can even make a new one. Anything mechanical."

"Steam engines?"

"Sure, why not? They're just another machine, only hotter and heavier than most. More ways to get hurt on them, too, and more ways for them to hurt themselves."

"Wow. I mean, that sounds like a fine thing to be. How does somebody get to be something like that?"

"It's a fine thing to be if people pay their bills like they should and if you don't get burned or cut or crushed or crippled and maimed in any of a hundred ways. Yeah, it's good stuff. I hate the money end of it, though. Farmers are tighter than a mouse's asshole."

"Just some of them, I think. The big ones, mostly. They think having a big spread and some machinery gives them the right to talk down to everybody else while they rob them."

"Sounds like you know the type, all right. What does it mean, that you're not exactly from around here? You following the harvest?"

"Well, the north half of it, anyways. I just started, about a hundred miles south of here. My brother says I'm on a vision quest." That, also, came out of his mouth with no conscious volition at all. Had he referred to his brother just because he didn't know how else to describe George Ravenwing? Whatever the reason, just as the Indian had predicted, he felt as if he had just stepped over a threshold, into a world where things were not what he had grown up with. And it felt as irreversible as it was exciting. He decided he had better say something else, quick, before he had to explain a vision quest.

"What's a vision quest? That anything like a holy grail?"

Too late.

"I think it's a lot like it. But I don't understand it all that well, so I don't talk about it."

"Except to me."

"Yeah, well, that sort of surprised me, too."

"How old are you, Charlie?"

"How old should an apprentice machinist be?" He was twenty-three. But he thought that might be too old for an apprentice, and he suddenly found that he wanted to be one. Could he pass for eighteen? Twenty?

"You can forget that apprentice idea. I have a hard enough time feeding the people I got now. I'm on my way to the Bjorkland spread, to put a planetary gear I welded up into a Case separator. You're welcome to tag along and watch, but after that, you're on your own."

"Fair enough." More than fair, in fact. *The people he's got now? What might that mean?* Did the man have sons who would inherit the trade? He decided not to ask. Not yet, anyway.

They rode in silence for another half hour, then turned into a driveway by a hand-painted sign nailed to a fence post. The top of the post also had a planter box with daisies growing out of it. "Oleanna Farm," the sign proclaimed. Charlie had a silent chuckle at that.

They pulled into the middle of a circular gravel area that had all the farm buildings arrayed around it — house, barn, granary, chicken coop, hog house, corncrib, and a three-bay machine shed. Beyond the barn, acres and acres of shocked wheat marched off to the horizon, and in front of it, sitting idle, stood a new dark green Case threshing machine and a black Minneapolis overmounted steam traction engine. The engine looked as if it had steam up, but nothing was moving. The thresher had a big flat panel removed on the side where the huge belt-pulley stuck out. Nearby, half a dozen wagons with two-horse teams hitched to them also sat idle, and at least twenty men were milling about. Charlie's mental arithmetic told him that meant at least a thousand acres of wheat to be threshed, as the usual ratio was fifty acres per worker. That was, if the farmer hired enough men.

A couple of the threshermen saw Avery's truck and began motioning him to drive over to the Case. But Avery stopped in the main yard, got out, and pulled a circular gear and a toolbox from behind the seat. Then he made a show of taking his time walking over to the eager group.

The farmer, Bjorkland, was easy to spot. He was the man with the best, newest-looking work clothes, the biggest belly, and the loudest mouth. By the time Charlie caught up, Avery was crawling into the guts of the Case and Bjorkland was in the middle of a major tirade.

"Who you think is going to pay all these men for standing around with their thumbs up their asses? Me? It's after eight o'clock already. We should have gotten fifty acres gleaned by now." He held up his pocket watch and pointed to it importantly, and Charlie wondered if he really cared about the time, or if he just wanted to be sure everybody knew he had a fancy watch. He also wondered if Mr. Bjorkland was really going to pay anybody, whether they worked or not. He looked an awful lot like the man whose bacon was in Charlie's backpack.

"I seem to recall asking if you wanted to pay the extra cost for having me work all night to fix your gear, Mr. Bjorkland. You didn't like that idea much."

"An extra two dollars, just for a little lamp oil? I'll see you in hell first."

"No, you see me at eight o'clock, which is exactly what I promised you. Charlie, bring me that crescent wrench, will you?"

Charlie was stunned at being asked to help. He ran with the wrench over to the disabled machine and poked his head inside the main chassis, where Avery had taken a very uncomfortable-looking position. It was a thrilling view, much better than he had gotten from the tiny panel on the top of the Case. He had seen plenty of threshing machines before, but he had never had a close look at the inside. All the parts he had read about or seen drawings of—the concaves, the shaker trays, the main cylinders, the transfer gears—were there for him to see, more wonderful than he had imagined but also somehow simpler, less mystical. Not hard to understand at all, once you knew the basic logic of it.

"You must be replacing the auxiliary gear that drives the Windstacker," he said.

"I'm impressed. How did you figure that out?"

"It's the only subassembly that isn't coated with chaff and dust, so it must have just been worked on. And nothing in that assembly but the drive gear ever breaks. I think Case didn't use good enough steel in the original casting."

"You seem to know quite a lot. Do you know where the power takeoff for the whole machine comes out?"

"Sure, it's right—"

"Go make sure this eager, oh-so-important, hot shot farmer doesn't engage it before I'm out of here, okay?"

"Absolutely." He left the wrench where it was, jerked his body back out of the wonderful innards, and climbed up on top of the machine, where a nervous-looking separator operator was already gripping the main clutch lever.

"I don't need anybody else up here, kid."

"Yes, you do. You have a man inside your machine, and I'm here to see that you don't jump the gun and get him killed. You want to fight me over that, we might as well start now. But either way, you're going to take your hand off that lever."

The man gave Charlie a hard stare and made no move of any kind. He was a good bit smaller than Charlie, and he looked like he realized that. When Charlie crouched down in a sort of linebacker position, arms wide and hands ready to grab, the man let go of the lever and settled into a defensive pout.

"Thank you," said Charlie.

"Go suck on a horseradish."

Below them, there was a lot of clanking and pounding, and finally Jim Avery emerged from the machine and began to bolt the cover back on.

"All right men, get to work!" Bjorkland made a broad circular motion with his arm, as if he were trying to dry off a towel, and people began to move. The steam engineer threw a lever and opened a valve, and the big reinforced rubber belt began to turn the idler pulley on the thresher. The separator man made a gesture toward the big lever but looked at Charlie first, to get permission. Charlie held up a hand in a gesture that said, "Just one minute."

"You all clear down there, boss?" It was obvious that he was.

"As soon as Bjorkland pays me, I am."

Well, there was that, yes. And Charlie saw an expression on the farmer's face that he knew altogether too well by now. He jumped down off the separator and quickly did some adjustments to the exposed gear and chain mechanisms on the far side of the box. "We don't want to forget to re-engage the swivett," he said. Nobody paid any attention to him.

"Crank her up," shouted Bjorkland.

"You owe me ten bucks," said Avery.

"Was I talking to you?" To the man on the separator, he yelled again. "Crank her up, you want to keep your job!"

The man looked at Charlie, who shook his head, no.

"Now, damnit!"

The man gave a shrug of helplessness and threw the lever. The machine shook, clattered, and clanked to life. A wagon pulled up alongside the apron and men began to pitch wheat bundles into it.

"Ten bucks," said Avery, holding out his hand.

"Are you crazy? You come here late, hold up my crew, and now you want to charge me enough money to buy a whole new gear, too? Highway robbery! I'll give you two dollars, take it or leave it. But either way, get off my farm."

So much for Oleanna and the land of good times, thought Charlie.

"Listen, you ten-cent chiseler, I can—"

"Take the two bucks," said Charlie in his ear. "Trust me, it'll be okay."

"You sure?"

"I'm sure."

Avery held out his hand again, Bjorkland triumphantly dropped two silver dollars into it, and Avery and Charlie strolled back to the truck.

"Walk slow," said Charlie. "It won't take long."

They strolled slowly back around the barn, and pretty soon they heard frantic shouts.

"Why in tarnation ain't anything coming out?"

"The feed belt on the apron don't move; it just shakes a bunch."

"It's got to be moving; it don't have a disengager clutch. The problem is in the collector gear coupling."

"No, it ain't. I already looked."

Very quietly, Avery said, "What the hell did you do?"

"Pulled a shear pin," said Charlie. "One that never breaks, so hardly anybody knows about it. No way they'll find it on their own."

Soon Bjorkland was back in their faces, first demanding, then asking, and finally begging that they fix his machine. Again.

"Seems to me, last time I fixed your machine, I didn't get paid."

"Ah, come on. That was just a little joke, see. I wanted to show off for the crew. I was going to pay you all along, you gotta know. You can't take a little joke?"

"Can you?" said Charlie.

"Look, here's the other eight bucks, see? You happy now? We all square?"

"Why, sure," said Avery.

"No way," said Charlie.

"But I paid…"

"For the extra time and the insult, you owe my boss another ten."

"Five," said Bjorkland. I'll pay the extra two you wanted for the overtime and another three to fix the new problem."

"Ten," said Charlie. "Up front. Or that swell Case machine of yours won't give out any wheat berries for another week. And that's if it doesn't shake itself to pieces before then."

"Okay, say seven, and I'll—"

"Ten," said Charlie, and began walking away. "Let's go, boss. This hayseed wouldn't know a good deal if it bit him."

"All right, then!" The man reached in his pocket and pulled out a ten-dollar gold piece, which he flipped at Charlie, along with a look that would wilt mustard plants. "Now fix my goddamn machine before I kill both of you."

"Why, I'd be happy to," said Charlie.

◇◇◇

As they were driving away, Charlie gave the gold piece to Avery.

"You get half of that, young friend. But what was that business back there with calling me 'boss?'"

"Did I call you that? Seemed like the thing to do, I guess. Seemed to work okay, too, didn't it?"

"Yeah. I guess it did. So. You're looking to be an apprentice machinewright?"

"I never heard the word before today. But I'm starting to think it's something I could like." Did that also mean it was his vision quest? He seriously doubted it. Still, it had a strange feel of *rightness* about it.

"Well, you certainly seem to have a knack for collecting the money, anyway."

"That's kind of a new thing for me, to tell the truth. I'd really rather make my money by working than by tricking somebody."

"We'll find out how you are at that, too."

"I won't disappoint you, Jim."

"The wages are horrible and the work can be terrible hard."

"Well, that doesn't make it a whole lot different from farm life, does it? Only it sounds more interesting."

"Well, there you are, then. Welcome aboard, Charlie Bacon. Let's go meet the rest of the motley crew."

Chapter Seven
The Ark

Midmorning, they rolled into the camp by a gurgling creek with willow trees and small birch groves. Avery had a traveling caravan that resembled some kind of carnival as much as a place to get machinery fixed. At one end was a wide, low-slung enclosed wagon that had rubber tires on wide steel wheel rims. It had a flywheel on the side of one wall, with a belt than ran to a shining black and red Peerless double-complex steam traction engine.

"What's the engine set up to run?" said Charlie.

"The flywheel? I've got a full machine shop in that wagon. Drill press, wood and metal lathes, milling machine, and band saw. Also a generator that makes juice for all the lights."

"Wow."

"Over there," he said, pointing, "is the cook shack. The big tent in front of it is a sort of café. Folks who come here to get their machines or tools or plows fixed can buy a meal while they wait, or just a cup of coffee. There's coffee brewing all day here. If they look like they can keep their mouths shut about it, they can also get a glass of beer and a shot of booze."

"Aren't most of the counties around here dry?"

"Very. And once the Eighteenth Amendment takes effect, every place will be. That makes this a pretty special place, wouldn't you say?"

"Sounds like you don't have much time for the law."

"It does sound that way, doesn't it?"

Several smaller trailers or wagons were strung out in a ragged line behind the machine shop. A McCormick reaper-binder with a broken cutter bar, a couple of Deere plows, and a sagging sheaf wagon were scattered around the site in no particular order. Charlie assumed they were waiting to be repaired. Above it all, a simple yellow flag fluttered on a tall pole, steadied by makeshift rope stays. Charlie had noticed it several miles before he could see the actual camp.

"What do you call this?"

"Call what, exactly?"

"All this." He swept his hand around in an expository gesture. "This, um *bunch* of trailers and machines and things. It's not exactly a carnival and it damn sure isn't a traveling salvation show, so what is it?"

"We call it the Ark," he said.

"Because…?"

"Because it's not the *Lusitania*. And maybe because it carries a little bit of everything. Most of the people who work in it are busy somewhere now. You'll meet them all soon enough. They're decent folk, mostly, but in one way or another, they are all orphans or fugitives of some kind. Fugitives from somewhere or something or maybe somebody. I won't even ask if you are.

"Jude the Mystic is off treating a sick cow somewhere. He's a not-quite vet, always one county line away from a charge of practicing without a license. He doesn't hang too close to the rest of us, because he doesn't think we're respectable." Avery let the Reo truck roll to a stop alongside the machine shop trailer, in the shade of a big elm.

"The women are probably cooking or doing wash right now, since we were lucky enough to find a site next to a little creek, and I never know what the hell Stump is doing. Probably off rounding up some more work for the shop. He's my right-hand man. He scouts the territory on our motorcycle, hands out fliers in the little towns, that kind of stuff. It takes a little tact. We like customers to be able to find us, but not necessarily people like sheriffs or aldermen, since we don't ever bother to get licensed, bonded, inspected, attached, or otherwise approved by anybody. Sometimes the unattached part is real important. It never hurts to camp close to a county line, either.

"Anyway, Stump is an ex-con from some hellhole down southeast in Dixie. Escaped from a chain gang. I don't know why he was on it in the first place, but any fool knows why he escaped. The women here are all running away from drunken husbands or fathers or uncles or pimps or cops who would screw them first and then arrest them anyway. You're blushing, Charlie. Does that shock you?"

"I guess I've led kind of a sheltered life. I always figured my own family had all the original patents on evil, and everybody else in the world was sort of normal and moral."

"Wouldn't that be nice, though?"

They got out of the truck and walked toward the machine shop.

"You know how to weld, Charlie?"

Charlie hesitated.

"Don't lie to me. Don't even think about it."

"No. Welding is one of those things I've read about every chance I got, but I've never actually had the chance to try it. Not braising, either. I'm pretty good with solder; that's as close as I've been."

"Well at least you know the difference between welding and braising. They say it takes about twenty hours of instruction and another eighty of practice to make a competent welder. But in my experience, you can see in less than an hour whether a guy is going to be any good at it, and if he is, he will pick it up fast. It's a knack. You either have a feel for it right off, or you never will. We'll find out today if you have the feel, on that cracked plowshare over there."

"I appreciate that, si…*Jim*, I really do." He could hardly say how much. Country blacksmith shops, in towns lucky enough to have them, still had traditional forges but they were coming to be fired up much less often than the more modern welding torches. If you were going to call yourself any kind of a metal smith in the modern world, you absolutely had to be able to weld and braise. Some people thought that the newly invented electric arc welder was about to eclipse both the torch and the forge, but he had never seen one and didn't know if he ever would. For now, it was all torch work, and he had always wanted to try it.

As they walked toward the gaping end of the shop, the screen door on the cook shack slammed against the wall and a woman came running out. She could have been anywhere from teens to early thirties. She had a long skirt that looked rough, almost like burlap, a puffed-out periwinkle blouse and a leather vest like Avery's, and large dangly earrings. Her hair was a mousy brown, but it had luster and shape, and it hung down just far enough to brush the tops of her shoulders, the same way her bangs brushed the tops of her eyebrows. Her eyes were also brown, but large and moist, almost like a deer's, and her mouth was wide and sensuous, too wide for her heart-shaped face.

"That's Maggie Mae," said Avery. "Maggie Mae Flowers."

"She looks like a lot of woman. I mean…" Charlie blushed again.

"If you want to tell her that, you'll have to learn to sign."

"Excuse me?"

"Sign language. She's a deaf mute."

Maggie Mae threw herself at Avery, wrapping one suede-booted leg around his thigh and arching up to kiss him hungrily on the mouth. For reasons he couldn't quite sort out, that seemed very appropriate to Charlie.

◇◇◇

Welding the cracked plow turned out to be trickier than Charlie had expected. The crack had to be filled in short, scattered beads of metal along its whole length, rather than a single, long one, or else the shrinking bead would warp the blade when it cooled. The last of the beads he put in were noticeably neater than the first, but he got them all done without causing any warpage, and Avery pronounced it a success. They ground the bead down with an emery wheel and then polished it with pumice and oil. Charlie thought it was beautiful.

At the end of the day, Charlie spread his bedroll out on the dirt floor in the back of the dining tent.

"That's all I've got," said Avery. "I offered you a job, not a cozy home."

"This will do fine, Jim." At least it wasn't the ditch that his father had predicted.

Chapter Eight
Dark Harvest

In Mercer County, people would have been all done with fieldwork for the year, content to let the land keep itself over the winter as best it could. But a pair of local machinery salesmen did not want to leave it at that. They convinced Djelmar Boysen to let them plow up one of his stubble-covered wheat fields in the fall instead of waiting for spring, so they could stage a spectacular contest. They would pit a Garr-Scott 18-50 double-simple steam engine pulling a six-bottom John Deere plow against a Reeves undermounted complex 15-45 (said to be highly underrated) pulling an eight-bottom plow of Reeves manufacture, made for the specific tractor.

The advantage to Boysen, besides getting a huge field plowed free, was that both the new plows cut deeper and did a better job of rolling over the soil than the more common models. At least, that was the claim, and he had no argument for it.

Nobody had ever seen an eight-bottom plow before. There were none anywhere this far east of the vast wheat fields on the banks of the Columbia River. The Dakota farmers had seen a few six-bottom Deeres, and they were a wonder and a monster at the same time. An eight-bottom was beyond imagining.

With the heavy work of the season over and the Mercer County Fair still two weeks away, people were ready for a party, and the event drew a huge crowd. The Ladies Auxiliary of the Lutheran church set up a table to sell pies and cakes and ham sandwiches, with a tent thoughtfully rigged over them to keep the sun from melting the cake frosting. At another tent, a café owner from Hazen sold cider and beer and quietly took bets on the outcome of the contest. Many people brought chairs from their homes, while others perched on the rail fence at the edge of the field, eventually breaking most of it. Sheriff Hollander and his deputy, Tom, were there, just in case the beer drinking led to something ugly, and the county's only doctor, Henry Curtin, was also there, just because in that size crowd, *somebody* was going to get sick or injured. The doctor and the lawman got their sandwiches and beer free.

The promoters let the crowd build through most of the morning, inviting people to look over the competing machines at their leisure. Finally, around eleven o'clock, Sheriff Hollander strode into the center of the field and fired his gun into the air, and the race was officially underway.

The two engines started out on opposite sides of an eighty-acre field, and the crowd was thrilled as the Reeves rig began turning over a swath of plowed land more than sixteen feet wide, laying back the stubbled sod in thick, rolling waves. It also plowed deeper than the rack of Deere bottoms. The Gaar-Scott only cleared twelve feet at a time, but it was noticeably faster than the Reeves. It was all heavy and exciting stuff, and people cheered, gawked, and placed more bets.

The Reeves ultimately stole the show, but not for the amount that it could plow. The operator found it amusing at first, when the big, unstoppable plowshare turned over a buried shoe. A girl's shoe, possibly. But his amusement turned to something else when he noticed on his next pass by the area that the shoe still had a foot in it, attached to a comely young ankle and leg. Or at least to something that used to be comely.

That was the end of the plowing contest. Technically, the Reeves was making considerably more progress than the smaller Gaar-Scott, but the operator stopped it adjacent to the makeshift grave. The Gaar-Scott operator made one more pass down his own row and back, and then also stopped, to see what the problem was. He thought the other engine might have broken down, which would give him a victory by default, and he walked over to the Reeves. When he saw the real problem, he froze, too horrified to move.

Soon, nobody cared about the plowing. The crowd became completely absorbed with the body, and the men jostled each other for the privilege of helping to uncover it completely. It took six men with shovels an hour to carefully excavate the body. When the face was exposed, Djelmar Boysen clutched his chest and keeled over. Four men carried him to a shady grove at the edge of the field, where Dr. Curtin elevated his feet, gave him part of a glass of lemonade with some cocaine powder mixed in it, and unbuttoned his shirt.

Mabel's body was taken into the dining room of the Boysen farmhouse and laid out on the table. As soon as he was sure that his patient, Djelmar, was recovering, Dr. Curtin went there to do a preliminary examination. The actual autopsy, required by state law, would be done later, in the barn.

It was an increase in business that the doctor did not relish. Most harvest seasons, he had a lot of major trauma cases, mostly from injuries involving harvesting machinery. It was a busy time for him, and the money he took in would pay for many of his charity cases over the coming winter. Acting as the County Coroner also improved his revenues, of course. But he had not become a doctor to get rich. Sometimes he wished he could be a bit less prosperous. And like most of the residents of the county, he had known and liked Mabel Boysen. He wept quietly as he wrote in his report that she had been sexually violated and then bled to death.

When Sheriff Amos Hollander read the report, he did not weep. He boiled with silent rage and told his deputy to get the pickup ready to travel again.

"You going to ask the County Board to authorize you to go out of your jurisdiction, Sheriff?"

"I'll ask. But if they can't come up with the right answer on the spot, we're going without waiting for it. Tomorrow morning, before first light. You don't have to come, if it worries you."

"I'll come. Don't I always back you up?"

"All right, then. Pack the tent and camp gear; we don't know where this is likely to take us. And be sure you pack both shotguns."

"Sheriff, we are figuring on taking this guy alive, aren't we?"

"Both of them, you hear?"

Chapter Nine
Life on the Ark

Breakfast at the Ark was flapjacks the size of dinner plates, molasses and butter, and fried ham. It had already started when Charlie opened his eyes, and he was grateful that he had fallen asleep too tired to undress, since his sleeping place was in the mess tent. He pulled his boots on, poured himself a cup of coffee from a big enameled metal pot, set it over by his sleeping pallet to cool, and went outside to look for a place to relieve himself. The others, at one of the big tables, ignored him.

Not finding a latrine, he settled for wetting the leaves of some scraggly looking bushes. Then he went down to the little creek, where he took off his shirt and splashed water on his face and torso. He had no towel, and he was about to dry his face on his flannel shirt, when a woman's voice stopped him.

"Here." A soft hand held a worn but large towel out to him. When he looked up he saw that the hand was attached to a soft bare arm and a small, dark haired young woman. She wore a tightly belted shirtwaist dress in a blue flower print and had a matching kerchief tying back her thick, dark hair. She had a pretty, heart-shaped face, with a prominent chin and a slightly upturned nose and large, hazel eyes that looked wise and a little bemused. She also had a scar that ran from the corner of one eye, down her cheek and neck, and into the covered area under her high collar. Charlie looked away from her face quickly, hoping he had not stared.

"Take it. Do a proper dry before you put your shirt back on, or you'll have a chill all morning." Was that an English accent? It was soft and lovely, whatever it was.

"Thank you," he said, a bit bewildered. He took the towel and buried his face in it. It was coarse and unevenly napped, but it felt good, and it dried him nicely. He dried his torso, also, suddenly feeling very self-conscious.

"I'm Emily," she said.

"Emily…" He made a palms-up gesture to indicate that he was still missing a surname.

"Just Emily," she said. "And you are?"

"Charlie Bacon." *A few more times, and it will be a genuine habit.* He wasn't sure if he should offer to shake hands, or kiss her hand, or what, so he awkwardly buried his right hand in the towel, suddenly finding himself awfully busy drying.

"It takes a lot of character to wash in a cold creek, Charlie Bacon. Are you a man of great character?"

"That's not a question I ask myself a whole lot. I do what I can, I guess."

"Then I'll tell you what you can do. You can stand guard while I take a whole bath in the creek. Are you comfortable with that?"

"Um, sure. I guess. Why not?" He wasn't at all sure whom he was guarding her from or what the job involved, but he couldn't imagine refusing.

"Do it then."

"Right." He draped the big towel over a bush, making a sort of screen and folded his arms over his chest, which reminded him he still hadn't put his shirt back on. He twisted part way around and bent down to retrieve it, and his eyes could not resist straying over to the creek, where a very naked Emily was settling down into the rushing water, her back to him. She was slim and athletic, and as unlike the soft, voluptuous Mabel Boysen as she could be. He had never seen a woman who looked like that before, or even dreamed of one.

"Turn your back, asshole!"

"Sorry." Besides sorry, he was also breathless, stunned, aroused, and very confused. Here was a young woman who actually used foul language but who was also so scrupulous about being clean that she bathed in an icy-cold creek. And she had kindly given him a towel before that. Clearly, she was a woman of great mystery and contradiction. She was nice. She was sweet. She was possibly wicked, with a hint of a violent past. But she was also modest. And in her own way, she was gorgeous, at least from the back. He concentrated on standing his watch and hoped his erection wasn't too obvious.

Looking back at the camp, he saw a tall, angular man with a horse face and bad teeth heading his way. He had been introduced to him the previous day, but he couldn't remember the man's name. Something odd. Stringbean; that was it. Stringbean Moe. He thought it was a stupid name, and he hadn't much liked its owner, either. When the man got within four or five yards, Charlie held up a hand, palm down.

"You can't come around here right now."

The man looked up and squinted. "Because you say so? Who the hell you think you're talking to, stiff?"

Charlie knew the look. He had seen it on the faces of two men who once tried to kill each other in a saloon in Hazen, one drunken Saturday night. This was not the look of his own bully of a father or of the farmer who had cheated him. This was the look of a man who liked to fight, liked the excuses that brawls gave him to hurt people. Charlie knew that if he had to fight him, he had better not quit until he had put him down, hard.

"You can't come here," he said again.

"Well, I'll tell you what, boy. I'm going to have some fun here. I'm either going to go down to the creek where that little British chippie takes her bath and get a piece of her ass, or I'm going to stay here and slice up a piece of yours. Or maybe I'll just do both. What do you think of that?"

He reached into a hip pocket and produced a folding knife with a straight, six-inch blade. He took his time opening it, spat tobacco juice on the ground, and went into an attack crouch, feet spread wide, arms out for balance.

Charlie slapped instinctively at his belt and felt the haft of his bayonet poking out of its sheath. But he couldn't pull it. He simply couldn't.

"Forget something, did you? Like, your nerve?"

"It won't matter."

"That's right; it won't. Hee, hee."

Charlie pulled the towel off the bush and quickly rolled it into a tube. Then he wrapped one end around each hand and put both hands in front of him, in a defensive vee, looking for a chance to snatch the knife hand in a wad of protective cloth. What he would do after that, he had no idea. And he knew that was bad. His brother had told him, "Always know what you're going to do in a fight. Otherwise, all you've got are your instincts, and you, little brother, don't have the instincts of a fighter."

The two men circled each other warily, with Stringbean making occasional false lunges and slashes. Charlie knew better than to react to them. *Don't let him learn how you move. Not yet, anyway.* He watched Stringbean's eyes, rather than his hands. And when he saw them suddenly get wider, he stepped smartly to his left and lunged with both hands, catching the knife hand in a vise grip. He pulled the hand to his right, twisting, and tried to trip the man as he passed in front of him. But all he managed to do was make him stumble a bit. The man's hand still gripped the knife, and now Charlie had no good way to hurt him. They froze in that pose for a moment and locked eyes, and the man spat again.

Then there was a muffled thud, and the knife fell from the hand. Emily, still naked, had come up behind them with a driftwood club and had smashed Stringbean's wrist.

"Don't let go!" she shouted.

Charlie continued to hold the man's hand and to twist, and Emily delivered two more blows, swung from over her head. At the second one, they could hear something crack, and the arm went limp. The man screamed, and Charlie let him go. He stumbled back toward the camp, cradling his smashed arm in his other one.

"I said don't let go, you bloody twit!"

"But he—"

"Somebody pulls a knife on you, you don't mess about. You put him in hospital or in the ground. I can't *believe* you don't know that!" She had tears streaming down her cheeks.

"Sorry," was all he could think of to say.

She seemed to realize quite suddenly that she was still naked, and she put a hand over her very ample tuft of pubic hair and an arm across her breasts. The scar that began at her eye ran all the way to her left nipple, which had been cut off. It made Charlie want to cry for her.

"Well, now you've seen it all, haven't you? Are you feeling satisfied, then?"

"I'm really sorry. I didn't—"

"You're feeling sorry for a lot of things, yeah? Try to be a little less sorry and act like a watchman while I get my clothes, will you?" She disappeared into the bushes.

In a few minutes she was back, once again dressed in the simple print dress and heavy shoes. She wrapped her thick dark hair in the towel she had originally given him, tied it in a sort of big knot in the back, and turned back toward the tent. Charlie fell in beside her.

"So much for my knight in shining armor."

"Sor— Um, well, I guess I don't have a lot of practice at it."

"No, I guess not. Why didn't you draw your knife? I saw you touch it."

"Because I knew if I pulled it, I could have wound up killing him."

"And just exactly what would have been wrong with that? Avery would have stood by you, you know."

"I wasn't thinking about getting caught. I just couldn't see myself doing that."

"Well." She sighed and wiped a cheek with the back of her hand. "I guess there's no help for that. If you haven't got the stomach for what has to be done, then you haven't got it. Let's go get some breakfast, Charlie."

"Sounds right to me."

But it didn't sound right, at all. As they walked back to the canvas café, a dozen different emotions washed over him, all of them heavily laced with self-recrimination. Why the hell couldn't he simply have pulled his bayonet? What was wrong with him, anyway? This woman had started out calling him a man of great character. Did he have to prove her wrong so quickly?

The adrenalin was wearing off now, and his legs felt unsteady. And he had the terrible feeling that he had only begun to get settled into the life of the Ark, and already he had botched his audition.

Chapter Ten
Searchers

Amos Hollander and his deputy caught up with the Yellow Fever thresher with the extra large Windstacker ten miles north of the tiny town of Bergen, in McHenry County. It was run and hired out by a man named Pat Flannery, who was more than a bit miffed at being questioned by a couple of uniformed law officers.

"Somebody trying to say I stole something?" he said, fists defiantly on his hips. "I never took nothing from no farm, I didn't, except as somebody give it me. Free and open, that's the way. Sometimes the farmwoman, she might not always tell her husband, but is that my fault? I runs a clean operation, I does. I don't even hold out any grain berries in the sorting trays, and I don't never—"

The sheriff cut him off with a "whoa" gesture.

"I'm more interested in your crew, Mr. Flannery."

"Like do any of them seem like killers?" added the deputy. Hollander shot him a look that would have dropped an ox in its tracks. If the deputy noticed, he made no sign of it.

"Me crew? I don't gots no regular crew. Just me and the engineer there, Freddy, who also so happens to be me brother-in-law, so I can vouch for him, all right. The others, the farmer goes out and hires his own self, from whoever's drifting about, you see."

"But some of them must follow your machine, surely?"

"Sometimes. A few as does. What's this getting at, here?"

"I'm looking for somebody who might have stayed with your rig after you worked the Boysen spread, about eighty miles south of here."

"Argh, I remember the Boysen place. Six hundred and forty acres, a full section, all in one big wheat field. A lot of fun, them kind are. Big crew, too, more than a dozen men."

"Forget about the fun. Think about the bindlestiffs."

"I mostly didn't know them by name. Some I got to know by sight after a while."

"Try for some names."

"Well, there was one that I heard his name later because he got into a row with one of the other farmers we worked for."

"What kind of a row?"

"Said the farmer didn't pay him, so he took a bunch of groceries and all. I believed him, me self. That farmer was one shifty character. Tighter than bark to a tree. Anyhoo, the farmer claimed he threatened him with a knife, though I never seen it." He waved the steam engineer over from his place at the rear platform of the big 20-50 Case. "Freddy, what was the name of that kid, back at the Bjorkland place? The one that faced down the fat, smiley bastard?"

"Oh, him? Um, Kringle? Craig? Chris Kringle. Crazy Craig. Not quite, but I'm getting closer. Keggler. Krueger! That's it. Somebody Krueger. Charlie, I think."

"Bingo," said Hollander, under his breath. Aloud, he said, "Could you point him out to me, sir?"

"Hell, no, I couldn't point him out. I mean, he walked away after that, didn't he? Pity, too. Hell of a good worker."

Sheriff and deputy traded looks of disappointment and exasperation with the crazy Irishman who had gone to the trouble of remembering a name of somebody who wasn't there anyway.

"Well, then, can you describe him, at least?"

"I can describe anything I ever seen, I reckon. He's a big guy, maybe six-two, six-three, built like a prizefighter. I seen a real prizefighter once, in Derry, back when—"

"You were telling me about Charlie Krueger, I think."

"Have a care. I'll get to him. He's maybe twenty-one or two or fivesome years, has near white hair that hangs in his face. I think he chews tobacco, right Freddy?"

"Well, he don't smoke, anyways," said Freddy. "Probably drinks a bit of the brew, though. Anybody works the apron has to have a drop of the brew, don't he?"

"I really don't care about any of that." To himself, he said *bullshit, all of it.* But at another level, Hollander was finding Flannery's description very interesting. He wondered if he knew this kid. Had he at least seen him a time or two? He began to think so. He knew most of the people in his county by sight, if not always by name.

"So you have no idea where this Krueger went?"

"There's maybe anywhere from fifty to a hundred custom threshers working the Dakotas right now. Could be with any of them."

"Great," said Hollander. "Just absolutely wonderful."

"Some days it's so goddamn, you can't even hardly," added Freddy, cheerfully.

"A course, there's Jim Avery," said Flannery, mostly to the engineer.

"That there is," said Freddy.

"What does that mean?"

"He's a guy runs a repair service for the machines, a kind of traveling smithy shop."

"He does at that," said Freddy.

"And therefore what?" said Hollander, writing the name in his pocket notebook.

"Well, he sees an awful lot of crews, or at least his runners do. You ought to go ask them."

"And just exactly where would I go to do that?"

"Dunno. Go to some town that has a rail siding or a grain elevator and ask around. Not the cops, he don't talk to them. But, like an elevator manager or a train hand. He hands out fliers and tells people where he's going to be for a while, asks if they know of any machines that's broke down."

"That's what I'd do, all right," said Freddy. Now that he was a part of the conversation, he seemed to feel obliged to always add a final word or two, even if there was nothing more to be said.

"Well," said Hollander. "Well, well, well. Gentlemen, you've been a great help." He started to walk away.

"What did this Krueger guy do?"

"Thank you for your time," said Hollander.

"We think maybe he murdered a young woman," said the deputy, "and had his way with her and maybe even—aagh! Ain't no call to kick me, Sheriff."

"I'd have shot you, but there were witnesses."

◇◇◇

They ate late breakfast at a diner on Main Street in Bergen.

"I haven't seen you boys in here before," said the heavyset waitress, pouring coffee for them.

"We're from Beulah," said Hollander.

"Yeah, and we're hot on the trail of a vicious killer," said the deputy. Hollander rolled his eyes. The waitress snorted and left them to study their menus.

"You couldn't shut your mouth if your life depended on it, could you?" said the sheriff.

"Well, it's true, isn't it? Where's the harm?"

"Did it ever occur to you that the Krueger kid might eat here some time, too?"

"So what? You think the waitress is going to tell him we're after him?"

"Who knows? If you can't keep your mouth shut, why should she?"

"Oh. I guess I didn't think of that."

"No. I guess there's a lot of things you don't think of."

"The hash is good today," said the waitress, returning to warm up their coffees.

◇◇◇

There was a small Great Northern Railroad office in Bergen, and Hollander sent a telegram from there to Western Union in

Beulah, asking if there were any urgent messages for him. But he didn't use a specific address, so the operator in Beulah didn't know who to give it to. He put it aside, to ask his supervisor about later. He had plenty to do, minding his own business, without running around taking a survey of who might want to communicate with a wandering sheriff.

Then the lawmen found a flier tacked to a tree by some railroad tracks, advertising Jim Avery's moving shop. It said he was set up by some creek, near the McHenry-Benson county line.

"So, we head east, then?" said the deputy, once again behind the wheel of the Model T pickup.

"Not just yet, Tom. First we're going to make a little detour, to the big city of Rugby."

"Whatever for?"

"To see if they have a newspaper."

◇◇◇

The lawmen wasted most of the rest of day in and out of Ipswich, which they were referred to by a shopkeeper in Rugby. It turned out that the *Ipswich Chronicle* had an old time reporter who used to draw his own illustrations with pen and ink, before the day when newspapers had the technology to print photos. They had wanted Freddy, the steam engineer, to go see him, but he flatly refused to take the time off from running his engine. So Hollander and his deputy took descriptions to the *Chronicle* reporter and got sketches, which they took back to the threshing site for critiques, then back to Ipswich again for corrections. Finally, they had a drawing that Pat and Freddy agreed was a reasonable likeness of Charles Krueger. And Hollander knew he had seen the kid before, though he had never talked to him.

The newspaper also did custom printing jobs, and they made up two hundred copies of a handbill with the picture and the caption HAVE YOU SEEN THIS MAN? It also had directions for contacting the sheriff's office in Beulah, though truth to tell, Hollander still had a much less than perfect system thought out for forwarding his messages. They had to wait a day and a half for the printing, which cost three dollars. Hollander paid it out of his own pocket. He would have liked to post a reward as well, but he couldn't afford it. In his home turf, of course, he probably needn't have bothered. Mabel Boysen was well liked back there. People had expected her to become fat, prosperous, and important someday, the wife of a banker or a wealthy farmer. They were devastated by her murder. And of course, a lot of them already knew what Charlie Krueger looked like. And the more those people thought about it, the more they thought they knew that he was guilty, as well. The poster only said "Wanted For Questioning." As far as the folks around Hazen were concerned, he was wanted for lynching.

As far as Hollander was concerned, Krueger was wanted as a candidate for getting "shot while resisting arrest." But he kept that to himself.

"So now we head east?" said the deputy.

"I do. You get on the next train that stops at that Great Northern station and head back home. Ask around at the farms near the Boysen spread, see if anybody remembers seeing anything strange."

"Aw, horse feathers, Sheriff. I want to stay on the chase."

"Stay in Beulah. Check the Western Union office several times a day, to see if I've wired in. If you find out anything useful, you can send me a reply, to wherever my last telegram came from. I'll wait around for one. You can do that, can't you?"

"Well, sure. I'm not stupid, you know."

"You fooled me. Get going."

"But I—"

"Argue with me again, and you'll go back without your badge. Understand?"

"Yes, sir." His tone indicated that he understood altogether too well.

Hollander, for his part, had no idea what a huge mistake he had just made.

◇◇◇

The search and the season wore on. People worked, made money, ate bountiful meals, nursed aching muscles, made babies, incurred horrible injuries, went to church, loved the land, sowed, reaped, and harvested. And here and there, one at a time, a few people disappeared.

Chapter Eleven
Sanctuary

The white bell tower of the First Unitarian Church loomed above the gently rolling prairie like a lighthouse in a golden sea. The Windmill Man had found it purely by providence, of course. He found everything by providence. His wanderings seemed random at times, but he had no doubt that they were all part of some great cosmic plan, even if he couldn't always see it. So he was pleased but not surprised when the church turned out to have a library.

In addition to the predictable religious tracts, there were works by Thoreau, Longfellow, and Wordsworth, plus books on modern farming and home medicine and even part of a set of encyclopedias. But most importantly, there were newspapers. Neatly folded and stacked, there were at least two year's worth of issues of the *Aberdeen Herald* and the *Huron Free Press* and even more copies of the *Minot Optic*, which somewhere in the middle of a stack changed its name to the *Minot Daily News*. Something from Rugby and maybe Devils Lake would have also been nice, but what was there was a treasure trove, anyway.

"I try to minister to the intellectual needs of our parishioners, as well as the spiritual," said the minister. He had a round face with sagging bulldog jowls and hair just going from brown to gray, but he looked fit and trim for his years, and his black suit coat hung from his shoulders with no major bulges. The Windmill Man shook his hand.

"Father, you are a beacon of knowledge in a dark sea of ignorance."

"We don't use the term 'father.' Just call me Pastor Ned, please."

"Well, Pastor Ned, I'm very impressed. This is exactly what I've been looking for. For my research, you see."

"Really?"

"Really. You might say it's a sort of a quest. It's hard to explain, exactly." He felt no need to say any more about it. The minister, he was sure, would fill in the rest.

"Well, feel free to spend as much time with our modest collection as you need. You'll stay to supper, of course?"

"If you're sure it will be all right with Mrs. Ned."

"She passed away three years ago, and our only daughter went to Minot to go to the Common School, in accounting. I live alone now."

"Oh, I'm so sorry." His heart leapt. The minister lived alone. "Then, I would be honored to break bread with you."

He had thought about killing the minister the moment he met him. That was normal. It was the first thing he considered about any new acquaintance. If the person was a man, he also thought about taking his identity. That was also normal, though it sometimes puzzled him. He seemed not to have a personality of his own, except when he was doing his holy work. Between the time he had killed his parents, at age sixteen, and the time he had started his holy work, almost fifteen years later, he couldn't remember who he had been, at all. That entire period was almost a complete blank, including the two years in reform school. But now he had a whole collection of identities he had taken from others, and he carried them with him at all times and could don any of them instantly. They were the invisible counterparts of the physical trophies that he took from his subjects, and he prized them just as highly.

But the minister would live a little while longer, while his guest learned his full persona and finished his research. Providence would tell him when it was time. It always did.

◇◇◇

It had begun in the early spring of 1914. He had gotten off the train at Enid, Oklahoma, literally in the shadow of the world's tallest grain elevator. He had joined a crowd of other bindlestiffs, high class hobos who had bought seats on real passenger trains and rode to the start of the spring wheat harvest, along with steam engineers and separator men and here and there a salesman from J. I. Case or Minneapolis Moline or International Harvester. They came on the AT&SF or the Rock Island Line or the Soo, or any of a dozen lesser known railroads, and they came ready to go to work, eager to claim their share of the enormous wealth that was about to be made from Big Wheat.

Also arriving on the trains were custom threshing contractors and their equipment. They normally owned a steam traction engine and a threshing machine and sometimes a cook shack or a traveling bunkhouse, and they would organize and supervise the coming operation, bankroll the crew, and scout out the advance bookings, so machines and men never sat idle. They never actually got their hands dirty, though they could do any job on the threshing crew, including working somebody else's horses. They had once done all such jobs, but now they were brokers and organizers, pure and simple, and proud of it. They traveled with a leather satchel, typically, and wore a three-piece suit. The satchel carried contracts, cash, and a large revolver. The vest for the suit would also hold at least one Derringer and probably a knife. And for reasons nobody ever figured out, they all seemed to wear bowler hats, even on the threshing field. By the time the mixed passenger and freight trains got to Enid, they had often already hired the full crew that would be with them for the rest of the summer.

Some workers who showed themselves to be prone to drinking or gambling or fighting during the train trip would be fired before the work of the year even began. Those who survived the scrutiny of the watchful broker would be given a ten dollar gold piece as earnest money, to seal their unwritten contracts. And any who thought to take the gold and then run off to join another crew would find themselves seriously regretting it. Machines weren't the only things that could injure or maim.

The Windmill Man had taken the gold on his first trip from Topeka. And he had looked at the three-piece suit and the bowler hat of the man who gave it to him and thought that the wearer was a fool, because he didn't make any effort to hide his power or his wealth. At that point in his career, the Windmill Man was fairly new at killing, and he hadn't yet discovered his true vocation, but he was an old hand at power games. He wore a slouch hat and a razor on a shoestring around his neck and rough work clothes that nobody would envy or even notice. And he found some large or small way to manipulate every single person he met, including the threshing contractor.

Every year, the start of the harvest was the start of a new world and a new life. The hobos and entrepreneurs getting off the train in Enid could just as well have come from another continent or another planet, for all the traceable past any of them had. They told stories of being from Alaska or Montreal or Spain or the North Pole, and their credentials were their straight faces and stories that didn't contradict themselves. They were from everywhere. They were from nowhere. They were chaff from last years harvest, and at the end of the season, they would become chaff again. The Windmill Man couldn't remember a life before the life of the moving harvest. In any way that mattered, there hadn't been one.

Early in that first season, he saw two bindlestiffs get into a fight over who got which job. One of them took a pitchfork and stabbed the other man several times in the belly, killing him. The killer ran away, and nobody chased him. That night, after the work was over, they buried the dead man in the farmer's field, "just deep enough so the plows won't disturb him." Nobody knew if he had any family, and there were no words said over the grave. The next day, it rained all day. And though he couldn't quite put it in words yet, the Windmill Man thought the whole incident, including the rain, was some kind of divine omen. He began to have intimations of being in exactly the right place at exactly the right time to achieve something great, something that would last forever. He began to feel his value.

He worked the entire harvest that year and killed and buried six people, including the contractor who had originally hired him. The following year, he had enough money to be able to follow the harvest without actually doing any of the work, and his body count went up considerably.

He couldn't remember what he did in the winter.

◇◇◇

The Windmill Man sat in the church reading room with his much-folded and wrinkled survey map of the Dakota territories and his pens and bottles of ink. As he reviewed the summer's issues of the newspapers, he made notes on the map, alternately in red or black ink.

MAN FALLS INTO BUNDLE CUTTER, BLEEDS TO DEATH. That was around the town of Norwich. That was good. Death by bleeding was good for at least a fifty-mile circle.

ESTRANGED HUSBAND STRANGLES WIFE. Not as good as bleeding, but still maybe valid, if the warring couple farmed the land. But no such luck. It turned out he was a shoe salesman and she was a seamstress, both from Minot. No good. The land around Minot still needed redeeming.

EXPLODING STEAM ENGINE KILLS THREE. Now he was getting somewhere. He dipped his pen in the red ink and drew a large circle with the town of Sawyer at its center.

He worked through the afternoon and into the evening. But he found his usual concentration flagging. Again and again, his eyes would drift away from the newspaper article he was reading and over to his map, where he had drawn a red circle around Hazen. Things were just not right in Hazen. He had done some of his best work there, had found a perfect subject. But the more he thought about the young man with the shock of light hair, the more he found the memory intolerable. It had been a huge mistake, letting the man live. He was sure of it. It was nothing less than a blot on his map, a stain on the log of his vocation. It was an ulcer on his soul. The man simply had to die.

But the man had a pack and looked like he was dressed for travel. He probably wouldn't still be in Mercer County any more than was the Windmill Man. So what was the best way to find him? Much as he hated it, he would have to wait for providence to show him. Meanwhile, there was other work to do. And more and more, the town of Minot seemed to beckon to him. Soon it would be time to kill the minister and go there.

Chapter Twelve
Ararat

After the incident at the creek, Jim Avery allowed Stringbean Moe to get his arm splinted and put in a sling by Jude the Mystic, but then he told him to clear out and not come back.

"But I can't work!"

"You were never too partial to it in the first place, as I recall. Anyway, you should have thought of that before you attacked my people."

"It was them attacked me! That little Limey bitch is crazy. I didn't do nothing, I tell you."

"Tell it to the marines, Stringbean. If I still see you here tomorrow, I'll personally break your other arm for you."

Moe spat, but not on Avery, kicked at the dirt, and sullenly walked away. Half under his breath, he said, "When I come back, somebody's going to be damn sorry."

"That's the second bad idea you've had today. Keep walking."

He did.

◇◇◇

Despite Charlie's initial failure as a bodyguard, Emily continued to let him stand watch while she took her morning bath. And if she was aware that he occasionally stole a guilty peek at her, she chose to ignore it. That and sharing breakfast soon turned into a daily ritual, though the conversation was often a bit on the edgy side. Charlie thought she felt safe with him because she knew he owed her for the incident with Stringbean. Whatever the reason, he was glad to have her to talk to.

One morning the breakfast was sausages, scrambled eggs, and cornbread with butter and honey. Charlie had never had real honey before, and he managed to make a sticky mess of his hands. Emily gave him her cornbread, saying that only in America did people think corn was fit for making bread.

"So why are you here, instead of someplace more civilized?"

"I don't know that you're ready for that story yet." She got a faraway look for a moment, then visibly shook it off. "What about you? What brings you out to the wild and lawless plains?"

"I guess you'd say I'm a voluntary orphan."

She gave him a raised eyebrow and cocked her head.

"My father is a mean drunk and a bully. I told him off, stabbed him in the hand with a carving knife, and left. I can't ever go back there." He wiped his hands on a wet napkin, but when he picked up his knife, his hand got sticky all over again. He decided the honey must be able to spread of its own volition.

"Well, don't let it bother you too much. Sometimes an orphan is not the worst thing in the world to be. In fact, sometimes it's the only thing."

"Are you one?"

She nodded. "Also voluntary." She got the faraway look again and sighed. "It was my father gave me the scar."

"Oh, my God."

"I was fourteen at the time. He said if I wouldn't give him and a few of his friends my crumpet, he'd fix me so nobody else would ever want me, either."

"Your crumpet? You can't mean…"

She nodded.

"Oh, my dear, sweet God."

"See, Charlie? I was right; you weren't ready for that. You're turning pale."

"Well, that's a hell of a thing to hear. I'm so sorry for you."

"Why?"

"Why? Because it's a terrible thing to do to somebody, especially your own child. And you could have been really pretty, too."

"Well, thank you so bloody much! You can tell that, can you, even looking at my bad side? I hope looking at me doesn't hurt your eyes too much."

"I didn't mean that the way it came out. I mean, you're something other than pretty, you're, um… Oh, hell, I guess I don't know what I mean. You're a fine person, even if—"

"Right; even if I'm ugly as a festering sore. Well, look on the bright side. It's kept me from a life of whoring, hasn't it? Paying customers want tip top goods."

"They do?"

"Well, you do, don't you?"

"Me? No. I mean, sure, but I don't go to, um…"

"God, you blush easily, too. Are you a virgin, Charlie?"

"Hell, no! I'll have you know I'm going to be a father."

"Really? When?"

"I'm not sure. Sometime in the spring, I think."

"So are we finally getting the real reason you left home? Did you knock up your girl and then panic and run away? Is that the kind of man you are, Charlie? Did you break her heart?"

"To tell the truth, she broke mine." He looked down at the table and spoke very quietly.

"Oh." Her expression suddenly softened. "I'm sorry. What happened?"

"She threw me over for a rich farmer."

"Ah. She likes the rich ones, does she? Well, then you don't want her. You only think you do."

"That's funny."

"Oh, I'm a riot when I get started, besides being *almost* pretty. You should hear me sing 'The Frozen Logger.'" The edge was back in her voice now, and she pushed on the table, as if she were about to leave.

"No, I meant it's odd. You're the second person who's told me that."

"Well, that's probably because it's obvious to everyone but you. They can tell that she's shallow and selfish. Vain, too, I'll bet.

"You don't even know her."

"Oh yes I do. But you don't." Her voice was much louder now, almost strident, and he wondered why.

"I think she just never realized how much I love her."

"*Still?* Why? Just because she's *pretty?*"

"Just listen, can't you? When she figures it out, and when she sees what an idiot her new husband is, she'll take the child and come looking for me."

"If you believe that, you're either round the bloody bend or just plain stupid."

"Now you sound like my father. She's—"

"She's a velvet nut cracker, you idiot. She probably kicks dogs when nobody's looking, too." She was practically shouting now, and people in the tent turned to stare. "And I'll tell you something else, mister wronged lover: the difference between you and me is that my scars show. But you let some mindless bit of fluff cut a huge piece out of your soul, and you're still trying to stuff the same failed hopes back in the same spot. It won't work." She slammed her coffee cup down on the table and got up to leave.

"Are you done now?"

"Yes."

"Well, I thank you for the corn bread, anyway."

"Choke on it."

As she turned away, he thought he could see tears running down her cheeks.

◇◇◇

Besides Maggie Mae the mute and Emily of the secret last name, there was one other woman attached to the Ark, a tall, willowy thirtyish slip of a thing with a sharp nose and blond hair that she cut short. She didn't look like a farmwoman, exactly, but she looked strong, if not too bright. She was called Nadine, and she seemed to do less of the work than the others and spent a lot of time going off into the bushes with the customers who were waiting for their repairs. Sometimes she went off with them in their trucks or cars. He didn't know for a fact that she was whoring, and he didn't figure it was any of his business anyway. But that was certainly what it looked like. He tried not to think about that, not caring much for the idea of living with a bunch of moral reprobates. And he couldn't stand the idea that Emily might also be selling herself, even though she had just told him otherwise. If she traveled with one, mightn't she also become one? It was all very troubling, and realizing that it was none of his business in the first place didn't help in the slightest.

Maggie Mae seemed to be a bookkeeper of sorts, and the keeper of the communal money. And there was no doubt that the Ark, whatever else it might be, was a commune. Whoever went into some town for groceries or supplies, she always went along. Charlie had heard somewhere that people with disabilities often had heightened talents in other areas, sort of by way of God making up for his own mistakes. He wondered if she might be a secret financial genius.

Whether she was or not, it was obvious that she was Avery's woman, completely. She lit up in his presence, and she hung on him shamelessly when he returned from some errand. The two of them lived together in one end of the biggest trailer. The other end of it was more a sort of bunkhouse, with a changing set of occupants. Jude the Mystic, the almost-vet, with wild hair and bottle-thick glasses slept there, as did Stump, the general roustabout whose name was also his description, and one or two other hangers on. Nadine seemed to sleep in a small tent, at least some of the time.

"I'm never sure how many I've got at any given time," said Avery. "Some of them help with the heavy repairs and the tents and such and some are just hanging around until they find a slot on one of the regular threshing crews. If they're not customers and they're here at mealtime, we mostly feed them, is all I know. As long as they do some kind of useful work and don't molest the women, I let them drift along. They're not really part of the family, though."

"The family?"

"That's right. Make no mistake about it, the Ark is my family in every way that matters."

Charlie wondered what he would have to do to be adopted by this strange family. But he kept his thoughts to himself, and Avery said no more about it.

"And food is cheap here in the farm country, of course. If you can't get rich fixing steam engines, you can at least eat good."

Hearing that, Charlie thought maybe he should have taken a couple of hams, as well as the side of bacon, from the farmer who tried to cheat him. He hadn't realized he was letting the man off easy. But he had other things to think about.

◇◇◇

The Ark had no shortage of work. Charlie found that he could weld reasonably well but not very fast and could use a lathe or a milling machine quite adequately. But he had an absolute gift for braising. He knew instinctively and unerringly when the metal was hot enough to draw the molten braise, and he never used too much or too little. It wasn't teaching him anything about steam engines, of course, but it was good to feel the new competence, all the same.

The work went on through most days and often into the night. Brass valves or regulators on steam engines got smashed or jammed, drive belts had to be re-spliced because they no longer ran true and would wander off the pulley, reapers tried to mow rocks and ruined their cutting teeth or their drive gears, and separators broke their concaves or their drums when something other than wheat was thrown into the works. And there were also farmers or steam engineers who wanted to modify their machines, to make them better or more specialized or just more personal. They paid premium price when the customizing machinist made house calls.

Charlie made a lot of house calls. He loved not being tied full time to one machine or one operation and he loved the challenge of figuring out why a machine did not do what it was supposed to or did not do anything at all. He didn't usually know what the man thought of him, but he was determined not to make Avery sorry he had taken him on. And at some level, he was starting to know his own worth. He mattered. Machines spoke to him. They told him all their problems, even the problems that had not emerged yet.

And like the preachers of the Wheat Belt evangelist circuit, he healed them by the laying on of hands.

His ongoing challenge was a cast iron bevel gear for a Pitman driver, from one of the many reapers that were everywhere on the prairie. It had several teeth broken off it.

"Defective casting," Avery had said. "So tell me, mister apprentice, how would you go about fixing it?"

"Do we have the pieces of the teeth?"

"No, but if we did, we probably wouldn't want to put them back on. If they broke once, they're most likely faulty iron, and they'd break again."

"Well, then, if we have the right setup, the best thing would be to make a mold, using this one for a pattern, and cast a whole new gear."

"You're right, that would be the best thing. The closest places you could get the right kind of crucible steel and a big enough retort to melt it in would be Kansas City or St. Paul. And if you were there, you could just go to a McCormick dealer and buy a new gear."

"Oh."

"So, what else can you think of?"

"Nothing. I can't think of another thing to try."

"Well, let me know when you figure it out." He tossed the broken gear into a drawer on the workbench and turned to some other job. "There's no customer waiting for that one. Take it as a training challenge. When you get it fixed, we'll call you a real machinist." The gear gleamed dully from its home in the drawer. Charlie had the distinct feeling that it was mocking him.

◇◇◇

And always, his thoughts drifted back to the question of Emily, the who and the what of her, the mysterious foreign roots and the troubled past. And the short temper. Why was he always saying things that got her upset? He could read crooked farmers easily, but he surely couldn't read her. In fact, he couldn't even read his own feelings about her.

Like most young men, he found the whole business of sex and love highly confusing. "Nice" young women weren't supposed to want sex unless they were in love. Young men, on the other hand, were expected to want sex almost constantly but not to take it too seriously. But in his own experience, it had been Mabel who had seduced him, not the other way around, and she was as "nice" and respectable as any woman he could imagine. And he had taken the experience very seriously indeed, while she seemed to be almost casual about it. Was there something wrong with both of them? And now, if he secretly lusted after Emily, did that mean he was being unfaithful to Mabel, even though she had said she didn't love him?

He realized with some surprise that he did want Emily, scars and all. At some level, he even thought he wanted her *because* of her scars, though the idea seemed crazy. Sometimes he imagined he could taste the salt on her skin, could feel her soft touch and the press of her firm thighs and belly. Then he would snap out of his reverie and feel slightly ashamed of himself. But if she really was a whore, despite her denial, or maybe just a "loose woman," whatever that meant, he did not want casual sex with her. He wanted something different, and he wasn't even sure if he could give it a name.

"Why don't you just get her name tattooed on your forehead," said Avery, one day in the machine shop, "so there's no chance she'll miss what's on your mind?"

"Who?"

"'Who?' he says. Mata Hari, that's who."

"Wasn't she some kind of spy?"

"She was a spy," he said, nodding. "She was also supposed to be one of the most desirable women who ever lived. You probably wouldn't like her as much as Emily, though."

"Then why mention her in the first place?"

"Fix that goddamn bevel gear, will you?"

"Listen, Jim, I have to ask you something. Is Emily, um, I mean…?"

"Why don't you ask her?"

"I did."

"Then believe what she told you. You should let people be who they say they can be."

"You can't be serious."

"Sure I am. I let you, didn't I?"

"Me? It's not like I lied to you, you know."

"You would have. You just didn't need to."

He had nothing to say to that. To get the life he had now, he would have been willing to lie, at that. But if that should tell him how to feel about Emily or how to treat her, it did not.

Chapter Thirteen
The Road to Minot

The next day, the café-tent smelled of bacon grease, toast, onions, and coffee. The first nip of real autumn was in the air. Plates of scrambled eggs and fried potatoes steamed on the tables, and cups of coffee cooled too fast. Charlie and Emily had tacitly agreed to avoid topics like scars, sex, and romance, and they were having a cordial if cautious conversation.

"Do you have any brothers or sisters back home, Charlie Bacon?"

"I have a sister, Ruthie, who's still there. I worry about her sometimes. And I had an older brother, Rob, but he died in France, in the World War."

"What on earth was he doing over there? I thought farmers were exempt from the draft."

"They were. But he was dead set on going. He volunteered, and nobody could talk him out of it."

"Ah."

"Ah again? What does that mean?"

"Oh, Charlie, you really can't read people at all, can you?"

"I have no idea what you're talking about."

"Think about it. Did you leave home because you wanted to go off and kill Germans or contract some horrible disease from a French prostitute?"

"Why are you always talking about prostitutes?"

"Did you, or not?"

"Of course not. I already told you—"

"Then why do you think he did?" She held up a palm in a gesture that said, "Is this obvious, or what?"

"My god, do you seriously mean…?"

"Pull it out, Charlie. Reach deep."

"You mean he joined the Army just to get away from my father?"

"More, I expect."

"More?" He had no idea what she was fishing for.

"I'm thinking he also left so you could inherit the farm. Or maybe so your sister could."

"But surely he wanted it?"

"No, he didn't. Come on now, you're almost there."

"He didn't want it because my father wanted him to have it?" And he nodded solemnly, as the truth of it began to wash over him.

"Hey, daybreak, after all!"

"And he thought I should feel the same way about it, didn't he?" Suddenly his dream made perfect sense. His brother wasn't beckoning to Charlie to come and join the war, he was just telling him to get out of where they had both grown up, no matter what it took. And he had done that, finally. He believed his brother would have approved. But he had also left his sister and mother defenseless.

"See? That wasn't so far to go, after all, was it?"

"For me, it was. You're an awfully smart woman, Emily. And you're right; I really can't read people at all." He got up from the table, leaving his breakfast unfinished.

"Where are you going? You're not mad, are you?"

"No. I have to go find Jim and tell him I need to leave for a few days."

"*Now?*"

He nodded. "I should have done it sooner, but I forgot for a while. I have to see if there's a letter waiting for me in Minot." Silently, he prayed that there was not.

"From your precious twit of a girlfriend? Trust me; there isn't."

"No, from my sister."

"Oh, really? I think I'd like to see that."

"Okay."

She got up from the table with him. "I'll pack you some food to take. Ask Avery if you can borrow the Indian motorcycle. It'll be faster, and he'll be wanting you back right away."

"I've never driven a bike."

"Can you ride a horse?"

"Sure. Everybody who grew up on a farm can ride a horse."

"Well, a bike is easier. It doesn't care which way you point it."

"Unlike some people."

"Unlike a lot of people. You better not be lying to me about where you're going, though, Charlie, or you'll find out where the saying, 'Hell hath no fury' comes from."

"Excuse me? Do I owe you something?"

"Apparently not."

◇◇◇

Avery showed him how to work the controls on the Indian motorcycle, where to put the gas and oil, how to set the kick-stand, and how to fix it if it threw a chain or a tire.

"Retard the spark at least three degrees to start it. Kick it over slow once or twice, with the ignition off, and listen to the tailpipe. When you can hear that you're in an exhaust stroke, fire it up for real. If you don't wait for that, it can backfire and break your leg."

"Emily was right; it's not like a horse. It's like a mule."

"It's just as temperamental, anyway. This gizmo here," he pointed to a handle near the front of the tank, "is the manual oil pump. Give it a shot every now and then."

"Every now and then?"

"If you're blowing blue smoke out the pipe, you're doing it too often. That doesn't hurt anything; it just uses a lot of oil. If the motor starts to sound like somebody is shaking a tin can with rocks in it, you aren't doing it often enough. Do that long enough, and you'll burn up the bearings. You'll get a feel for it quick enough.

"This is Indian's Powerplus V-twin model. Sixty-one cubic inches. She's five years old now, but she'll still do an honest sixty miles an hour on a hard road. Don't try it in soft dirt, though, or she'll get real unforgiving, real fast. It's a good idea to take it out in some grassy field or soft sand and deliberately dump it at low speed a couple of times, just to teach yourself what it feels like when you're on the verge of losing control. You can get a hell of a lot of speed out of this baby if you learn how to keep it just below that point. You want a demonstration?"

"Thanks Jim, but I think I can handle it."

"Why doesn't that surprise me? You always did prefer to learn by doing, didn't you?"

"Seems to be the only way I know, yes."

"I don't suppose you'd care to tell me what it is you have to do in Minot?"

"Not really."

"Fine, then. Just remember how to find your way back."

"Thank you for saying that. I will."

"There's a snap-brim hat and a pair of goggles in the saddle bag. You'll want to wear them. You'll get bugs in your teeth anyway, but at least you won't go blind. Wear the hat backwards, like Barney Oldfield, or it'll blow off."

He put on hat and goggles, kicked the starter pedal five or six times, and drove off the stand. As Avery stood and watched him fade into the distance, Stump came up beside him and watched, as well.

"You figure he'll come back, or just take the bike and keep on going?"

"He's one of us now. He'll be back."

◇◇◇

Some forty miles to the north and west, Amos Hollander read the telegram from his deputy, back in Beulah.

FARMERS NEAR BOYSEN PLACE SAW NOTHING STOP POSTMASTER IN HAZEN SAYS KRUEGERS SISTER SENT HIM A LETTER TO MINOT FOUR DAYS AGO STOP COUNTY BOARD

NOW OFFERS 50D REWARD BUT ONLY FOR CONVICTION
STOP

He was impressed. All those years, he had seriously believed Tom was a hopeless idiot. He obviously still hadn't grasped the art of composing messages for a sender who charged by the letter, but he had done a good enough job of investigating that Hollander forgave him that minor shortcoming. He composed a reply on a Western Union form and gave it to the telegraph operator: GOOD WORK DON'T STOP.

"But that doesn't make sense, sir. See, the way it works is—"

"Your trouble, boy, is that you have no sense of humor."

"No, sir. But still—"

"Just send it." He walked out of the office humming a little tune.

◇◇◇

Charlie got the hang of riding easily enough. As Avery had suggested, he took the Indian out in an unfenced pasture and deliberately skidded it out a few times. He also taught himself to do a crude power slide, which he had read about in a *Popular Mechanics* but had never seen. He found that the Indian had an amazing amount of accelerating power, as long as he paid attention to his spark setting. But on the rough and rutted country roads, it still took him over four hours to get to Highway 83, a raised, Macadamized highway that ran straight into the heart of Minot. Darkness was falling before he had the city in sight, and he went off on a side road and made camp for the night at the edge of a cornfield. He picked the ears off three cornstalks and laid them in a neat pile for the unknown farmer to find. Then he made a campfire with the dried stalks and leaves. It wasn't as good as the wood in the Turtle Mountains, but it was enough to heat a can of beans and roast a coarse sausage link. He pitched his tent and went to bed. He slept fitfully, dreaming of riding the Indian at breakneck speed, pursued by a strange, black, swirling cloud.

Chapter Fourteen
Mail

A sign at the outskirts of Minot proclaimed that it now boasted a population of over nine thousand souls, making it the biggest city Charlie had ever seen. As he got near the center of town, he saw buildings of four and even five stories, and he felt that he was riding through a man made canyon. He found the effect strangely exhilarating. Downtown, he found a Red Crown service station on a corner next to a Ford dealership, and he filled up the gas and oil tanks on the Indian and asked directions to the main post office.

"Ain't got but one'" said the attendant, and he directed him down a wide street called Central Avenue. It paralleled a set of several railroad tracks that neatly divided the city into a north and south side, and it was easy to see that the north side was the "wrong side of the tracks." Crooked, often unpaved streets were lined with saloons, gambling halls, and seedy-looking two-story hotels. Behind them were as many tarpaper shacks as real houses, and the people on the streets looked dirty and tough. The south side of Central Avenue could have been a different country. Streets were paved with granite cobblestones, buildings were stately and large, and both the place and the people looked prosperous and respectable. Charlie went five more blocks west, turned left, and crossed Main Street. Two blocks later, he was at the building he sought.

The post office was a large, important-looking building of smooth gray stone, in the Federal style, with fluted columns on the façade and a grand staircase up to the main entry, which was half a level above the street. There was a real concrete sidewalk leading to it and real curbstones along the street, something Charlie had never seen in Hazen or even Beulah. He nosed the bike into the curb, then turned it around, facing out, and put it up on the kickstand. He pulled his goggles down around his neck but left the hat where it was.

Parked next to the bike was a Model T pickup, which caught his eye because it was painted brown. He had never seen a Model T painted anything but black before. Henry Ford himself had supposedly once said, "People can have them any color they want, as long as it's black." When he looked closer, he saw a gold star painted on the door, and the title MERCER COUNTY SHERIFF.

He had never met the sheriff back home, but he was intrigued that someone else had come all the way from there to the big city of Minot. If the man was inside, he thought he would introduce himself and see if there was any news from Hazen.

Inside, the building looked like a big bank, except that half of the back wall was covered entirely with locked brass letter-boxes with tiny glass windows in them. The other half had a high marble counter with tellers' windows, each with its own polished brass security grille. At the one farthest from the entry, a square, solidly built man with a tan uniform and a pistol in a holster was busy chatting up a pretty redheaded teller with thick glasses. If that was the Mercer Sheriff, Charlie guessed he didn't want to be bothered just then.

Opposite the tellers, along the wall with the main entry, were raised writing stands. At one of them, a boy of about ten was carefully placing a stamp on a big brown envelope. On the wall behind him, a big cork bulletin board displayed various postal regulations and public service announcements. It also displayed the flier with Charlie's picture and the bold headline HAVE YOU SEEN THIS MAN?

His jaw dropped. As he got closer and could read the finer print, it dropped farther. He was a wanted man! At a quick scan of the text, though, he couldn't quite figure out for what. He turned his back to the lawman and the teller in the far corner and leaned over to talk quietly to the boy with the envelope.

"Hey, kid."

"Hey, yourself, mister. I don't talk to strangers."

"Sure you do. There's four bits in it for you."

"I don—for true?"

"Cross my heart." Which he did.

"Okay, maybe. Who do I got to kill?"

"Nobody. Go over to the window that says general delivery and ask—"

"Which one is that?"

"Not the closest one, but the one right after it, okay? Go over there and ask the teller if there's a letter for Charlie Krueger. Can you remember that?"

"Sure. I'm a smart kid."

"Say it."

"A letter for Charlie Krueger."

"Okay. You are a smart kid. If the teller asks you to prove it's for you, say you don't have anything on paper, but you know the return address on the letter. It's Ruth Krueger, Rural Route 16, Hazen."

"That's a lot of stuff to remember. How come you don't just get it yourself?"

"For fifty cents, what do you care? Think of Ruth in the Bible."

"We don't do much Bible in our house. What's a turn, um, dress?"

"Return address. Like you've got on that envelope of yours, in the left corner, see?"

"Oh, the send-it-back."

"If that's what you can remember, fine. So you've got three things to remember: You're Charlie Krueger, the letter will be from Ruth, and she's at Rural Route 16 in Hazen. Say it back to me."

He made the boy repeat it three times and them gave him a quarter.

"When you get the letter, go straight outside with it. I'll be sitting on a motorcycle out front, and I'll give you the other quarter."

"Wow, a real motorcycle? Can I have a ride?"

"Sure."

"What if there isn't any letter?'

"You still get the two bits, but no ride."

"Okay, here I go!"

Charlie stole a quick glance back to the far teller's window and saw that the law was still busy dallying. The teller was now idly twisting a lock of her hair around an index finger and smiling as she batted her eyelashes. As quietly as he could, he pulled the flier off the bulletin board and headed for the side exit. He forced himself to walk normally, but he held his breath. The kid was already at the general delivery window, and he wasn't pointing back at Charlie.

"Sir?"

The voice came from behind him, and it sounded like an older woman than the one the sheriff was flirting with. He ignored it and kept walking.

"Sir? You can't take things from the bulletin board, sir."

He kept walking.

"You just stop right there, sir!"

He did not. As soon as the exit door closed behind him, he stuck the flier in his back pocket and ran as fast as he could to the bike. He kicked the engine into life, put his goggles back over his eyes and held his breath again. Nobody was following him yet. On a sudden inspiration, he left the bike up on its stand, motor idling with its signature pop-pop sound, and ran over to the official Mercer County pickup. He lifted the hood on the driver's side and yanked the main ignition wire off the magneto, stuffing it in a pocket. He closed the hood again, went back to the bike, and rolled it off the stand, ready to go. Then he forced himself to wait.

After an eternity of white knuckles on the handlebars, he saw the boy come out the main door. He squinted in the bright sunlight for another eternity, then finally spotted Charlie and came trotting over to him. He had a white envelope in his hand.

"Four bits, mister!"

"You already got two," said Charlie. He handed him another quarter and took the envelope.

"And a ride! You said!"

"A promise is a promise. Hop on, but be quick about it."

The boy eagerly jumped up on the passenger seat, Charlie gunned the motor, and they were off. As they cleared the parking lane, the door of the post office flew open and the lawman came running out, gun drawn.

"Stop or I'll shoot!" he shouted, taking a two-handed marksman's stance.

"Will he really?" said the kid.

"Beats me," said Charlie, and he opened the throttle as far as it would go. Almost immediately, he heard six gunshots behind him. Two of them ricocheted off cobblestones ahead of them. He had no idea where the rest of them went. He kept the throttle open. But there were no more shots and nobody was following him. Half a mile later, he slowed to a more reasonable in-town speed and started obeying traffic signs again.

"So, where do you want to go, kid?"

"Um. I think this will do fine right here, mister, if it's all the same to you."

He jumped off the bike without waiting for it to stop. Charlie hit the brakes and looked back. When he could see that the kid was getting up, apparently unharmed, he kept going. He didn't stop until he was five miles out of town. He took a gravel side road until he was out of sight of the Macadamized highway, parked in a little grove of poplars around a windmill, and allowed himself to breathe normally again.

Then he read the letter from his sister.

Dear Charlie,

I hope your travels have been kind to you and this letter finds you well. I have terrible news, I'm afraid. Or mixed news, anyway.

First, you don't have to worry about our father hurting Mother or me. He died two days ago. We think he was beating the horses out in the barn, and one of them, probably old Barney, kicked him to death. He lived for a day or so after that, but there was nothing Dr. Curtin could do. He had too many internal injuries. I know it's wrong of me, but I did not cry.

So the farm is yours now, if you want it. But you can't come home to claim it. Maybe you can't come home ever again. Somebody has murdered poor Mabel Boysen. I know that you loved her, and I can imagine what a shock that must be to you. But because you left right after she died, everybody thinks you did it. The sheriff is out there somewhere now, hunting for you. If he catches you, I do not believe you will get a fair trial.

So keep moving, wherever you are, and don't talk to any law officers. Remember that we love you, and if you never come back, we will understand. Maybe I will try to send another letter to you, at general delivery in Winnipeg, if they have post offices there. You might think about turning Canadian.

Be brave and be well.

> *Your loving sister*
> *Ruth*

He read the letter three times, feeling waves of sorrow, relief, fear, and shock wash over him. The only easy item to take in was about his father. He felt nothing at all about his father's death, and unlike his sister, he did not feel ashamed of that fact. He had heard it said that a boy never really comes into his manhood until his father dies. If that was true, he should be feeling liberated and empowered, but he didn't even feel that. He didn't feel anything. *Maybe that's because I never really had a father in the first place*, he thought.

His beloved Mabel, even if she wasn't his anymore, was a different matter. He had a lot of feelings about her death, most of them very confused. *I've lost her twice now*, he thought, *and this time, it's permanent.* Who would do such a thing? Killing a beautiful young woman who was also pregnant was beyond evil. It was unthinkable. It was a huge tragedy and a personal hurt, and it made him angry and sad at the same time. But at some level, he also began to think that it meant the end, finally, of an entire chapter of his life. There would be no more waiting for her to have a change of heart, no more agonizing over what he ought to do differently. The disaster of his first love affair was over, through no fault of his. Did he dare call that a relief?

And he was wanted by the law. Oh my, oh my, oh my.

He kicked over the motor on the Indian and headed back south and east, toward the Ark. He kept to the gravel roads and country lanes, avoiding all other traffic. As he rode, he thought about the possibly endless trip ahead of him. There was not only no reason to go back to the farm near Hazen now, there was also no possibility that he could, ever. And if he told Jim Avery the truth, he probably couldn't stay at his newfound second home, either. After he returned the borrowed Indian, he would surely be told to leave. And what the hell did he know about being a fugitive? He had only just learned how to be a bindlestiff. And as footloose as that role was, somehow the law had found him anyway.

He didn't know what to do about any of it. But he just bet he knew someone who would. If his choices were bitter, she wouldn't sugarcoat them, but she would know what to do. He decided not to stop for the dark.

Chapter Fifteen
Sanctuary

Charlie rode all night. But the single headlight on the Indian was about as effective on the dark road as a candle lantern, and he didn't dare go very fast. It was past dawn when he found the Ark again and parked beside the machine shop. He put the goggles and hat back in the saddlebag and headed for the mess tent, where he poured himself a cup of coffee and sat down to read the letter again. He was still trying to grasp the enormity of it when Jim Avery came up behind him.

"So how'd the Indian treat you?"

"Didn't see him," he said, not looking up.

"Huh?"

He looked up, his concentration broken. "Oh, you mean the bike. Fine; no problem. She's a real thoroughbred."

"That she is. But you seem to have left your wits on the far side of nowhere. Is there anything you want to tell me about?"

"Something I have to show you, anyway." He sighed deeply and scratched the back of his head, feeling as if he were about to deliver his own execution order. Then he handed Avery both the letter and the flier. "Read the letter first, I think."

"Why don't you read them to me? There's nobody else around to hear." He handed the papers back, and Charlie read both of them aloud. When he read his sister's letter, his voice faltered at several points, but he pushed on to the end. When he read the flier, he sounded more astonished than upset. And when he finished both, he looked up to see that Avery had been studying him intently.

"Well," said Avery. "Not your average trip to the big city, was it? Anybody following you?"

"No. At the post office, I ran into the sheriff from back home, but his pickup wouldn't start, and I got away from him, clean. No way he could tell which way I was headed. And on the way back, I stayed off the main roads."

"His pickup didn't start, huh? I don't suppose it was missing a shear pin, or something?"

"Could have been something like that, yes."

"Did you kill her?"

"Excuse me?"

"The girl, Mabel whatever. I have to know. Did you kill her?"

"No. I swear—"

"Don't swear, just say it."

"All right. The first I knew she was dead was"—he paused to get control of his voice—"when I read my sister's letter. I have no idea who killed her."

"But somebody did. She didn't just walk off a cliff. And whoever did her in must be real happy, about now, that this sheriff is after you."

"I would say that's true."

Avery went and got himself a cup of coffee, then sat down across from Charlie, put an elbow on the table, and buried his chin in his hand for a while. When he spoke again, it was with a different tone.

"Okay, here's what we're going to do. First—"

"I expect you want me to leave. I won't argue with you. But I should go right away. That pickup isn't going to stay broke down forever."

"You talk like a fish, Charlie. You're my people now, and I don't give my people up."

"What else can you do?"

"You ever hear the saying, 'hide in plain sight'?"

"No."

"Well, you're about to do it. Come with me. And bring a folding chair."

Outside, Stump was checking over the Indian, and Avery asked him if he had seen Emily.

"Cook shack, last I saw. Looks like this machine's been through some mighty rough and dirty country."

"You don't know the half of it."

At the cook shack, Emily was washing up the last of the breakfast dishes.

"Let somebody else do that," said Avery. "You go get your bottles and brushes. We need to make Mister Bacon, here, into a different man."

"He been a bad boy, has he?"

"No, but somebody thinks so. We need to make him hard to see."

"I can handle that, right enough." To Charlie, she said, "Take that chair down by the creek and find us a nice sheltered spot to work. I'll meet you there. Here, take a couple of dishtowels with you, too."

He had no idea what they were doing, but he did as told. He picked out a spot by the biggest tree he could find, set up the chair, and sat down to wait. Soon Emily joined him, carrying a small wicker hamper. She seemed to be suppressing a smile, like a poker player who can't quite hide the fact that he had just filled his inside straight.

"I need to talk to you, Emily."

She put down the basket, tied a dishtowel around his neck, like a bib, and began circling around him, peering intently at his hair.

"First the length, then the color."

"What are you talking about? Didn't you hear what I said?" He started to get back up, but she put a hand on his shoulder and pushed him down again. He realized with some surprise that it was the first time she had ever touched him, and he found the touch oddly exciting.

"That shock of hair on your forehead is like a white flag. We change that, and nobody looking for Charlie Bacon will glance twice at you." She produced a comb and scissors from her basket and went to work. "Hold still, will you?"

"I'm not sure I—"

"I am."

"Do you really know what you're doing? I mean, where—"

"I worked in the theater for a while."

"Really? I thought—"

"You've already made it very clear what you thought, Charlie. I didn't go on stage. I was what they call a dresser. I worked with costumes and makeup and hairdos. You'd be amazed what you can do with stage makeup. You can even make somebody like me look like a real woman."

"I never thought you looked like anything else."

"Than what, a dresser?"

"No, a real woman."

"Oh, really? Well, you certainly took your sweet time saying so."

"Well, you said it first: I'm no good at reading people. I guess that means I'm no good at knowing what I should say to them, either."

"Hmm. Well maybe that's not such a bad thing, at that."

"How do you figure?"

"If you don't know any guile, then you're stuck with honesty. Sometimes honesty works, you know."

"Unless you're talking to the law."

"Too bloody right. Or unless I'm trying to tell you I'm not a whore, yes?"

"Excuse me?"

"Being honest didn't help me a bit there, did it?"

"What are you saying? I never called you a liar."

"I could tell you wanted to."

"You could *not* tell, because it wasn't true!"

"I'm the one who can read people, remember? At the very least, you weren't sure about me."

"I might have had a small doubt somewhere, but that's not—"

"Right. So small that you just had to tell somebody else about it?"

"Oh, my God. How did you—"

"Just forget it, Charlie. You had your chance to give me your trust. And fool that I am, I might give you another one. But not today. Will you *please* hold still?"

"I'll try."

She spent a long time cutting his hair, not merely getting rid of the forelock but making the entire style different. "Your neck and shoulders are one big, tense knot," she said as she worked. "Did you get in some trouble in Minot?"

"More like I found out about some trouble I was already in."

"You promised me I could see a letter, I believe."

He wouldn't exactly have called it a promise, but he pulled the letter out of his pocket and handed it over his shoulder to her, all the same. She made no comment on it and he couldn't see her face, so he didn't know what her reaction was. She passed it back to him and went back to her clipping. After a while, she started humming a little tune as she worked.

"That'll do for a first cut," she said, finally. "Now get down on your hands and knees by the creek, with your head hanging over the water."

He did as she said, and she hunkered down next to him and poured creek water on his head with a big enameled saucepan. Her knee and shin pushed up against his ribcage, and she made no effort to move farther away. Her shin felt hot, even through his flannel shirt. She put down the pan, picked up a bar of soap, and worked thick lather into his hair with both hands. She took her time, stroking the strands almost sensually. Or was that his imagination? She let her fingers wander over his neck and the backs of his ears.

"I'm about to transform you completely, Charlie. Have you ever been so totally in a woman's hands before?"

"Not that I can decently talk about."

She gave a surprised little laugh, high-pitched and lilting. "Aren't we the racy one, though?"

"We? You're the one who can't keep her hands to herself."
He grinned. He could no longer tell if she was just lathering his
hair or was deliberately kneading the back of his neck, working
out the knots of tension with skilled, soap-slick hands. But if
she was doing more than necessary, he didn't worry about it.
It was surprisingly easy, being touched by this woman. In fact,
everything was suddenly easy with her. It was as if she made him
real. He had never felt that with Mabel Boysen.

"Close your eyes tight."

He did. She poured a deluge of cold rinse water on his head,
and the soapsuds disappeared downstream. She lathered him
up a second time, more slowly than the first, and the feel of her
hands was again charged and faintly erotic. She rinsed again
and then let him sit back on his haunches to dry his eyes while
she toweled his hair off and applied some kind of dye from an
evil-looking dark glass bottle.

"That looks like poison."

"It probably is, but I wasn't going to ask you to drink it, you
know. Now get back in the chair. We'll do a final cut while the
dye takes."

"Takes?" He went to the chair and sat down.

"That's what I call it, anyway." She combed and snipped,
this time doing a lot more looking than cutting. He saw that
the hairs falling on his dishtowel-bib were pitch black. "You'll
have to touch this up from time to time, but the basic job will
last for months. You'll also have to start using some pomade,
to hold it in its new shape. I'll teach you how to do all that."

She turned her attention to his eyebrows, which she colored
using a toothbrush. Then she took an artist's brush and painted
a pencil moustache on his upper lip. "You'll quit shaving in that
spot, right away. When your real moustache starts to grow out,
we'll do that with the toothbrush, too."

"I can't believe this is happening. Is Jim really meaning to
hide me? He could get in a lot of trouble, doing that."

"He doesn't worry about trouble all that much. He's been in
and out of it all his life. He's an old hand at slipping past the law."

"I hope he's better at it than I am."

"Trust, Charlie. Remember that word?"

"Yes."

"Good. Now, let's have a look at you, and then we'll do a final rinse."

She took off the dishtowel and produced a mirror. He looked at himself from every possible angle. His hair was short enough to reveal a widow's peak, and slicked back on the sides and top. His eyebrows were thick and brooding, and the moustache really looked very believable, from anything more than a couple of feet away. He looked for a long time, scarcely daring to believe his eyes. Looking back at him from the mirror was the exact, unmistakable image of his dead brother.

"You like it?"

"I'll let you know when I get over the shock."

Chapter Sixteen
New Horizons

Avery was greasing a bearing journal on the big Peerless steam engine when Stringbean Moe, still wearing his sling, walked back into camp. Avery wiped his hands on a rag, picked a two-foot crowbar out of the toolbox on the tractor platform, and strode out to meet him.

"I don't give second warnings, Stringbean."

"Now don't go getting yourself all worked up. I got business here."

"No, you don't."

"You seen this?" he asked, holding out one of Sheriff Hollander's fliers.

Avery took it from him, looked at it for a moment, then tore it into pieces and threw it on the ground. "No," he said, "and neither have you."

"I run into some kind of sheriff on the road yesterday. He give it to me."

"And you told him what?"

"Told him I hadn't seen this guy, was all, but I'd be looking out for him. I told him I used to work at this place, and he said as how he'd be heading this way."

"You told him where we are?"

"He'd a found you anyway, I expect."

"But you just couldn't resist helping him, could you? Did he say when he'd be here?"

"A day or so. He had to go to some church first, he says. I could be watching for him, seeing as how I know his rig now. I could warn Bacon, or Krueger, or whoever he is. For the right fee, that is. I figure he's been making some good money, doing all that fancy metal stuff and all. For the right fee, he ain't never been here ay-tall. Or if you fellas druther, I seen him headed south on a fast coal rattler."

"You would do that, would you?"

"Yes, sir, I surely would."

"You would lie to the cops, but only for money, and if you don't get your money, you would rat out a fellow traveler, is that about it?"

"Aw, come on. It ain't such a bad thing as you're making it out to be. Everybody's got to live, don't they?"

"No, not everybody." Avery suddenly had fire in his eyes and an intimidating set to his jaw.

"Jesus man, don't get all riled. I just—"

"Stump!" When there was no immediate response, Avery went over to where the Peerless engine was chugging away at a smooth idle and blew the whistle once, a full ten-second blast. Soon the whole population of the Ark began to gather in a loose circle around the engine, where Avery now stood on top of the boiler, on a wooden catwalk he had installed there.

"This man," he said, pointing at Stringbean, "is a backstabbing fink. He wants to rat one of us out to the law, unless he gets a bribe."

"Hey, it ain't like that!"

"If the skipper says it is, then it is," said someone in the crowd that was now pressing in on him.

"Stump," said Avery, "take this turncoat up in the mountains, as far as the truck will go on one tank of gas. Take his damn razor away from him, tie him to a tree and leave him."

"Hey, I ain't going to—" But Stringbean never got to finish his protestation. Emily, with her arms still wet and a kitchen apron clinging to her front, hit him solidly on the back of the head with a cast iron skillet. It made a lovely, resounding "blong." The man rolled up his eyes briefly, then closed them and collapsed in a heap. Stump picked him up in a fireman's carry and headed for the truck.

Still perched on top of the big engine, Avery began to shout orders.

"All right, pay attention here, please! Fold up the tents, bury the garbage, fill the water tanks, and get everything secured," he said. "I want us hooked up, packed up, and ready to travel in two hours, tops. You know the routine, people. Time to part the Red Sea."

Chapter Seventeen
Providence

If Sheriff Hollander found the Unitarian church by providence, he was not aware of it. But then, he didn't usually think in those terms. He pulled into the graveled front drive and filled his canteen and the radiator of his official Model T pickup from the church pump and then went up to the big front door. Inside, the man who greeted him had dark hair, wide eyes, and a nose that looked as if it had been broken. His black minister's suit was nicely tailored, but it hung on him like a sack.

"I'm Pastor Ned," he said, extending his hand. "Ned Thorn. How can I help you, sir?"

"Amos Hollander, Pastor." He shifted his leather satchel to his left hand. The pastor's handshake was firm but brief, and Hollander noted that his eyes wandered. "I'm the Mercer County Sheriff."

"Mercer? I'm not even sure I know where that is. You must have come a long way. Come in, please. I have coffee in the kitchen in the basement. I can reheat it in no time."

"I could do with a cup of coffee, all right. Are you sure it's no trouble?"

"On weekdays, I'm glad for the company." He led the sheriff through a door in the side of the nave and down a narrow set of stairs that smelled of floor wax, snuffed candles, and the kind of rat poison that people with no pets or small children put in their pantries. "I live alone these days, you see. What about you? Are you traveling all by yourself?"

"Afraid so. I had a deputy with me, but I had to send him home."

"Oh?"

"Couldn't keep his mouth shut."

"Ah. I'm sure that could be a problem in your line of work."

The kitchen turned out to be small, but it had a full-sized wood stove with an enameled coffee pot on top of it. The pastor put four or five corncobs and some wood shavings into the firebox, added a splash of kerosene from a tin squirt can, and lit it with a Diamond safety match. Then he rummaged in a cupboard until he found a ceramic jar full of sugar cookies. He placed it on a small table, produced plates and cups, and gestured to the lawman to sit.

"So, Sheriff, if you are free to say it, what brings you half way across the state, to my humble church?"

"Half way? I thought you said you didn't know where Mercer County was."

"Um, I don't. Well, not exactly. I was just using a figure of speech."

"Hmm. I'm looking for a traveling machine shop that's supposed to be about thirty miles east of here. But I stopped here because I was told you have a sort of public library."

"More like a reading room, actually, but yes."

"I was hoping I could leave some of these fliers in it. I realize it's not what you would usually find in a church, but it's important that as many people as possible see them." He opened his bag and pulled out a stack of papers.

"May I see?" The pastor took one of the fliers, and his face momentarily froze. "And, ah, what is it you want with this person, exactly, this—let me see—Krueger?"

"He's wanted for questioning in connection with the brutal murder of a young woman. I'd prefer it if you didn't say that to your parishioners, though. I only told it to you because it's important that you don't get any misguided notions about sheltering this man."

"No, no, of course not. Terrible things you deal with, Sheriff."

"Sometimes, yes. You look a little pale, Pastor."

"It will pass, it will pass. I don't often think about murder, you know. Why did you say you're looking for this machine shop, exactly? Does that have something to do with the murder?"

"I guess it wouldn't hurt to tell you, as long as you understand it's in strict confidence."

"Yes. Surely."

"The guy who runs it is named Avery. He sees a lot of vagrant harvest people, so I'm hoping he might have seen my man Krueger. It's also possible that Krueger is traveling with him. I narrowly missed him in Minot yesterday. He had a motorcycle that had some kind of advertising painted on the gas tank."

"Advertising for this machine shop?"

He shrugged. "I wasn't close enough to tell. But stranger coincidences have happened. Anyway, it's the only lead I have right now."

"The coffee should be hot by now, sheriff. Will you take a little something in it?" He moved the two cups to a sideboard, grabbed the pot handle with a heavy towel for protection, and poured. His back was to Hollander.

"I drink it black, thank you."

"I meant a shot of brandy and a bit of sugar. You look like you could use a little bracer."

"Technically, I'm on duty. But then, I've been on duty nonstop now for more days than I care to remember."

"Do I take that as a yes?"

"All right. But just one."

More cupboard doors opened and closed and finally the steaming cups were carried to the table. Hollander took a small sip to test the temperature, and then drained his cup in three long gulps, relishing the sudden jolt from the alcohol, even though he thought it tasted like a pretty poor brand of booze. The sugar helped a bit.

"Providence."

"I beg your pardon, Pastor?"

"Absolutely, unmistakably, the hand of Providence, sheriff. The beauty of it is unbelievable."

"I don't understand."

"You won't need to find this machine shop, after all. The young man you want is in my reading room, upstairs."

"You mean now?"

"Even as we speak."

"Judas Priest, man, why didn't you say so?" He stood up so fast that his chair went skidding across the stone floor behind him. "Show me the way," he said, drawing his revolver. "But once we get there, you stay clear, understand? This is a very dangerous man."

"Just as you say. It's this way."

He led Hollander up the stairs and across the nave to a side door, which was closed. Hollander stumbled on the top step, and when he came to the reading room door and made a shushing gesture with his finger, his movements seemed slow and exaggerated. It occurred to him that he shouldn't have had the alcohol on an empty stomach.

As smoothly as he could, he motioned the pastor out of the way, threw open the door, and rushed inside. There he saw a table and two chairs and shelves with books and newspapers but no Charlie Krueger. Sunlight streamed in through a lace-curtained window and illuminated lazily floating dust motes. The air in the room smelled musty.

"Empty. How long ago did you say he was here?" He holstered his pistol, fumbling with it a little. Then he felt something smooth and cold at his throat. Had the Krueger kid somehow managed to sneak up behind him? He looked down and saw that his shirt was bathed in blood.

"Wha...?" When he tried to talk, he choked.

"Actually, I lied."

Not Krueger, after all. The pastor. But why? Hollander clasped both hands to his neck, but he couldn't stop the blood.

"I was telling the truth, though, when I said that you wouldn't have to bother going to find the machine shop. I'll take care of young Mister Krueger far better than you would have. And you're right; he does have information about the murder of that young woman."

"Y—?" He choked again.

"Me, yes. And he knows, I'm afraid."

Hollander managed to turn around and gape at him.

"But what a wonderful fool you turned out to be. I put rat poison in your coffee, by the way."

Hollander's vision narrowed and everything turned gray. He began to feel very cold.

"It's a little slower than I would have liked, though. I decided not to wait for it. I have a pressing appointment thirty miles east of here, you see. Be sure to say hello to Pastor Ned for me. You'll be meeting him shortly."

Hollander just had time to think *oh, shit*. Then his world went black.

Chapter Eighteen
Pulling Up Stakes

"You're pretty good at bashing people when they're not looking," Charlie said to Emily. "If I didn't know better, I'd think you were a professional killer."

"If you didn't know better? You don't. For all you know, I have a bloodier past than Lizzie Borden."

He shook his head. "I'll never believe it. Even if it was true once, it's not when you're here."

"What, do we have our own private Jesus on the crew, to wash away all my sins?"

"Maybe. Sometimes the only thing we can be is what the people around us are willing to believe in."

"That's a twist, coming from you. Where did you get that notion?"

"From Jim, maybe. Or maybe I just invented it; I don't know."

"Well you don't know what other people believe about me, either," she said.

"I know what I believe. That's enough."

"And what is that?"

"I believe you're some kind of fine woman."

For the first time since he met her, he saw her really smile. It was a smile that took up her whole face. He had never thought of that face as plain, exactly, but at that moment, it was positively radiant.

She sidled up to his shoulder, holding the skillet behind her back, as if to put all weaponry away. She was about to say something into his ear when they were interrupted by Avery.

"You two don't have anything to do besides pat each other on the back? Pretty soon it won't just be the back, either, by the look of it. We've got a caravan to get rolling here, and that's not going to happen by itself."

"Sorry, Boss."

"Don't be sorry, be busy. Emily, I need you in the cook shack, helping get it secured for travel. Charlie, you get the Peerless backed up to take the trailer tongue on the shop, and get the power-takeoff belt stowed. Move like you've got a purpose, people."

Charlie couldn't believe what he had just heard. *Get the Peerless backed up.* He would definitely do that as if he had a purpose, all right. It was the opportunity he'd been dreaming of.

If life around the camp sometimes seemed random and lackadaisical, now the entire group moved like a well-oiled machine, perhaps even thinking of that dreadful pun. Tent poles were pulled out and canvas dropped, hardly hitting the ground before well-practiced hands folded or rolled it up. One man went around pulling tent stakes with a long-handled shovel, a job he had obviously practiced many times. Charlie noted it approvingly as he made his way over to the Peerless engine. He was always interested in seeing new ways to use old tools. His own broken shovel wouldn't have worked for the job, though.

He smiled, thinking of that. How long ago had he left his home of twenty-three years, carrying a broken shovel and an inadequate backpack? Not that long, by the calendar. A lifetime, in other ways. And for somebody who was homeless and orphaned by his own hand, he could be feeling pretty good about it, if it weren't for a few nagging little questions like being wanted for murder.

The wagons and trailers were still in the line they had come to that place in. They had arrived from the west and would therefore leave going east. The caravan could be turned, of course, but it was not a trivial maneuver, and they would get the train cruising smooth and straight before they tried it. They would also cross the nearby county line before they changed direction.

Though the wagons and trailers were already in the proper line, they were not hooked up anymore. The wagon tongues had been disconnected and dropped, so nobody would trip over them, and now they had to be reconnected with great attention and care. Each one carried the load of the entire train behind it, and as they got closer to the traction engine, the strain on the connections was monumental.

Charlie climbed up on the operator's platform on the Peerless and took a quick inventory. He blew the sight glass to be sure of its reading, noting that there was plenty of water over the boiler breaching. The reserve tank behind him could stand topping off, though, and he buttonholed a passing roustabout and asked him to see to it.

"You got it, Boss."

Boss? Wow. What a day this was turning into. He shoveled a little more coal into the firebox, being careful not to add enough to bank the main fire, then cranked the big worm gear that moved the timing assembly from forward to reverse. Then he threw a big lever to disengage the main clutch. It had been driving the power takeoff pulleys on either side of him, mounted up at his shoulder height because the main propulsion gears were using up the space below the boiler, the mark of an "undermounted" machine. One pulley had been running the power shaft in the shop trailer, and when it coasted to a stop, he leaned over and dropped the heavy belt off the pulley, making sure it fell where it would clear the main wheels. Running over your own belt was a famous rookie mistake among engineers. That done, he took a very, very deep breath, engaged the main drive gear, engaged the clutch, and eased open the throttle valve. If the big engine failed to recognize the master's hand, it gave no sign of it. It moved in reverse slowly and smoothly, with a grace that belied its huge size and mass.

The brakes on the Peerless were almost a joke, really only usable for parking, rather than maneuvering. Stopping was done by simply cutting off the power to the wheels. And since all the speeds involved were slow, it worked well enough. It took Charlie three tries to get the engine in just the right spot for hooking up the main hitch, which had a short-coupled chain winch for making the final adjustment. He did it without help or supervision. And just like that, he became a steam engineer. *Easier to learn than sex.* Well, easy anyway.

In an hour and a half, the whole complicated string of people and trailers was ready to roll. Jude the Mystic, the almost vet, usually plied his trade on the Indian bike, but he had it lashed to the side of the cook shack now, and he rode inside with all his medical implements and bottles of potions, making sure they didn't get tossed around. Avery and Maggie Mae climbed up onto the engine platform, and she made a playful tough guy face as he put a striped railroad engineer's cap on her head.

"You did all right, your first time as an engineer, Charlie."

"Thanks. It was—"

"Even if it did take you three tries."

"Um…"

"But now you're demoted to fireman."

"Sure." He grabbed a shovel. "Seems to me everybody is going to an awful lot of trouble on my account."

"Trust me, they like it. It reminds them of when we did it for them. My people are my people, and the Ark is the Ark, and nobody, lawman or anybody else, comes and snatches them. Lest you get to feeling too important, though, it was about time to move anyway."

"Do we know where we're going?"

"I go wherever Maggie Mae tells me."

"And how does she know?"

"I have no idea."

He eased the Peerless ahead slowly, taking up all the slack in the complicated tow. Behind him, wheels groaned, hitches clunked into new positions, and a few items that hadn't been properly secured came crashing down inside trailers. Finally everything was moving at the same speed and in the same direction, and Avery eased open the main throttle.

"Tell me something about this woman who was murdered. Was she your girl?"

"I thought so for a while. Turns out somebody else thought so too, and I'm starting to see that it was maybe a good thing she dropped me when she did. But she's a real charmer, let me tell you. Or was, I guess. She was a woman who was so special that I think even if you had cause to hate her, you'd still love her a little. I think she must have been killed by a total stranger. Nobody who knew her could do it."

"A bindle, you think? A drifter?"

"Who knows?"

"Well, at least one person does. And if it wasn't somebody who knew her, then it's somebody who's still out here, floating around just like we are. I'm thinking we ought to try to find him. Too bad we don't know who to watch for."

"I'd tell you if I knew."

"Maybe you'll think of something. For now, let's settle for making some tracks."

"Well put."

"Shovel some coal, Longfellow."

Avery leaned over the right-hand cleated wheel and looked back along the string of odd shapes lined up behind the engine. At the far end of the string, the woman named Nadine swung a lantern, exactly like the conductor on a train. Avery waved a kerchief in response, and as the Ark picked up speed, she climbed into one of the trailers. Charlie noticed that even though it was still broad daylight, lanterns had been attached to the roofs of all the trailers, as well. Not yet lit, but ready.

Avery checked the same gauges and valves that Charlie had, then opened the throttle still farther and took the train across the land, ignoring all roads. A mile later, he made a sweeping left turn and headed north.

"I notice Stump didn't make it back from his errand with Stringbean yet. How will he know where to find us?"

"He'll know. He always does."

The Peerless could make as much as nine miles an hour, but with such a long string of unsprung carriages behind it, that wasn't a very good idea. They dropped into a steady pace of just over four miles an hour, and they ran for over six hours at that rate. Then they stopped for a meal and a rest break, lit the lanterns, and set out again. This time, they only ran at about three miles an hour. Or so they thought. The Peerless was not designed for road travel and therefore had no speedometer.

Charlie and Maggie Mae led the way, walking out in front with lanterns, thirty yards ahead and on either side of the engine. They picked a route with subtle but important maneuvers around the few rare trees and the somewhat more common ravines, through the endless landscape of wheat stubble and shocked crop.

They had started out on government land, a place where the soil was so poor, nobody had ever applied to own it, even as free homestead property. But soon they were back in working farmland, and they were careful to respect the crops that were mowed and headered or shocked, waiting for the threshers. When they came to a barbed wire fence, they pulled the staples and laid the wire down, then put it back behind themselves. Their trail would still be easy enough to spot, but at least they weren't leaving behind a string of angry farmers.

Sometime after midnight they intersected an east-west gravel road, and Maggie Mae signaled Avery to stop.

"What's she telling you?" said Charlie, back at the engine.

"She's thinking we should turn here, and so am I. The road already has plenty of tracks on it, so ours wouldn't stand out. And the fields are hard packed here, too. If we make a really wide turn, we should be able to get up on the road without leaving much of a trace. As far as anybody can tell, we went north from our last camp and then we vanished. I like it."

"So now we go east or west?"

"West. Toward the Indian nations."

"And into them?"

"Maybe."

"Is that legal?"

"Maybe."

They took half a mile to make the turn onto the road, overshooting first, and then doubling back. On the high, hard surface, they expected few or no obstacles. Jude the Mystic untied the motorcycle and replaced Charlie and Maggie Mae as pathfinder, with an extra lantern strapped to his rear fender. Avery looked back at the trailers from time to time, and once they were tracking smoothly, he took the Peerless up to seven miles an hour. All through the night, the bizarre, oddly lit string of shapes rolled steadily across the black prairie. Charlie shoveled coal into the firebox and wondered if somewhere behind their own swaying lanterns was a pair of dim headlights attached to a brown Model T pickup.

Chapter Nineteen
The Wine Dark Prairie

The Ark continued on through the moonless night, the lanterns on the roofs like a wobbly string of fireflies following each other to some mystical safe haven. Around seven in the morning, the sky behind them began to lighten with the first false dawn. Avery let the caravan roll to a slow stop, stretched his back and arms, and climbed up on the catwalk on top of the boiler. He motioned to Charlie and Maggie Mae to come and join him.

"That's far enough for now," he said. "Time to look for a likely place to stop for a long rest."

They scanned the horizon in all directions. They were still in wheat country, but they had climbed up into more rugged terrain. Already, the land was hard and barren looking, with large areas so gravelly that it was hard to tell the difference between the fields and the road. Mainly, the fields had some stubble from cut wheat. There were no sheaves, though. This was rough, uneven ground, and rough ground was invariably header country. In the dim distance they could see a few of the monstrously big loaf-shaped stacks of cut wheat, drying and ripening and waiting to be threshed.

"Where are we?" said Charlie.

"If you have to ask, that's a good sign. Generally, if you're lost, that means nobody else can find you, either."

"And are we lost?"

"Only sort of. I haven't got a map that goes this far west, but I think we're within a dozen miles of the Indian nations. Lakota, most likely, as if that mattered."

Maggie Mae shook Avery's arm, and when she had his attention, she pointed off to the south, where a cloud of dust was coming their way.

"Should I kill the lanterns?" said Charlie.

"Not much point anymore. We've probably already been seen, and if we haven't, we will be. There's no place to hide out here."

"No cover on the rocky road to Canaan," said Jude the Mystic, who had pulled his bike back by the engine after they stopped. "Want me to go check them out?"

"They'll come to us, soon enough."

"Then maybe I should go break out the artillery and be ready to give some cover while you folks parlay?"

"I didn't hear that, Jude."

"Right you are. You didn't hear it." He disappeared toward the back of the train.

As they watched, the cloud of dust got closer and eventually revealed a dark rectangle at the bottom. The rectangle grew until it turned into a Model T pickup truck with a flatbed box on the back. A man and a woman sat in the front seat. The truck came to a squeaking stop ahead of the big Peerless engine, and the dust cloud continued to move, enveloping it. Ignoring that, the two figures jumped out and went over to the engine.

"Glory be to God," said the man.

"It's a miracle," said the woman. "Just like you said, Pa. It surely is."

"Would either of you folks care to let me in on this conversation," said Avery, "seeing as how this is my machine you seem to be so excited about?"

"You folks been sent here to us by God," said the man.

"In answer to our prayers," said the woman.

"Jesus Christ," said Avery.

"That seems to be who we're talking about, all right," said Charlie.

Maggie Mae made a series of gestures that clearly indicated she thought the new arrivals were crazy.

"I'm Jonas Wick," said the man from the dust cloud, "and this here's my wife, Annie. She's a little goofy with all the God stuff, but don't pay that too much mind. Most of the time, she knows which way is up pretty good."

"I'm Jim Avery, and this is my traveling city. We call it the Ark. Good to meet you, Mr. and Mrs. Wick. I'm afraid you're mistaken about me being sent here by God, though. We have a long trip ahead of us yet. Right now, we're just looking for a place to stop for a day or so. Out of the traffic, if you get my drift." He climbed down off the engine and shook Jonas Wick's hand. When he offered his hand to Mrs. Wick, she crossed herself before taking it.

"Oh ya, ya. I get lots of drifts, not like my crazy wife. You could stay right where you are, on the road, as far as that goes, and you wouldn't see enough *traffic* to wake you up. But better you come to my farm."

"I'm afraid we really can't."

"Oh sure, you can. I got a big barn and two big corncribs with wagon alleys in the middle. You can put all your wagons inside, out of the rain, if you get *my* drift. And they can stay there as long as you want; only then you got to use your big steam engine there to help me get in my crop. I used to have two sons and two daughters, God bless me, and I built up a big spread with them, enough for all of them to take over some day. We used to bring in the whole harvest by hand."

"So why do you need me, then?"

"The two of my boys was damn fools enough to go off to the big war, thought they could look out for each other. One of them's in a hospital, out east. He can breathe okay, long as they don't take the tubes out of him. The other one is buried in the mud in some damn French place called Ye Pray, or something. And then this year, both our daughters died of the influenza. I told Annie she should birth stronger children, but she don't listen to nothing, don't you know?"

"I'm very sorry for you, Mr. Wick."

"Call me Joe. Be sorry some other time. Right now I got five hundred acres of wheat all made up into header stacks, but I got nobody to help me thresh it. My banker, old man Puckett, owns the only steam engine in thirty miles, and he decided not to let me use it this year. He says it's too busy, but it's really because he wants to foreclose on my place."

"That's quite a story, Joe. Can I offer you something to drink before you go?"

"Nope. No time. You and me got to get back."

"Do we, now? Look, your offer sounds just fine, except for one thing: this is not a traveling custom threshing operation. I have a steam engine all right, but I don't have a threshing machine."

"Oh, I got one of them. I got one of the first Gaar-Scotts ever made. Puckett wanted to foreclose on that one time, too, had a contract deputy come and impound it in a big machine shed. But we fooled him. My boys and me snuck over in the dead of the night with a team of six horses, and we stole the thing back. Then we brought in a bumper crop, even though it was a dry year. We could do that, see, because we got a lot of good bottom land."

"Sounds like you also have a lot of scorn for authority."

"It's okay in its place, I guess."

"And where might that be?"

"Back in some town."

Avery smiled. "I might have enough people here to handle that size crop. What's the yield around here, something like fifteen or twenty bushels to the acre?"

"Fifteen for sure, sometimes more. Eight or nine thousand bushels altogether. I'll give you nine cents a bushel for the use of the machine and another hundred or so to split up amongst your crew. That's a nice chunk of money for you. And a good place to hide out, too."

"Not that I said I was looking for one."

"Nope. And not that I heard it, neither."

"Sounds to me like we can work something out," said Avery. "Just exactly where are this big barn and the corn cribs?"

"You just follow Annie in the pickup."

"I can only make about three miles an hour on this kind of ground."

"That's okay. I tell Annie, keep it in low."

"You're not going with her?'

"No, I ride up with you, I think."

"The hell, you say. And why would you do that, exactly?"

"Cause I ain't never rode on a big honker of a steam engine before. Is that okey-dokey?"

"We'll try it that way, anyway."

"Ya, sure, then!" He shook everybody's hand enthusiastically, ran over to talk to his wife who had already gotten back in the pickup, and then ran back to the engine, grinning broadly.

"Here we goes, then!"

"Praise God," said Jude the Mystic. He headed back toward the Indian.

"Ah, you don't gotta say that stuff. That's just for when I'm in front of the old woman."

The dawn was still nothing to brag on, but the Model T had newly wiped-off headlights, and they could see it easily as it turned south. Avery cranked the steel steering wheel into a fifteen-degree turn, and the whole chain of rigs headed around into a broad left arc, finally straightening out on a heading roughly south by southeast. They drove for an hour and ten minutes before the rising sun lit up a cluster of buildings on the horizon.

"Looks like a mountain pretending to be a barn," said Charlie.

"Looks like just what the doctor ordered," said Avery.

"Hey, I'm the only thing resembling a doctor here, and I say it looks like heaven," said Jude the Mystic, now riding his bike alongside the engine.

Maggie Mae gave an unequivocal thumbs-up.

◇◇◇

Later that day, the Windmill Man looked with dismay at the abandoned campsite of the Ark. He had decided not to look for it on the same day he killed Amos Hollander. Instead, he disposed of Hollander's body in the church cistern, where it joined Pastor Ned's, cleaned the floor of the reading room with a rag mop, and spent the rest of the evening altering Hollander's spare uniforms to fit himself and moving provisions from the church pantry to the Mercer County pickup.

How could he have been so stupid?

Even on the hard, dry, autumn ground, the tracks from the big, cleated steel wheels of the traction engine were easy to spot. But there was one set going east and one set going west, and no way to tell which was newer. Which one should he follow? Would Providence forgive his moment of pride and show him the way? He had been given a perfect setup and had frittered it away. Surely, he would be punished for that.

He followed the tracks to the west for a while. They turned north and then went straight into wheat land. The first barbed wire fence they ran under was still intact. Or intact again. That seemed to argue for this being the older set of tracks, since the farmer had had time to repair the fence, which would certainly have been smashed down.

He reversed his course, going back to the campsite by the creek and then east for a few miles. But the tracks in that direction didn't encounter any fences, so he couldn't draw any new conclusions.

He decided to find out just how angry Providence was. He took an empty bottle from the back of the pickup, laid it down on a bit of hard, smooth ground, and spun it, saying, "Show me the way." The bottle whirled, wobbled, and finally came to rest pointing straight south. Damn, damn, damn!

He got back behind the wheel and continued east, cursing himself and fuming with impotent rage.

Chapter Twenty
The Hungry Rooster

Annie Wick led the procession past the house and the other farm buildings, straight to the barn, which now had one side bathed in golden morning sunlight. It wasn't quite the size of a mountain, but it was big. She pulled her own vehicle off to one side, got out, and swung open the twelve-foot high doors.

"You could cut up one of those doors and build three chicken houses," said Charlie. Looking at the looming gable, he thought of a picture he had seen in one of his *Popular Mechanics*, of a Zeppelin hanger.

The barn was built in the classic Midwest manner, with a shed-roofed section on either side of a center bay that had double doors on both ends. Above all that rose a hayloft big enough to put most farmers' houses inside and still have room left over for a flower garden. The open center was a throwback to the pre-machine harvest days, oriented to the prevailing wind.

Before the machines, workers like Charlie and his brother would use the hard floor to flail the wheat, to get it to let go of its wheat berries. Then they would pitch the cleaned straw up into the loft and would open both sets of big doors, letting the wind blow through while they tossed the grain into the air with canvas tarps. Unless it was a dead still day, the chaff would blow away and the clean grain would land back on the tarp, where it could be scooped up and bagged. Then they would bring in a fresh pile of wheat from outside and start all over again. It was backbreaking, unnatural labor, for an output of about a bushel per hour per worker. Charlie had done it many times, and the thought of it made his muscles sore. The changeover to machine threshing made it easy to believe in progress.

"If that barn had a bottom," said Avery, "it could be a real ark."

"I think it could be several of them."

The farmyard was also big, and the maneuvering was smooth and easy. Avery made a wide, shallow turn to straighten out the caravan in the right direction, and then pulled right into the center of the barn and out the other side. He stopped with only the small supply trailer poking out the back end. Completely inside were three other trailers. Jude the Mystic undid some hitches at that point, and the engine and cook shack proceeded to follow Annie Wick around to an open-centered corncrib.

A couple of roustabouts unhitched the small trailer, pushed it by hand into the barn alongside the others, and closed both sets of doors. At the corncrib, they left enough of the cook shack poking out for the smoke stack to clear the building. Then they unhooked the last of the hitches and Jude stowed his bike alongside a sheltered crib of new corn. The Peerless engine was now free to do what it did best: run other big machines. As a long-distance, cross-country vehicle, it was not likely to have a big future.

They followed the pickup back out into the fields, to a pile of unthreshed wheat that was the shape of a loaf of bread, fifty feet long and twenty feet high. A ladder leaned up against one end, for the pitchmen to climb up on top. The next time any of them did so, they would not have to climb back down, as the pile would have all been fed into the thresher before they needed to.

Around the back side of the pile, looking dusty and old and very much in need of a coat of paint stood a threshing machine.

It was one of the early wood-bodied machines with a steel angle-iron frame. Most of the drive mechanisms were chains or belts, rather than gears or shafts, many of them with no guards of any kind. All the transporting runs were canvas conveyor belts. It did not have a Windstacker. The body was painted dark green, or used to be, and on the side was a faded picture of a rooster, the trademark of the company, and the painted legend:

The Hungry Rooster
Gaar-Scott
Number 14

"I think they might have built that to harvest grain for the Civil War," said Charlie.

"Well, you know," said Avery, "that's one of the great things about heavy machinery: you can always fix it. If it was worth a tinker's damn when it was brand new, it still is. We can make it run, if it doesn't now. We have power, we have a repair shop, and we have talent and expertise."

Maggie Mae grabbed his shoulders from behind and did a quick, deep massage, working up to his knotted neck muscles and finally giving him a little kiss on the back of the neck.

"What Maggie Mae is telling me at the moment, though, is that we do not currently have the stamina. And she's right. God, do I need a rest."

"Then take one," said Charlie. "I'll get the engine secured. I know how. You can't make an engineer out of me one day and then the next day pretend it never happened."

"Best offer I've had in ages. She's all yours."

He and Maggie Mae climbed down the operator's ladder, and Charlie began to tend to all the simple but terribly important things that an engine needs to have done to keep it from destroying itself. He decided to top off the water in the boiler and let the fire burn itself out for the time being. This could be the last chance they would get for a while to empty out the ash pans.

Once he was satisfied that the engine could be left alone, he climbed down to take a better look at the thresher. Annie Wick came walking across the field to join him.

"You figure she'll work? It wasn't new when we bought it, you know."

"To look at it now, you wouldn't know it was ever new. Listen, Mrs. Wick…"

"Annie, praise God."

"Yeah, listen, Annie Praise God, I need some strong coffee and something to eat before I bring this thing back to life."

"You see, how the Lord provides? I can't make that machine run, but I can make you a breakfast you'll remember in your prayers and then you can make it run."

"Could you bring it out here? I want to get started on this monster."

"Could Moses lead his people out of Egypt?"

"I guess."

"Well then, how can we do less? Coffee first, then food?"

"That would be great."

Annie Wick went scurrying off toward the farmhouse, and Charlie walked the rest of the way to the threshing machine. He pulled a small Crescent wrench out of his back pocket and took off the lug nuts that held on the main side panel. Inside, there were nests from small animals, cracked and frayed canvas belts that had holes eaten in them, and quite literally a ton of old straw that could be fossilized by now, for all he knew.

"Rooster, you and I have got a lot of work to do."

He found a pitchfork leaning against the nearest wheat header, and he used it to pull the dried, brittle straw out of the maw of the Rooster. He got as much out as he could from the outside and then lifted one leg to climb inside the main drum. He stopped when he felt a tug at his sleeve. When he turned his head to look, Annie Wick was pushing the biggest coffee mug he had ever seen into his hand.

"Praise God," she said, beaming at him.

He took a sip of the steaming brew. It was hot enough to scald his tonsils, and it contained thick cream, a lot of sugar, and quite probably some brandy. It went down his pipes like liquid fire and blew the cobwebs out of his soul.

"Praise God," he said. "Absolutely too damn right."

He was still looking over the inside of the machine, organizing his plan of attack, when Annie Wick brought him ham and eggs and fried potatoes on a blue and white china plate, with utensils he thought must be the good family silver. He stuffed his mouth shamelessly, savoring the flavors that mixed on his tongue. Quite a lot of the food simply seemed to evaporate, though. He had been awake for about twenty-six hours, a lot of it spent working, and he was at a point where food and drink didn't go to his stomach at all. They were simply *absorbed* somewhere south of the esophagus. But as tired as he was, after another cup of coffee and the short rest that eating gave him, his interest in making the machine work overcame his need for sleep. He had slept many times. He had never before been inside the guts of a Gaar-Scott threshing machine.

He went to the machine shop trailer and got canvas, heavy thread and a sail maker's needle, a grease gun, an oil can, and some assorted wrenches and screwdrivers. He threw the tools in a bucket, took everything back to the Gaar-Scott, and went to work.

There were a lot of grease zerks inside the machine, which didn't seem like a very good idea, and they were all totally dry. The outside ones were dry, too. But generally, the machine was not in bad shape. He cleaned out the rest of the straw and the leaves and animal nests, greased everything that had a zerk and oiled everything that didn't. Then he went over to the two-foot pulley that would take the belt from the steam engine, put a wrench on its center hub, and twisted. And gasped. It moved! With the clutches all engaged, he was actually running the internal machinery of the whole thresher with nothing but his own muscle power and a little leverage. Furthermore, he found it really not very hard to do. *This is one hell of a well-designed machine*, he decided. He thought of all the seemingly unnecessary counterweights and over-center pivot points he had seen on the interior, and he vowed to remember them, for some day when he might be designing machines. Whoever Gaar and Scott were, they were some damned smart cookies.

He turned his attention to fixing the canvas belts. The sail maker's needle was an unfamiliar tool for him, and he found that he was clumsy and slow with it. The internal belts took him two hours to patch and mend He didn't want to think about how long the main feed belts would take. He remembered an itinerant master carpenter telling him once, "You never, never count the number of boards in the pile that you still have to nail up." That seemed like good advice.

He bolted the main side panel back on, stood up, and stretched his aching back muscles. He suddenly felt tired almost to the point of delirium.

"How are you getting on, Charlie?" Emily. Maybe he was delirious, at that.

"Hello, Emily. How come you aren't sleeping, with the others?"

"I'm slept out. I slept some on the trip, and besides, it's dark and stuffy in that big barn. So I thought I'd go out and take a chance on finding you."

"Take a chance?"

"Mmm. I've been thinking a lot about that."

"I'm not sure I know what that means."

"It means I'm a little scared, but don't worry about it. How's the work going?"

He shook his head. "I've got the machinery in pretty good shape, but some of the canvas still needs to be mended. I don't know if I can get that done before Jim wakes up."

"He won't expect you to. If you've got the metal guts basically ready to run, you've done quite enough."

"How would you know that?"

"I heard him say so before he and the Silent Princess went off to hibernate. He'll be surprised. In fact, he'll be delighted. Leave the canvas and the needle and thread out where anybody can see it, and he'll know that part still needs to be done. You go have a bit of a lie down. You've earned it, as much as anybody here."

"A bit of a lie down? I've never heard it called that before."

"That's my mother tongue sneaking up on me, actually."

"That's an English way of saying 'nap?' You know, I've never known an Englishwoman before. It's a pretty accent for a woman, sort of soft but ringing."

"Hah. And you must be Irish, from the way you dish out the blarney."

"I don't think so. My mother's people were Poles, and my father's were German and Danish, I think."

"It was a joke, Charlie."

"Oh. I'm not very good with those, I guess."

"Jokes?"

"With women, anyway." He looked away and set to work cleaning the grease from his hands with a rag.

"You're a mess, Charlie. Dirty, I mean, not any other way."

"Yeah, well, greasing machines will do that to you. And I don't think we have a creek here to wash in."

"Tough luck for you. You won't get to steal any peeks at my naked bum anymore. I found something else, though, just as good."

"Really?" *What else could be as good as your naked bum?*

"Come." She held out her hand, and he took it and followed. She led him behind the barn, where a windmill ran a well pump and dumped water into a cascading series of big galvanized metal tanks.

"This one's for cooling down the cans of milk, you see," she said, pointing. "And this big one is for watering the horses. The last one is just overflow, for when somebody forgets to shut down the windmill. It's been sitting here, full of water, soaking up heat from the sun all morning."

"Nice," he said.

"Nice for you. Get your dirty clothes off and get in."

"You can't be serious."

"I already asked Mrs. Wick about it. She gave me a bar of soap and a towel for you. You've made a pretty big impression on her, somehow or other."

"I called her Annie Praise God. That was probably it."

"Well, that would do it, wouldn't it? This time, I stand guard for you. Strip and get in there, before I start tearing your clothes off."

He was way too tired to argue with her and didn't want to, in any case. He looked to be sure her back was turned and then took off everything, laying it in a neat pile on a spot where he thought he wouldn't be likely to splash on it. Then he vaulted over the side of the tank, making a huge splash. It wasn't exactly hot, but it was a lot warmer than the creek.

"You said something about soap, as I recall."

"Just relax there a bit, and I'll bring it to you."

He put one hand on each side of the tank and lowered his torso into the water, as far down as he could get, willing his fatigue to flow out into the water. It felt like floating to paradise. He closed his eyes. Soon he felt Emily's hands soaping his neck and shoulders, and he sat back up. Then her hands were smearing soapsuds down his chest and around his torso and farther down still. He was amazed at his own lack of shyness, and he made no effort to hide his nakedness from her. She rinsed him with a big cooking pot and then, to his utter astonishment, he felt her mouth on the back of his neck, just the way he had seen Maggie Mae kissing Avery.

"My God, Emily, are you—?" Her small hand closed his mouth.

And suddenly she was in the tank with him, first with her clothes still on and then as naked as he was. She rubbed and soaped him some more from behind, then stood up in the tank and walked around to his front. She let him have a long look at the body he had once "guarded," then wrapped her legs around his waist, sat back on his thighs, and put her arms around his neck. Their mouths found each other, hungry, yearning, and he wrapped his arms around her waist and pulled her to him greedily, feeling her single erect nipple against his chest.

"I can't possibly be doing this," he said. "I'm way too tired."

"Your body doesn't seem to know that, does it? It looks to me like it wants my crumpet."

"It does look that way, doesn't it? Do you think Annie Praise God would approve?"

"Oh, yes. I've not a doubt that's why she gave me the soap and told me about the tank. You can't tell me the Bible lovers don't screw. They just can't bring themselves to call it that."

"I don't think I care what we call it."

"Charlie?"

"Yes."

"Just shut up and fuck me, all right?"

Chapter Twenty-one
Side Tracked

Sheriff Amos Hollander had kept his vehicle in good repair; the Windmill Man had to give him that. It would do almost forty miles an hour on a flat grade, and it only burned about a pint of oil for every tankful of gas. It also had the new-fangled No-Skid tires that looked hardly worn. But that was the end of the good news. By the time he saw the spire of the Unitarian church off in the distance to his right again, the Windmill Man had to admit that he had lost the trail of the traveling machine shop. He didn't approve of profanity, as a rule—it showed a terrible lack of self-control—but he uttered some, under his breath.

He stopped in the middle of the single-track lane he had been following and opened Hollander's leather satchel, hoping it might contain some kind of notes about the hunt for the fleeing Krueger kid.

The first thing he came to was a telegram from somebody named Tom.

COUNTY BOARD AUTHORIZES BACK PAY AND TRAVEL EXPENSES FOR YOU STOP SEND NAME OF FIRST WESTERN UNION OFFICE YOU FIND TO THIS SENDER STOP MONEY WIRED AT ONCE STOP

He had no experience with telegrams, and he puzzled over it for a while. Could they really send money over a telegraph wire?

Maybe they just sent authorization, and the office paid cash out of their own till. Even so, it was a remarkable innovation. But the message implied that it had to be a Western Union office. And even he knew that there were a lot of places with telegraphs that were not Western Union.

The message was dated two days earlier, and it was printed by hand on a lined yellow form. Not a Western Union form. That probably meant that Hollander had not yet collected this marvelous over-the-wire money. Should he? Was providence again guiding his steps? It had been the first piece of paper he pulled out of the satchel, after all. And while he didn't need the money all that badly, it gave him a new direction. And new directions were never to be ignored.

So where would he find the right kind of telegraph office? He would find somebody to ask.

"But not at the church," he said out loud. And he chuckled at his own joke.

He started the pickup again and continued west. Five miles later the road got a little wider and was paralleled by a set of railroad tracks. He stayed with it. Some fifteen miles later, he came to a grain elevator on a short spur line. There were a few other buildings around it, but he couldn't tell if they were offices.

Several wagons were lined up at the elevator, waiting to unload. There were two lines, one for farmers who had their grain in bags and a longer, slower one for those whose crop was in bulk, in high-sided wagons. He picked a farmer at the back end of the slow line to chat with.

"You been here long?"

"I ain't got any gray hairs yet, but I'm working on it."

"You sell your grain here, or just ship it?"

"Both, I reckon. Pillsbury Company, from over Minnesota, has an agent right here, buys it off you smack dab on the spot."

"How do they know what the going rate is?"

"Oh, they're real fancy. They got one of them little machines that makes a lot of clickity noises and spits out a skinny paper ribbon with all manner of numbers printed on it. If they're cheatin' you, they at least put on a good show about it. You can sell on the futures market, too, if you want, store it at the elevator here and don't ship 'til the middle of the winter, when the price is up. Course, then you gotta pay the elevator a bigger fee. Personally, I don't hold with it. I sell my crop now, I get paid now, and I let somebody else worry about when to put it on the Great Northern R and R."

"Can you send a regular message on this Pillsbury machine?"

"You can't *send* anything. It *gets* numbers, is all. Prices."

"So they don't have a regular telegraph office here, then, just the machine with the prices?"

"What in tarnation would anybody want with a real telegraph office here?"

"Law enforcement business."

"Oh. Well, we don't get a lot of that out this way. Law is mostly a Bible and a shotgun. Specially the shotgun. You most probably want to go where there's a county courthouse and a Western Union, I expect."

"You expect right."

The farmer said nothing more for a while. Then he clucked at his horses and moved his wagon forward ten yards or so. The Windmill Man considered slapping him alongside the head, but he wasn't sure if that was how a real sheriff would act. If it came off as just petty anger, that would be no good. Mostly, people who saw him angry had to die. He tried another question.

"And just exactly where would I find a county office and a Western Union?"

"Oh, you don't know? Huh! Some lawman. Well, Fort Thompson would be one, but that's about sixty miles west and a little south."

"How interesting. Try again."

"Oh, well, Ithaca is one, I guess. You follow these here train tracks sorta northwest, you'll get there all right, just so long as nobody shoots you for trespassing along the way."

"How far?"

"How far will they shoot you? All the way until you're plum dead, I'd s'pose."

"How far is Ithaca, you brainless hick?"

"Oh, that. Twenty miles, tops. Maybe eighteen, if you hurry."

"If there is a god, your own horses will step on your head before I get there." He forced himself to walk calmly back to the Model T.

"They tried that already. It didn't work. Nice talking to you, though. Surely was."

◇◇◇

Three hours later, he pulled into the town of Ithaca, identifiable by the name painted on the side of a shiny new water tower, the sure mark of a rising metropolis. He guessed it was a town of somewhere between one and two thousand people. There were few buildings more than one story tall, but Main Street was seven blocks long and there were storefronts on side streets as well. It looked prosperous and new.

Even in the towns, he noticed, the people of the high plains used the land as if there were an unlimited supply of it. In a city that was unlikely to see fifty cars on Main Street on the same day, the streets were sixty feet wide, some with planter islands in the center. He couldn't decide what was worse, growing wheat or growing unnecessary pavement.

He ignored the County offices for the time being and went straight to the railroad depot, which also had a Western Union office. With the help of the clerk, he composed the briefest, and therefore cheapest, message possible, to be sent to Tom, whoever he was, back in Beulah:

SEND BACK PAY THIS ADDRESS STOP HOLLANDER

"You can tell by the original message where to send it?"

"I send it to everybody on the line who's close enough to pick it up, but only the Western operator who hears his call sign will copy it. That's here on the message, see? If he's too far away, somebody else will forward it."

"Good. And how long will it take to get a reply?"

"How should I know? They're your people, not mine."

"Let me put that another way. When you get a reply, how soon can I get some money?"

"On the spot, Sheriff. That's unless it's such a big amount that I gotta send somebody to the bank. But even then, real soon."

"Excellent."

The telegraph key rattled, and he strode out of the office to look for someplace to get something to eat. Maybe they would give him a cup of coffee at the County courthouse. Sooner or later he would go there anyway, to ask if anybody had any leads on the Krueger kid.

But before he found any government offices, he was taken in by the aroma of a small bakery and café. As he got closer, the air was filled with the smells of cinnamon, yeast, bread, and lard-and-sugar frosting. He went in, took a small round table with wrought iron legs by a window, and ordered a frosted long john, two kinds of Danish rolls, and six sugar cookies, which he dipped in strong dark coffee.

His waistline did not reflect his fondness for sweets. He didn't apologize for it and certainly never called it a weakness. In fact, he had never understood why so many people referred to their appetites as weaknesses or sins or bad habits.

He himself had very few appetites, but he respected all of them. Smoking and drinking did not appeal to him. He generally felt comfortable being around other people, but he had never craved either friendship or love, wasn't even sure what those words meant. Money did not interest him, in and of itself. As for sex, if he wanted a woman, he would wait for the right moment and take one. And the pleasure of throwing her away afterwards was at least as great as the pleasure of sex, which was, after all, just a reflexive body function, like sneezing or letting gas. But power was another matter altogether. To have another human being utterly under your control, desperately seeking your approval, even begging for your mercy, was a pleasure not to be rivaled by anything else he had ever known. Still, a good maple long john was not to be scoffed at, either. As he was paying his bill, he chatted up the teenage girl who was working the cash register.

"That was a real banquet, darling."

She blushed a bit at the "darling" and mumbled something like, "Glad you liked it, sir."

"Yes indeed. You know, they say the wild, barren prairies produce the most beautiful flowers ever known. Jewels of the wilderness, so to speak."

"Um, I guess I never heard that. Sir."

"Did you make the cookies?"

"Yes, sir. Well, I helped, anyways."

"Well, I think they are jewels of the wilderness, too."

"Um. Thank you." She blushed and gave a bit of a nervous giggle.

"You don't know what to say to that, do you? You think I'm just a funny old man who's talking nonsense."

"Oh, no, sir."

"You're polite as well as beautiful, I see. It becomes you. It's Amos, darling. Just Amos, not 'sir.' And you are…?" He began to hold her eyes with his, with gentle intensity. It was an old tactic. The reference to being old, which he definitely was not, put them at ease, while the intense and very sexual stare drew them in.

"I'm Darlene."

"What a lovely name. Where are you from, Darlene?"

"I was born here. My pa owns the shop."

"Does he, now? Well, I must say I'm amazed at that, I truly am. I figured you for a transplant from some big, glamorous city like St. Louis or Chicago, you have such genteel and sophisticated beauty."

"Oh gosh." She giggled again. "You shouldn't say things like that, sir."

He continued to hold the eye contact, and when he gave her the coins for his tab, he made a point of touching her hand longer than necessary. She was obviously embarrassed and a little scared. But just as obviously, she was interested. They always were.

"Amos, remember?"

"Oh gosh, yes, I forgot." She giggled again.

Wait until I shove you up against the wall in the back room, he thought. *After that, it'll be a long time before you giggle again, and you will never, ever forget my name. Or rather the one I'm using.*

Violence for him was like whiskey to a blackout drunk. The drunk could make a rational and conscious decision to buy a bottle of liquor, could even make a conscious, if hardly unbiased, decision to open it. But once the first of the alcohol was in his blood, all free will disappeared. He was on a road that had only one direction, and he could no more turn back than he could stop breathing.

The Windmill Man knew he was like that with violence, and the thought did not bother him, any more than did his other appetites. He could make a rational decision to make this silly girl into a senseless, quivering victim, based on a cool assessment of the odds for success. But once he made that decision, he crossed a threshold that could not be uncrossed. The outcome could be delayed and the strategy changed for unforeseen circumstances, but the end of the game was absolutely set. It would enforce itself. And like the drunk, he would go farther and farther into the throes of it until he reached a state where he did things that afterwards could not be remembered at all. He would remember being on the brink of a delicious blackout and loving it, but that was all.

That was partly why he always had to collect a memento.

He looked at the foolish girl's neck and saw no locket or necklace. She had no bracelet or earrings, either. She did have an unusual tortoise-shell comb in her thick blond hair. He considered it.

But fate was not having it just then. The bell on the front door jingled and a couple of men with stiff collars and ties, probably shopkeepers, walked in, chatting with each other. They looked like the types who would sit down for coffee and stay a long time. The Windmill Man made one last bit of eye contact and spoke very softly, so the newcomers couldn't hear.

"I'll be back to see you later, Darlene, my little prairie flower."

Now she had gone from giggling to staring, transfixed, like a chicken looking at a fox. And he knew, absolutely, that he could own her, could do anything he wanted with her. It was almost too easy, really. He would think about it a while longer. Of course he would, just as the drunk would consider whether he really wanted that next bottle of whiskey. He spun on his heel and marched smartly out, tipping his hat to the two interlopers on the way.

"Gentlemen."

"Officer." They nodded. "Lovely day for a fresh doughnut."

You have no idea.

Out on the street, strolling down one of the boardwalks that were everywhere, it occurred to him that what he had just considered doing was dangerous. Working at breaking down and raping a girl in her father's own shop in the middle of the business day was sheer madness. Very dangerous indeed. How delicious it would have been. He might go back again, at that, and ravage that little bit of giggly fluff. But it could never again have the same thrill of a completely spontaneous act of great risk, great danger. And that, he admitted, was the fourth appetite that he did not call a weakness or a sin. Danger. Power, danger, violence, and sugar, more or less in that order, were the only things he ever craved. He definitely had enough of the last one for the time being. He wondered if the day might yet bring him one or more of the other three.

He went back to the Ford, had a last wistful look at the bakery, and cranked up the trusty four-cylinder. Then he got in and took a leisurely cruise through the town. It was the biggest town he had been in since he had started the harvest season just outside of Enid.

In what looked like the middle of Main Street lay a formal town square featuring a large green area in front of an ornate brick and copper and stone courthouse, a Civil War cannon on a pedestal, a small bandstand gazebo, and a couple of poor-quality statues of people the Windmill Man had never heard of. A crowd had gathered in front of the bandstand where a speaker with a megaphone was standing on a box, shouting and gesturing. The crowd was all made up of men in work clothes, and over by the cannon, there was a bunch of bindles stacked up. The speaker was waving a red card in the air, and now and then somebody in the crowd would wave one, too.

Wobblies, he thought, *honest-to-god, card-carrying members of the International Workers of the World, or IWW.* They claimed to be a labor union, and some of their slogans and philosophy actually seemed very practical and reasonable. But underneath all that, they weren't really unionists at all, they were communists, with the occasional anarchist in the mix as well. They would sometimes pretend to be striking for better wages, but they didn't really want their demands to be met because at the core, they didn't believe in wages in the first place. A lot of people thought they didn't believe in work, either. Shopkeepers, bankers, businessmen, public officials, cops, and even farmers hated them. In fact, just about everybody who didn't have a red membership card hated them. The Windmill Man found them pathetic. Secret saboteurs who advertised the fact in advance and even carried distinctive red identity cards. What a bunch of complete idiots.

He took his time, scanning the crowd, looking for a tall young man with a shock of near-white hair. Nobody came close.

As he watched, a group of three uniformed law officers and four or five men in suits came out of the courthouse and moved purposefully toward the bandstand. They had some kind of armor on their shins and forearms, and they carried sidearms, billy clubs, and stern looks.

This ought to be good.

The center invader was almost certainly the local sheriff, and as he moved into the crowd, leading the others, he repeated the simple command, "Disperse!" His followers were more elaborate.

"Get out of here, you red bastards!"

"We're good Americans here. We don't need your kind!"

"Go back to Bohemia, you worthless bums!"

"See how your rights are trampled on?" said Mr. Megaphone. "See how they ignore *your* constitution?"

But the crowd was, indeed, dispersing, running away from swinging billy clubs, shielding their heads with their arms, scrambling to get their packs and get themselves elsewhere. Only the man with the megaphone stood his ground.

"I am a native born American!" he proclaimed. "I have the right to free speech. I have the right to organize a peaceful assembly. I have the constitutional right to disagree!"

He was a forceful speaker, but his audience was running away, and the cops and their suited friends weren't listening. They stormed the bandstand and pummeled Megaphone, who went down in a defensive fetal posture. They took turns kicking him for a while, and then the sheriff pulled him back up and leaned him against one of the columns of the gazebo. He held out a pair of handcuffs.

"Put your hands out," he ordered.

The man stuck his hands in his pockets and spat at the sheriff. There was more blood than spit, and it stained the crisp uniform shirt with an obscene-looking splotch. The sheriff looked down at it, then back at the agitator, who seemed to have no more spit left, or at least none that he could propel. His face was a bloody mess.

"You know what a new uniform shirt costs?"

"Damn right I do. It costs you your soul."

"Goddamn commie traitor."

"Capitalist goon. Where's your dog collar and your leash?"

The sheriff smiled slightly and pulled his straw cowboy hat down a notch on his forehead. Then he drew his sidearm and calmly shot the agitator through the head.

Jesus H. Assassin. And I thought I was cool and remorseless. I had no idea being a sheriff had so many possibilities. He really would have to meet this man. First, though, he would see about a place to stay, in case the kid at Western Union didn't come through right away. And even if he did, the Windmill Man was starting to think he had more than one day's work in this town.

Chapter Twenty-two
So Shall Ye Reap

Something changed in the pattern of sunlight on his eyelids, and Charlie woke with a start. When he opened his eyes, he saw a red-tailed hawk soaring far above him, a stark silhouette against the wispy cirrus clouds. He turned his gaze back down and looked around to find himself utterly alone, floating in the stock tank with a warm and flowing sense of well being. He couldn't believe he had gone to sleep there, but all things considered, he couldn't think of a reason in the world to regret it. As the sleep cleared slowly from the corners of his mind, he thought of Emily and her smooth, white body that was soft and firm at the same time, the loins that yielded but enclosed. A thing of many mysteries was a woman. Had he dreamt the whole incident? Unlikely. He had never had a dream in his life that was that fine.

He pulled himself up to a standing position, flicked water off his chest and belly and legs, and stepped out of the tank. His clothes had been replaced by a stack of different ones, clean and neatly folded, with a couple of towels on top of the stack. He spread one of them out to stand on and dried himself with the other, sitting on the first one when it was time to put on his socks.

The clothes seemed fairly new, and they were a reasonable fit. He assumed they must have belonged to one of the Wick boys who had gone off to the terrible, tragic foreign war. They were also good quality, for work clothes: the wool union suit that everybody wore, year around, crisply ironed denim trousers, a blue chambray shirt and a leather vest. He liked that vest.

He wondered fleetingly if their paths might have crossed with that of his own brother, before they all met their solitary rendezvous with death. *Why should they have? There were five million men in that war.* Because he wanted them to meet, that was why. He wanted some kind of a connection with this fine farm and even with crazy Annie Praise God. He would never, he knew, be part of a loving and settled couple like Annie and Joe, looking out upon their homestead with its memories. But maybe he could be somehow connected, all the same. He could fix their thresher and he could bring in their harvest and he could even wear their son's clothes. Maybe that was as much as he could hope for. He pulled on his shoes and went off to see how much of the day he had slept away.

Something caught his eye over at the barn. Up on top of the high ridge sat a wrought iron black weather vane in the shape of a rooster. He had noticed it when they first came to that place. But now there was a long yellow pennant trailing from its base, coiling and looping lazily in the light breeze. And that, he assumed, was how Stump would find the Ark again. If he found it, that is. He had been gone far too long.

As he walked toward the barn, he heard a screen door slam and looked over at the house, where Annie Wick was emerging with a tray. He stopped and let her intercept him, and saw that the tray carried sandwiches and another steaming mug of coffee.

"No brandy this time," she said. "Time to sweat out the demons and make the straw fly. You missed the regular lunch, so I made you some leftovers. You have a good sleep?" And to his utter amazement, she gave him an exaggerated wink.

"I had a wonderful sleep," he said. "What time is it?"

"Around two."

"Oh, lordy. How could you let me sleep so long?"

"You seemed to be pretty dead to the world, so we all let you be. The others can do a few things without you, you know."

He didn't know. "Are they threshing yet?" he said.

"Only for a couple of hours. I don't think the machine is working real good. The wheat's maybe too wet yet. Anyway, there'll be plenty of work left when you get there. Eat your sandwiches."

He took one off the tray and took a big bite, tasting coarse bread, butter, roast beef, and pantry pickles. And despite his big breakfast, his body seemed to want it all.

"She's a lovely young woman."

"Yes, she is." He didn't insult her or play coy by asking whom she meant.

"You gonna settle down with her?"

"I wish I could. I don't have any land. I don't know if I'll ever be able to afford anything called settling down."

"That's too bad." She shook her head slowly, looking down. "It surely is. But land can be had or lost, you know. It's just a thing. Love, now that's something else. You don't need land for that, you just need a heart."

He stopped chewing and smiled. "That's nice," he said. "I'll always remember you said that."

"You do that, Charlie Krueger."

"I will, and— what did you call me?"

She held up one of Hollander's fliers.

"The hair job is good," she said, "but I have an eye for faces, and I figured it out. You'll be harder to spot when your real moustache grows out. It's okay. Nobody here's looking to turn you in. We're grateful you came, praise be to God. I'm just telling you, the word is out. Keep in the habit of looking over your shoulder. And if you got to run, you take that sweet young woman with you."

"How could I ask her to do that?"

"You can ask. And she will go. And I will pray for both of you. Trust me on this. You ain't much of a man if you leave her. The course of true love didn't never run around the rocks. It's in the good book."

"Well then, I guess it must be true."

◇◇◇

When he got over to the threshing operation, the Peerless was spinning the flywheel on the Gaar-Scott smooth and fast, but the straw was coming out of the rear hood in uneven clumps and a couple of the pitchmen were leaning on their pitchforks and looking at it dejectedly.

"What's the story, boss?"

"I think the old green rooster ain't what she used to be," he said, "and maybe never was. No reflection on all your good work, but she keeps wanting to jam up."

Charlie nodded. "The Gaar is known for getting every last kernel out of the wheat. That's why they have the rooster for their label. You know, no dropped kernels left for the hungry bird? But that also means it's sort of like a cow. Every now and then, you have to stop and just let it chew. Who's running the separator?"

"Nobody. I figured it could run by itself until you got here."

"Not if you want it to put out fifteen bushels a minute, it can't." He couldn't believe a smart man like Avery didn't know that. "She'll put out that much and more, but only if you've got an operator who understands how to control the feed."

"Well, there you go, then. Take your position, Mr. Operator."

Charlie climbed up on top of the Gaar Scott, grabbed a lever in each hand, and proceeded to make grain. When the sun began to set, he was still making grain. He had no way of telling for sure, but he thought they must be putting out something close to fifteen bushels a minute, or one every four seconds. They had moved to another header stack by then, and the operation was going so smoothly that they had to shift one worker away from pitching raw wheat and set him to bagging cleaned grain.

At sundown they broke for supper, then cranked up the operation again and threshed by lantern and moonlight. Avery had somebody put a lantern up on the barn roof, too, to light up the wrought iron rooster.

Sometime near midnight, Charlie looked up and noticed a rocket flare off on the northern horizon. Then he saw Avery take a Very pistol out of a toolbox on the engine and fire one off in reply. Charlie left the separator to talk to him about it.

"Stump?"

Avery nodded.

"What does a flare from him mean?"

"It means he is in very, very deep shit."

Chapter Twenty-three
The Missing Man

Charlie ran back to the Rooster and shut down all its functions. Back at the engine, Avery disengaged the main power takeoff, and the wide, heavy drive belt coasted to a stop. Then he ran the water pump and refilled the boiler to its regular startup level, closed the draft on the firebox, and blew the main pressure relief valve. A huge cloud of live steam gushed out of the side of the engine and floated upward until it became lost in the black night sky. He held the valve open until the pressure gauge showed something less than five pounds, where the readings were no longer accurate. All that done, he climbed onto the catwalk on top of the boiler.

"Shut it all down, people!" said Avery. "Shut down everything. We're done here for the night. Go get some sleep."

On top of what was left of the header stack, where he had been doing the very unaccustomed job of pitching wheat, Jude the Mystic said, "Well that just makes me want to weep, let me tell you. I was having *such* a good time here."

"No rest for you, doc," said Avery. "We're going to need you, your bike, and your little black bag, pronto."

"I saw the flare. Stump?"

Avery nodded. "He's in trouble, maybe hurt. We're going out to find him."

"Oh, shit."

"Very likely. Charlie, go tell whichever Wick you can find that we're going to need to borrow their pickup. Then meet me with it over by the barn. If they have a gun you can borrow, that would be good, too."

◇◇◇

Charlie was back at the barn in less than ten minutes, with the Model T pickup and Joe Wick's double-barreled shotgun. He left the motor running for a minute while he dashed into the barn and up into the haymow, where he fumbled frantically through the loose straw, looking for his pack.

"What are you doing up there, Charlie? We need you, now!"

"On my way, boss." The pack was buried farther down than he had expected, but he found it at last, pulled it up quickly, and rummaged inside it for the Luger.

It wasn't there.

He knew he was looking in an agitated and inefficient state, but even so, the familiar odd-shaped lump of heavy metal wrapped in cloth, the item that had been such a bother to carry, simply wasn't there. He dropped the pack and hurried to join the others.

Avery did not chide him for the delay. Charlie had noticed that he never wasted time talking about things that couldn't be helped,. They hurried back outside, where Jude the Mystic now had the Indian sitting up on the kick stand, next to the Model T, its engine pop-popping irregularly.

"Did you see the flare, Charlie?"

"The last of it, anyway."

"What bearing would you say it was?"

"A little west of due north, I thought. Not much."

"Jude?"

"I agree. North by northwest plus another five degrees north."

"That's what I thought, too. That's the way we will go. Let's hope he still has the truck. If he's lost on foot, or worse yet, if he *was* on foot and now he's down, he's going to be damned hard to find in the dark. I have a compass, so I'll hold our main course in the pickup. Doc, you zig zag around both my flanks, so we get your headlight swept back and forth. Charlie, you take my shotgun and ride in the passenger seat, with me. Major alert here, crew."

Major force, too, Charlie thought, noticing that Avery now had a holster on his belt with some kind of big semiautomatic pistol in it.

"You'll need blankets." Emily emerged from the dark jumble of shapes and people in the barn. "If he's hurt, he could be in shock. You should take these blankets."

"Good thinking," said Jude the Mystic. "Don't know why I didn't think of it. I guess it's been a long time since I thought like a real doctor."

"Riding a bicycle, and all that," said Avery. "Throw the blankets in the back."

"I'm going along," said Emily. "You can use every set of eyes you can get."

"Absolutely not."

But Charlie remembered, suddenly, what Annie Praise God had said about him running off without her. He fully expected to be coming back to the Wick farm, but who really knew? Who really knew anything about what life held in store?

"Let her come," he said. "If it comes to that, I'll be responsible for her."

Avery looked into his face, hard and long, and apparently read something there that was convincing.

"All right, then. Let's move. If she gets hurt, Charlie, it's on your head."

"That's exactly where it is, all right."

They drove through the main farmyard, found the remnants of the trail they had made when first coming there, and steered off into the darkness, over the rocky, stubbled fields. Avery held the Ford in low gear to give Jude plenty of time to make his sweeps, and all eyes pressed hungrily into the night, trying desperately to see what might not be there at all. The man called

Stump was out there somewhere, they knew, one speck on the huge ocean of prairie. And God help both them and him if they missed him by not paying close enough attention.

"Not much left of our original tracks," said Charlie. "Just interrupted bits here and there."

Avery nodded. "That's good and that's bad. It's good if you're hiding from somebody. But if you are Stump trying to get back to the Ark, that's horseshit."

"Why would he be trying to find us at night?" said Emily. She was riding in the back, kneeling on the folded blankets she had brought, leaning into the passenger cab through the opening of the missing window.

"I'm thinking because he couldn't wait until first light."

"That doesn't sound good."

"No. That, it does not."

When they came at last to the gravel County road, they stopped to confer and consider.

"Could he have missed our tracks completely and turned north off the road?"

"Seems unlikely," said Avery. "He knows how to track. Stump once told me that he could follow a careless man across ledge rock or sheet ice."

"That's good for him, but we've got prairie."

"And we're not Stump."

"You had to remind me."

"Let's assume for a minute that he got this far on the main road and then saw a bit of our track headed south," said Emily. "How does that help?"

"Try this," said Charlie. "When we were following Annie, we were going a bit east of south. If Stump lost the trail, he would have tried instead for a direction that at least made some kind of sense."

"Which is?"

"A right angle to the road. Due south."

"Let's try it out," said Avery.

◇◇◇

Fifteen minutes later, Emily spotted the Reo truck, a quarter of a mile off to their right. Avery turned, motioned to Jude to take his motorcycle off on a wide flank to the left with his lights off, and headed for the Reo. He stopped fifty yards out, left the lights on, and jumped out, drawing his pistol.

"Charlie, you take my right flank," he said. "Emily, you stay here for now. Get behind the wheel and be ready to come in hot and fast, to rescue us."

Hot and fast, in a Model T? But somehow, Charlie could see her doing exactly that. He cocked the shotgun and ran out wide to the right, while Avery approached from just to the left of the headlight beams. They couldn't tell where Jude was, but they could hear his bike in the darkness, purring smoothly now. Soon they also heard his voice.

"It's just him. Come on up. Bring some light and my bag."

Charlie walked warily up to the darkened truck, while Emily drove the Model T up to join him. In its feeble yellow head-lamp beams, they could see a figure, slumped in the driver's seat, clutching the steering wheel with one hand. His hand was covered with blood, and on closer inspection, so was he.

"Hey Stump."

He looked up through eyes that were starting to glaze over.

"Thanks for finding me. I really didn't want to die alone. Now it'll be okay."

"You can quit that kind of talk right now," said Avery. "Jude the Mystic is here. You're going to be okay. Let's get you out where he can work on you."

Stump shook his head, grimacing from the pain of the effort.

"He can't do nothing, skipper. I ain't never going to be okay again."

"Sure, you will," said Jude. "Do you know your blood type, by the way? I could try to rig up a field transfusion, but I have to know the type of blood." He was gently peeling back the front of Stump's jacket, trying to get a better look at his wounds.

"Won't matter," said Stump. "I'm gut shot, see? That lousy little rat shit, Stringbean had a gun. You believe that? A goddamn German pistol. What do you call them?"

"Luger," said Charlie, his heart in his boots.

"Yeah, them. Funny-looking thing. I can't believe I didn't check him for that. Took his razor and thought he was disarmed. How could I be so damned stupid?"

"Will you please shut up and let me do some work on you?"

"Won't matter. Won't matter at all."

Jude finally managed to pull open the jacket and saw that Stump's lap was full of dark, purplish blood and gore.

"Hard to drive this damn Reo when you got to keep one hand on a gut wound all the time, you know? Got another wound in the back of the shoulder, too, but I mostly been ignoring that one. Damned unforgiving truck though, that Reo is."

Quietly and off to one side, Avery said to Jude, "What can you do?"

"Damn near nothing. Both wounds are hours old, he's lost an ocean of blood, and either one of the shots would probably be fatal by itself. Do *you* know his blood type?"

"No. Could we try a transfusion anyway?"

"Bad idea. Really bad. And anyway, he's most likely going to be dead before I could get it set up."

"I'm really cold," said Stump. "You got anything for cold?"

Emily was weeping bitterly, but she controlled herself well enough to wrap him in the blankets she had brought. Jude got a syringe out of his bag and gave him a shot of something.

"That's better. Thanks, doc, Emmy. Thanks to you, too, skipper. It's been a hell of a ride, it really has. If you find that little ratfink turncoat, though, kill him for me, will you?"

"Count on it," said Avery.

"Okay then, I will. Gonna sleep a little now, okay?"

If it wasn't okay, it would have to do. He closed his eyes, gripped the steering wheel convulsively one last time, and slumped into death. Charlie reflexively pulled Emily to him and wrapped his arms around her, as if he could shield her from death by keeping her from the sight of it.

◇◇◇

The sky was the color of slate, undulating and boiling with streaks of fire where the dawning sun tried to break through. They wrapped Stump in a rough canvas shroud, stitched it closed, and buried him in Annie Wick's tiny flower garden, alongside her prematurely departed children. The Wicks produced a bible, and to Charlie's surprise, Jim Avery read from it, the Twenty-third Psalm and another passage that Charlie hadn't ever heard before, something that sounded as if it were written for a burial at sea. And he added some words of his own.

"On an ocean of troubles, across a sea of wheat, a vessel called the Ark carries its lost souls toward an elusive and distant safe harbor. Today she has lost a faithful crewman and a constant friend. Into the darkness of the rich earth we commit his body. His soul sails on with us." He picked up a handful of dirt from the side of the hole, the dark black loam that loomed just under the familiar gravelly clay, and tossed it onto the shroud.

"Ashes to ashes, dust to dust," said Joe Wick, and did the same.

"Safe Harbor, Stump," said Jude the mystic.

"God speed," said Emily.

"Amen," said Charlie, and a chorus of amens followed. As he turned away from the grave, Emily took his arm. It made him feel proud, and he wondered if he should thank her.

"Would he be wanting a marker?" said Joe Wick.

"If there's a flower bed over him, I think he would have liked that," said Avery. "Something short."

"Nasturtiums?"

"Perfect."

Away from the others, Emily said to Charlie, "You'll be taking over the operation now."

"Me? We just lost Stump, not Avery."

"He'll be going after Stringbean. He never abandons his own people, even in death. You should have figured that out by now."

"Well, he damn sure stood by me, all right."

"And he always will. If he wasn't going to, he wouldn't have taken you on."

He nodded his understanding, his acceptance of a contract that was only then becoming clear to him. He left Emily and the others who were covering the grave and walked off toward the threshing field, surprised to find that he had tears running down his cheeks.

◇◇◇

Everybody else slept for about four hours after that. Annie Wick and the other women woke them with a huge meal that could have been breakfast or lunch or both. By then, the sky had turned, if anything, even darker than at dawn, and the northwest wind had a distinct bite to it. There was a bit of clear sky to the south and east, but it was an eerie, green color.

"Tornado weather," said Joe Wick. "I seen it too many times not to know."

"Where do you go if a tornado hits around here?" said Charlie.

"Straight to hell."

There wasn't much to say to that.

Charlie walked over to the Peerless and lit off the boiler. If a tornado hit the farm, it wouldn't matter much if they had finished the threshing first or not. But if what they had coming was merely a big storm, it would matter tremendously. People manned their pitchforks.

Avery climbed on top of the catwalk again, blew the whistle, and announced to the crew that Charlie would be in charge of the Ark in his absence. Then he stepped down for some final words of advice.

"You figure you can handle the engine and the separator both at the same time?"

"Well, it won't leave me very much time for scratching my ass or sneezing, but it's not like I have a whole lot of choice, either."

"Atta boy. Today is Tuesday. Put all of our rigs and gear out of sight after the crop is in, and wait for me here, until the end of the day Saturday. If I'm not back by then, take the Ark west, into the Indian nation. Find something to fly a yellow flag on."

"I know a place west and south a bit. Big cottonwood tree in a small grove."

"Good. If you still haven't seen me by the end of the month, it's up to you where to go next. The heat should be off by then, no matter how I make out. Small town law enforcers have a long memory but a short attention span. If you want to stay with the harvest and pick up the repair work, you should be someplace north and west of Winnipeg by then. You can get a good run along about the fifty-second parallel, almost all the way to the Pacific Ocean. You'll get another two months of work there."

"Two? The harvest will be over in one."

Avery nodded. "And afterwards, people catch up on the tricky repairs they didn't want to stop for sooner. It makes kind of a nice cycle, don't you think? You start the year a hundred miles from the Gulf of Mexico and end up a hundred miles from the Pacific. If I make it, that is."

"If you don't, I'm going to be mighty pissed off at you."

"Yeah? Well, I'll do what I can to see that doesn't happen. See you, Charlie."

"Listen, boss, there's one other thing I have to get off my chest."

"Spit it out, but make it quick."

"I think Stump was killed with my gun. It's a German Luger, and it's missing from my pack. Stringbean must have taken it."

"Ah, shit, Charlie. Just shit."

"That's what it feels like, all right."

"I'm sure. Stump is just as dead, wherever the gun came from, but that's a heavy load for you to carry. Keep it to yourself, though, okay? You are going to be in charge around here, and you don't need a rumor going around that will undercut people's faith in you. They need that, you understand?"

"Okay, if you say so. But there's another reason I brought it up. It was a German officer's pistol, okay? My brother sent it home from the war."

"I hope you're not going to tell me you want it back, for sentimental reasons?"

"No, I'm going to tell you that I know this gun, really well. And if Stringbean didn't clean and oil it damn carefully after he shot Stump, it could be next to useless by now. Lugers will rust up and jam up if you give them too long a dirty look."

"That's good to know. I wasn't planning on giving that asshole a chance to use the thing, but it's mighty good information, all the same. Anything else?"

"That's about it."

"Show me a bare field when I get back."

"Get back."

They shook hands and then Avery kicked the Indian into life and rolled it off its stand. Maggie Mae ran over and gave him a fierce embrace and kiss, and then he was off, with a pack on his back that contained a rifle with a scope sight. Charlie climbed up on the catwalk where Avery had stood so many times.

"All right, people, lend an ear! We've got bad weather moving in. We've only got about a hundred acres' worth left to do, so let's see if we can get it all put away before it gets nasty out here. But if you see the wind shift around to the southeast, drop whatever you're doing and run like hell for any kind of shelter you can find. Don't wait for a funnel to hit us."

Emily, who had appeared at his side without his noticing, stood on her tiptoes to whisper something in his ear. "You're probably right," he said.

Shouting again, he said, "Let's make Avery proud of us, folks. You know how it's done. Let's make some wheat!"

The sky boiled, the Peerless undermounted double complex engine chugged, and the Hungry Rooster spat out bushel after bushel of clean, hard wheat kernels. It would be a race.

◇◇◇

In the City of Ithaca, Stringbean Moe walked into the office of the County Sheriff. A big, blunt-featured farm kid in an ill-fitting uniform sat with his feet on top of a large desk, reading a Pink Police Gazette. He did not look up until Stringbean cleared his throat.

"Yeah, what do you want?"

"I was hoping to talk to the sheriff."

"He's out making his rounds. I'm one of his deputies. Whatever's on your mind, you can tell me. You a Wobbly?"

"No. I was a bindle, 'til I hurt my arm, but I was never a Wobbly."

"Doctor's office is down the street, thataway." He hooked a thumb over his shoulder.

"I was wondering if you folks are looking for a guy named Krueger. There's supposed to be reward money for him."

"You got him?"

"No, but I seen him. He's with an outfit's got a Peerless steam engine. I might could—"

"You see any reward posters for him up there? Up there, on the big wall, is all the wanteds and all the rewards we got. You don't see it there, we ain't got it. Get it?"

"I don't read so good. Maybe you could help me some."

"Life's just a goddamn vale of tears, ain't it? Get out of here before I book you for vagrancy."

He strongly suspected that the deputy didn't read so good, either, but he knew it was time for him to leave. Maybe the real sheriff would have a different attitude about what he knew. By God, he was going to find *somebody* who did.

He noticed that the sky outside was darkening, fast.

Chapter Twenty-four
The Open Bottle

Over the blue plate lunch special at the Sunshine Café on Main Street, the Windmill Man learned from the counter man that the sheriff of Lewis County, of which Ithaca was the county seat, was named Delbert Drood, and that anybody who thought that was funny quickly came to regret saying so.

"Likes to assert his authority, does he?"

"You didn't hear it from me."

"I think I saw him shoot a Wobbly over in the park yesterday."

"Yeah? Well, I wouldn't say anything about it, if I was you, unless he brings it up first." He leaned low over the counter and dropped his voice to a near whisper. "More often, he just takes 'em over to the county line, kicks their asses a little and tells 'em never to come back. If he shoots 'em, too, I guess I don't know anything about that. With the Wobblies, though, it's good riddance, either way."

"Sounds like a tough guy in a tough job."

"That, he is. Bet your tintype on it. More coffee?"

"No thanks. I think I'll just go meet this tough guy."

◇◇◇

Sheriff Drood was back in his office at the county jail, having relieved the heavyset deputy, whose name was Clete, for the day. His reaction to the sheriff from far away Mercer County was noticeably cool, though he shook his hand firmly enough.

"You're kind of a long ways out of your jurisdiction, aren't you, Hollander?"

"I'm chasing a young man who murdered a woman back in my county. Maybe you've run into him?" He passed Drood a copy of the wanted flier, which he'd been carrying folded up in his hip pocket.

"Can't say as I have." He passed the flier to his other deputy with a blatant show of disinterest. "How you figure on finding him?"

"I was hoping you might have some ideas in that department, Sheriff."

"Uh huh. Like I don't have enough of my own business to take care of? I don't see anything on that flier about a reward."

"There's a reward of fifty dollars. But of course, lawmen like us can't take rewards."

"I think you got too small a hat, Hollander. Pinches your brain. Makes you think funny. A lawman can damn well take a reward to pass on to the unnamed person who helped him out."

"The person who wants to remain anonymous, maybe?" *That's it. Keep going.*

"Could be something like that."

"The reward only gets paid if this Krueger guy gets arrested and convicted. That could take some time." *Now put in the last piece.*

"Well maybe that could all be done without. Like if he was to get shot while resisting arrest, say."

"Maybe it could, Sheriff Drood. Just maybe it could, at that."

"I'll give some thought to finding this guy. How long you figure on staying in town?"

"At least another day. I'm waiting for a telegram."

"I see. You got a place to stay, out of the rain? It looks like some nasty stuff blowing in off to the west. You're welcome to sleep in the jail, if you want. It ain't very fancy, of course. But then, folks ain't supposed to like it." He snickered at his own joke, and his deputy dutifully grinned.

"I got a room in the back of a saloon down on the other end of Main Street." *And I really don't want you knowing when I come and go.* "But thanks for the offer."

"Any time. Maybe I'll see you in the morning. I usually eat at Merle's, down West Main."

"Maybe you will."

They shook hands again, and he headed back out to his pickup. *Nice guy, this Drood,* he thought. *Not a moral fiber in his body, and he'll do anything for you if you let him think it was his own idea.*

But he didn't think the man was quite highly motivated enough yet. After dark, he would go back to the bakery. And if the giggly little blond just happened to be the last one in the place, he would give Sheriff Drood a powerful new reason to find Charlie Krueger.

Fat drops of rain were beginning to splatter on his windshield as he drove back toward the saloon he had mentioned, with its rooms in the back. It was two storefronts down from the bakery.

He had a brief image of a hand reaching for a whiskey bottle.

Chapter Twenty-five
Storm Clouds

North of the Wick farm, Avery picked up the tracks of his own Reo truck. When he came to the main road again, he headed east, back the way the Ark had come from, looking for their original turning point. The cool gray light of the threatening storm made all the tracks easy to see, and he could hold the Indian at a nice steady thirty-five without fear of losing them.

If he wound up retracing the trail of the Ark all the way back to the campsite by the creek, he would have failed. Stump had known roughly where they had been headed, and even in a wounded and confused state, he would have tried for an intercept route rather than a direct trail. Avery was looking for the place where the truck tracks first joined the caravan tracks, coming in from the west.

He found it sooner than he had expected, only about five miles south of the big road. Any farther north and he would have missed it, and indeed Stump probably would have missed the Peerless tracks in the harder, unplowed ground. But this was solid wheat stubble, and the prints were easy to read. He turned the bike and opened up the throttle. Now that he had only one set of tracks to watch, he could afford to get a little careless.

After another five miles, he lost it. He stopped, retraced his path slowly, and then found a spot where the Reo had made a hairpin right turn. So Stump had never made it to the mountains at all. Another mile or so, and he found some oddly matted stubble along one side of the tracks, and that was enough for a picture to emerge.

Stump had not bothered to tie up Stringbean before he had left with him. Avery knew that much, because they had argued about it briefly. Stump assumed the guy was out for a long count and didn't need to be bothered with. But the stiff must have revived early and got the gun out from wherever he had it hidden and shot Stump then and there, with little or no preamble. But afterwards, Stump had managed to push the guy out the passenger door and get the hell out of there.

He stopped to look more closely at the matted down stubble. Was it consistent with a body falling out of a moving truck? He thought it was. So the man with the Luger would have gained his freedom but nothing else. No truck, no money, and not even his pack, which was now back at the Ark. So where would he have gone? Back the way he had come, most likely. Back where he knew the lay of the land. Avery got off the bike and looked more carefully still. And sure enough, there was a set of footprints making a dashed line through the loam, pointing back to the east. He got back on the bike and followed them, more slowly now.

When the first heavy drops of rain threatened to wipe out all tracks of any kind, he opened the throttle, fighting hard to keep control of the bike on the rough field. There was a farm up ahead. As the drops were joined by even more, he looked up at the sky and saw a fast moving black bank of clouds that went from horizon to horizon and swept over him like God's eyelid closing over the sky, turning day to night. The few drops turned into a shower, then a full rain, cold and driving, and he headed for the farm, driving the bike into the center bay of the barn just as the black clouds opened up into a full-blown deluge.

"I believe," he said, "that's what is known as 'rain like a cow pissing on a flat rock.'" He wondered what it was like back at the Wick farm.

"That's what we call it, all right. And just what the hell do you think you're doing in my barn?"

The voice belonged to a big, square-faced man with a Scandinavian accent and a heavy canvas barn coat and knee-length rubber boots. He looked as if he, too, had run into the barn unexpectedly to escape heaven's wet wrath. He looked more bemused than hostile.

Avery gestured at the door and said, "Getting out of the rain."

"I'd say that's a pretty good answer, all right. I always did like a man who knows what he thinks he's doing. I guess you'll stay to supper, den?"

"If I'm invited."

"I just said so, didn't I?"

"Then I accept. I'm Jim Avery" He held out his hand.

"Arlan Gustafson. Good ta know ya. Last guy I caught in my barn, he wouldn't stop and visit at all. Took off hitching a ride with the creamery truck driver, who also don't never visit."

"Oh, really? What did this last guy look like?"

"Tall, skinny drink of ink. Smart-alec smirk on his face all the time. Called himself Beanpole or Beanbag, or something."

"Stringbean?"

"Yeah, just like what I said, den."

"And just where would the creamery truck have taken him, I wonder?"

"Nearest big town, he said he wanted. That would be Ithaca."

And once the rain stopped, that would be Avery's destination as well.

◇◇◇

Charlie ran back and forth between the Peerless and the Gaar-Scott, doing his best to tend to the needs of both. The last header stack of grain must have been at the perfect moment of ripeness, because the separator worked flawlessly. He figured they were putting out something between fifteen and twenty bushels a minute, one every three or four seconds. After an hour or so, he had to stop and let the baggers catch up. The product bin on the thresher could hold a hundred bushels before it started to overflow. An auger drive would empty it periodically into either of two wagons that could hold another three hundred each. They should have had three more. Once they were full, they just had to stop the feed for a while and wait for the discharge end of the production line to clear itself out. That gave Charlie time to add water to the boiler, fine tune the pressure a bit, oil a few bearing journals, and add some coal to the firebox. It was an exhausting routine, but the results were spectacular. By eleven o'clock the header pile had been replaced by a less orderly straw pile, and they had suddenly run out of things to thresh.

Charlie went back to the engine and held down the lanyard for a long, gleeful blast on the whistle. As he did, he looked up at the clouds that continued to boil overhead, getting darker and more violent by the minute.

"Beat you, you bastards." He shut down the power takeoff, climbed down from the platform, and took a long swig from a gallon stoneware jug that Annie Wick had carried out to the crew. It turned out to be beer, and it tasted like heavy, dark, homemade brew. Jesus-loving Annie was just a bundle of surprises.

Off to the north, a dust cloud announced another car coming to join the party, both faster and bigger than the ubiquitous black Model T. Something with wide, fat tires, a long hood, and a shiny, dark blue coach body. Charlie picked it for a LaSalle.

"My banker," said Joe Wick. "I'd give a pretty to see the look on his sour puss right now."

"Maybe he'll come over and share it with us."

He did not. Instead, he stopped some hundred yards away and glowered. So the whole crew walked out to meet the big banker's car, surrounding it in a loose picket of men and women with bemused smiles on their faces and pitchforks in their hands. Joe Wick led the group up to the car window, and the banker, who was alone in the car, rolled it down.

"Howdy, Mr. Puckett. Nice day for a drive out in the country. Gonna rain in a bit, though."

"Think you're pretty clever, don't you, Wick? Just exactly where did that steam engine come from?"

"Tell him, Charlie."

"I believe the manufacturer's plate on the boiler says Racine, Wisconsin," said Charlie, stepping up a bit closer.

"Another clever fellow. Is that your engine?"

Charlie caught the eye of Maggie Mae, who was standing to one side with her arms folded over a pitchfork handle. She nodded to him. She may have been mute, but it was becoming increasingly clear that she was definitely not deaf.

"Yes it is. You looking to hire it?"

"I don't need your antique hunk of scrap iron. I've got my own Case. What I want to know is where you stole it."

"I'd be careful about irresponsible accusations if I were you, Mr. Puckett." He did not fidget, and his voice was steady and serious.

"I'll be careful, all right. I'll take the serial number of that machine to the sheriff, and when it turns up on a missing list, I'll be back here to have it seized."

"You might do that, if you had a warrant to go get the serial number in the first place. Of course, this isn't my farm. If Joe, here, wants to let you wander around it where you will, I guess I can't stop him. Joe?"

"Get off my land, you ink-stained thief."

"You better be careful, too, Joe. You'll need a good crop if you're going to pay me back my note."

"And I've got one, too, by dad."

"Looks to me like you've still got two headers left to thresh over there."

Charlie furrowed his brow at that, and Annie Wick, behind the banker, pointed to her eyes and made a gesture showing a tiny distance. Apparently the banker was nearsighted.

"Let me talk to this man," said Puckett, pointing to Charlie.

"Talk."

"A little more private, if you don't mind. Would you get in the car, please?"

Charlie looked at the others, shrugged, and got in the car on the passenger side, making a point of not brushing the dust and dirt off his clothes first. Puckett rolled his window back up, pulled a roll of bills out of his inside jacket pocket, and stuffed some in Charlie's hand. "That's shut-down money," he said, under his breath.

"What does that mean?"

"It means you're all done threshing here. Okay? We have an understanding?"

Charlie snorted once and counted the money. "Sure," he said. He put the money in his pocket and got out of the car, a wry smile on his face.

Puckett rolled down his window again and talked to Joe Wick.

"That note is due now, Joe."

"No, it isn't. It's due on the first of November, like everybody else's."

"Look at the fine print. If I want to take a twenty percent discount, I can call it whenever I want. And if you don't have the cash from selling the crop yet, that's just too damn bad. I can have you thrown off your land. You think the sheriff doesn't work for me?"

"But he don't seem to be here, does he? And somehow, I don't think you'll find any other witnesses to your calling the twenty percent clause." All the others in the group shook their heads, no.

"I'll come back with the sheriff, then."

"You think so? Might be kinda tough to make it back to town in the rain that's moving in, what with all those holes in your tires."

"What holes?"

"The ones these here pitchforks are about to make."

Puckett looked around the car in a panic, put it in low gear, and floored the gas pedal, throwing dirt and rocks as he careened wildly, making his escape. The threshing crew laughed, clapped, and cheered.

"Maybe we should have punctured his tires and made him stay here, at that," said Joe. "He will be back with the sheriff, you know."

"Then we'll just have to give him something to see when he gets here, won't we! How much do you need to pay off that note he's talking about at the twenty percent discount?"

"The note is for five thousand."

"Discounted to four, if he wants it right away," said Charlie. "Maggie Mae, can we swing that kind of transaction?"

She held out her splayed hand and rotated it back and forth, then held out three fingers, meaning they had three thousand, more or less.

"He won't really do it," said Joe. "That's less than the original principal, and even he won't lose money just for spite."

"But you should be ready to call his bluff, all the same."

Maggie Mae made some other gestures that Charlie didn't understand. He looked over at Emily for a translation.

"She says maybe we could make up a Philadelphia bankroll."

"What's that?"

"A great big wad of one dollar bills with a few hundreds on the outside, so it looks like a fortune.

Joe nodded. "A bluff, you're saying. That's a pretty dang high-stakes game."

Charlie shrugged. "You can only do what you can do."

"Maybe what I can do is sell the crop. I'll go out first thing in the morning and see. If Puckett comes by before I get back, everybody hide. You, too, Annie. He can't call the note if there's nobody to talk to."

"What did the banker give you money for, by the way?" said Emily.

Charlie pulled out the wad of bills and fanned them for the group, grinning. "Wait until you hear this. He gave me two hundred dollars to promise not to thresh anymore here."

"But there's nothing left to thresh," she said.

"He's nearsighted from counting all that money, I think," said Annie. "He must have thought those last two piles of straw were headers still waiting to be threshed."

"We should leave them there, just so he can feel stupid when he comes back."

"And just so he can see that I don't have to give him back his two hundred bucks," said Charlie. "But I've got an even better idea. Besides showing him what a fool he is, let's make the engine disappear."

"I got no more sheds big enough," said Joe.

"Not sheds. He can look inside them, anyway. Lets put some tarps over the engine and bury it in the straw, make it look like the header he thought he saw anyway. I promised Jim I'd wait for him here until Sunday, and it might not be such a good idea to have the Peerless out in plain sight that long. Whether it has a checkered past or not, the sheriff and the banker together might be able to cook something up. Let's just make it go away."

"This whole game just gets better and better," said Joe. "God, am I glad you folks came along."

"It was a miracle," said Annie, for the hundredth time.

"I sure hope we don't have to change your mind on that score."

They pulled the Hungry Rooster over to the last empty machine shed first, put it inside and shut the doors. Charlie made a mental note to grease and oil it one last time before they shut it up for the year. Then he ran the Peerless over alongside the last big straw pile. He opened the emergency valve in the shelf above the firebox, flooding the box with steam and completely smothering the fire. Soon there was nothing anywhere on the engine any hotter than the temperature of steam. He blew off the last of the boiler pressure and they draped tarps over the entire machine, using wooden props here and there to form a tunnel under the machine and onto the control platform.

Then they all pitched straw until the whole mass was completely covered, making a very plausible imitation of a header. Over at the next straw pile, the only other one that hadn't yet been burned off, they tidied up the shape a little, making it more loaf-like. There was no way to blow the whistle anymore, so they all joined in a huge cheer.

They were answered by rolling thunder from all directions. The sky turned the color of dirty dishwater, and the clouds seemed to be going in all directions at once, twisting around one another like colossal snakes, backlit by chain lightning. Over at the bogus header, some of the straw was floating upward into the sky.

"This," said Charlie, "does not look good." The others looked up in silent awe.

As he was debating where they should go if a tornado hit them, Maggie Mae tugged on his sleeve and pointed to the west, where a wall of rain was marching across the prairie.

"We are delivered again," said Annie.

There were a few hushed amens, because they all knew that if they had a severe rainstorm, then the heart of the twister, if there was one, was someplace else.

Three minutes later, it hit them, with gale force winds and raindrops the size of quarters. They stood there for a while, letting it drench them, laughing like idiots. Then they ran for the shelter of the big barn.

"You just had to name that thing the Ark, didn't you?" said Charlie to Maggie Mae. She grinned.

The noise on the roof of the barn was terrific, but it was not the noise of a tornado.

"Them's thick-sawed cedar shingles up there," said Joe. "The rainstorm ain't been made can rip any of them off. I think it's time for a celebration here."

"Oh yes," said Annie. "Yes, indeed."

"I've got a fiddle," said somebody.

"I've got a jaws harp."

"I've got a jug of sipping whiskey."

What else could they possibly need?

◇◇◇

A bit later they were gathered around a circle of lanterns on the old threshing floor, a glass of booze in every hand.

"A toast," said Charlie. They all stopped talking and turned to him.

"Here's to Jim Avery, wherever he may be. Godspeed home, Jim."

"Hear, hear."

"Amen."

"To Jim. You bet."

"And here's to Charlie Bacon," said Annie, "and to the bounty of the good harvest. Praise God." And she took as deep a drink as anybody.

The fiddle screeched, somebody let out a whoop, and the party began.

◇◇◇

Twenty miles away, Emil Puckett was taking a drink from his silver flask and fuming. His big LaSalle was stuck in the mud up to the hubcaps after his windshield wipers had been utterly unable to cope with the sudden downpour and he had lost sight of the road and driven into the ditch. He had half a pint of gin and five tailor-made cigarettes to last him through the night and the storm. It was going to be a long night. Somebody was definitely going to pay for this.

◇◇◇

Farther away still, Jim Avery sat at the dining room table of what had to be the most boring man he had ever met. While they drank elderberry wine, he listened to the merits of dry cultivation, the best way to build a cluster of corn shocks, and how to dispose of a stillborn calf, and he seriously thought about riding back out into the storm.

"You a gambling man, Mr. Avery?"

"We're probably all gambling men. Some of us just don't know it." *I'm gambling with my sanity, right this minute.*

"What I mean is, would you fancy a little friendly game of poker?"

"Sure, why not?" It had to be better than the conversation.

Two hours later, he was the owner of a 1917 Chevrolet flatbed truck. The Indian would fit on the back very nicely, and if the windshield wipers worked, he could continue on his way in spite of the rain.

◇◇◇

The Windmill Man stood in the shadow of a storage shed in the alley behind Ithaca's Main Street bakery. He was wearing his nondescript bindle clothes again, and water poured off the brim of his slouch hat and onto the front of his rubberized range coat. His trousers were soaked, and the water had dripped down and filled his boots, as well. But he paid no attention to his body's discomfort. In the back room of the bakery, the foolish little blonde was taking loaves of bread out of a big oven, dumping them out of their pans, and dabbing butter on the top crust of each one. She worked by the light of two kerosene lanterns, and he could clearly see her through the single back window of the shop.

She was alone.

Soon she would be locking the place up for the night. If she left by the back door, he would have her at once. If she left on the street side, by the front door, things would get a bit more difficult. He might have to shadow her for a while and look for a different place to take her. But either way, her fate was sealed. He had crossed the threshold.

The storm would hide most of her cries, and his hand would muffle the rest. He could beat her into unconsciousness if she screamed too loudly, of course, but he would much rather have her awake when he raped and slashed her. And when he was done, her body would look just like the one that had been found in the field back in Mercer County, the one that was now attributed to Charlie Krueger.

He wondered fleetingly where her "pa," the one who owned the shop, was. Whether he was sleeping blissfully or engaged in his own dark adventures of the night, he would soon regret leaving his daughter alone, probably for the rest of his life.

His temples throbbed, and despite the cold rain, his face and body felt hot as the power flowed into him. Soon it would possess him utterly. It was a feeling like no other. Maybe this time he would manage to remember it.

The blonde wiped her hands, hung her apron on a peg on the wall, and then blew out both lamps. The Shadow Man moved to the side of the door and waited for the knob to turn. The blood fugue was about to begin.

But the knob did not turn. After an endless minute, he went back to the window and saw the girl leaving by the front door. A fat man with a lantern was with her. The father, no doubt, come to see his little girl safely home. Damn! Damn, damn, damn it all! Never before had he gone this far and then had to abort. Was he still being punished for his carelessness back at the abandoned campsite? Hadn't he suffered enough already?

He fumed with impotent rage as he watched the front door close and the shop go utterly black. Then he limped off into the night. He was surprised at how cold the rain suddenly felt. His bad ankle sent shards of pain up his leg, and he did not smile. *Somebody* was going to pay for this debacle.

◇◇◇

Four blocks away, Stringbean Moe huddled miserably under the inadequate shelter of a makeshift tent tied to a tree by the Courthouse. It didn't matter that his tarp kept out most of the rain, because water was flowing in sheets across the lawn. His clothes were soaked, and he shivered uncontrollably. Sleep was impossible.

He decided to take the sheriff's deputy up on his offer of jailing him for vagrancy. How much worse than this could it be? First, though, he had to hide the Luger somewhere. He looked around for a likely place.

Chapter Twenty-six
Gray Dawn

The party at the Wicks' barn went on all evening and well into the night. The fiddler played every tune he knew and then started over, and anybody who didn't know how to dance learned on the spot. They drank whiskey and hard cider and homemade wine and ate pickles and hard-boiled eggs and ginger snaps, and they laughed and danced until they collapsed.

The rain went on longer than the party. In the morning, it was reduced to a misty drizzle but still showed no sign of being ready to quit. The wind had shifted to the north, and it had a distinct bite to it. The golden days of the long harvest were rapidly drawing to a close.

The farmyard and fields at the Wick spread were a greasy, soggy mess, and beyond the usual morning chores of picking eggs and feeding the livestock, people put their ambition on hold for the day. There were still eighty acres of corn to be cut and shocked, but that could wait.

Charlie and Emily woke in each other's arms, in a corner of the hayloft over the horse barn, where they had a small measure of privacy. The night before, she had brought them two blankets, a bottle of wine, and a chamber pot.

"How romantic," he had said.

"Practical. I'm planning on us having our clothes off for a good long time here, and I don't want to have to run out to the loo that way."

"A thoughtful sort, my woman is."

"Your woman? That better not be somebody else you're talking about."

"Not on your life. You want to get married?"

"I can't ask you to do that, Charlie."

"You didn't ask, I did. It's a symbol, in a way, and I guess I'm asking if you need that. As far as I'm concerned, you're my woman, absolutely, until the day I die, whether we have a certificate and a ceremony or not. But if you need those things, you can have them. You just have to say so." He looked over at her face and saw that she was crying.

"What in the world is wrong, Em?"

"Oh, Charlie, Charlie, you idiot. You really don't know a damn thing about me."

"I know enough. I know who we are when we're together."

"What if I told you I was a fallen woman?"

"Then I would say, 'Well, now you have somebody to pick you up.' If anybody else says that to me about you, though, they had better be ready to duck."

She laughed softly, though the tears still flowed. "If this is all a big lie, I don't ever want to hear the truth. Please, Charlie, don't break my heart. If you're going to leave me, kill me first."

"That might not be so easy. You're a wicked hand with a cast iron skillet, as I recall."

"Well, just see that you remember that."

"You do realize that I have nothing to offer you? I have no land and no family that I can ever go back to. I have no education and no money, and according to that flier that I took off the post office wall in Minot, I'm also wanted for murder. I could wind up swinging from the end of a rope most any time, and I have no idea what to do about that. My life is a real mess."

"Charlie?"

"Hmmm?"

"Shut up and make love to me again, okay?"

"You didn't say 'fuck' this time."

"I'm a lady now."

◇◇◇

At first light, Emil Puckett, stiff and cold from sleeping in his car, slogged through the mud to a nearby farm where he hired the farmer and his team of mules to pull the car back up onto the road. It cost him five dollars.

"I would 'a done it for two," said the hayseed, "but that was back afore you said I hadda do it afore morning chores."

"Well, my time is important. I'm—"

"A banker, yeah. You told me that already. To tell the truth, that didn't help you much, neither."

As if that weren't a big enough disaster, there turned out to be something wrong with the steering on the big car. It consistently pulled to the right, and he thought there might be a vibration in the front end, too. So now instead of going home to his nice, warm bed and liquor cabinet back in Waltham Corners, he had to drive all the way back to the LaSalle dealership, where he would demand that they fix his defective machine. He would not, of course, mention that he had driven it off the road. The LaSalle dealer was in Ithaca, some forty miles away.

◇◇◇

Stringbean Moe had managed to spend the night indoors, in the Ithaca jail, without actually being arrested. The night deputy, as it happened, was a person who had a bit of compassion and a passing resemblance to a human being. He had let Moe sleep in an unlocked cell.

In the morning, the deputy did not offer any breakfast, but he did give Moe a cup of coffee. Having his spirits thus lifted, he decided to have another try at the Krueger reward.

"I haven't heard anything, but I'll ask Sheriff Drood about it when he comes in. So you know where this Krueger guy is, do you?"

"Well, not exactly," said Moe. "I just know who he's traveling with."

"And who would that be?"

"Hey, I ain't telling you that until we talk about some reward money."

"Oh, yeah?" And suddenly Moe learned that the new deputy was not such a swell guy, after all. Faster than he could have believed possible, he found himself pushed back up against a cinder block wall, with a beefy forearm pressed hard against his wind pipe and a very hard-looking set of eyes staring into his.

"You're saying you only want to do the right thing, which is also your legal duty, if somebody pays you? Is that what you're telling me here? That better not be what you're saying, because if it is, then I'm going to have to leave some big, ugly marks on you, just so the sheriff can see I'm doing my job. You understand me?"

"Hey, a fella's gotta eat."

Whap! A hand made for wringing chickens' necks slapped him on the ear, so hard he thought the drum must be ruptured.

"While you still have one good ear, you want to try that again?"

"Hey, I just—"

The meaty arm cocked itself to fire again.

"Okay, okay! This Krueger guy is with a traveling machine shop, belongs to a guy named Jim Avery. He has a Peerless steam engine."

"And?"

"And?' That's it. That's all I've got."

"And you think that piss ant piece of information is good for some kind of money? Get the hell out of here, before you use up all my good will"

And once again, Stringbean Moe found himself walking away from the sheriff's office with nothing to show for his trouble. He went back to the dense shrub under which he had hidden his pack. The stick was just poking out enough for him to see the end of it, and he grabbed it and pulled the pack to him. Inside it, he found no Luger. It wasn't possible! He rifled through the pack again, with growing frenzy, then crawled under the scratchy bush, thinking the gun must have fallen out of the pack. It had not. He couldn't find it anywhere.

"Son of a *bitch*!"

He climbed back out on his hands and knees and found himself looking at a pair of black leather boots and some canvas trousers. Looking up, he saw the familiar face of Jim Avery. In his hand, pointed squarely at Stringbean's forehead, was the seven-millimeter Luger.

"Looking for this, Stringbean?"

◇◇◇

Joe Wick headed in a totally different direction from Ithaca that morning. The roads were still greasy and soft, but the Model T was designed for bad roads, and its high clearance allowed him to go down secondary trails that his banker's LaSalle could never navigate. He headed north and east, to the grain elevator and rail siding at a place called Meeseville. It wasn't really a town, but somebody apparently thought it never would be one unless they gave it a name and a sign. What they also gave it, more importantly, was an agent who could buy Joe's grain. If he would, that is.

The elevator operator was an authorized agent for Wilcox-Crosby, General Mills, and several lesser milling companies, all located in Minneapolis. The elevator man worked on a straight commission, so it was in his interest to get the farmer the best price for his crop. That is, except when he was acting as an intermediate broker, which was most of the time.

"You're kinda late, Joe. Most folks hereabouts have already sold their crops this year."

"Ya, well, I had to fight a little war, sorta, with my banker before I could get together a crew."

"Anybody beats a banker is a friend of mine. Trouble is, though, my elevator's full up. And nobody's calling for me to ship anything for another two months. They made enough money this year and they want the profits from milling the rest of the crop in 1920, is what I figure. And you can't argue with high-powered strategies like that. You want coffee?"

"That's what you figure, is it? Seems to me you figure a little too much sometimes, and every time you do, I lose money. I got eleven thousand bushels of Turkey red in perfect condition. What can you do on it? And your coffee is always lousy."

"You want some, or not?"

"Sure."

"Is the grain bagged or bulk? Help yourself. Over there, by the counting desk."

"It's about half and half. You want it all bagged, it'll cost you another nickel a bushel."

"You got enough space to store it, out of the weather?"

"Well, I might have to tell the old woman to sleep in the outhouse, but I can find enough room, sure. Sour owl shit, this really is bad coffee."

"How about I give you a contract now for buying it in December?"

"For how much?"

"Oh, I think about eighty-five cents would be fair."

"And they say all the big-time highway robbers are dead and gone."

"Hey, I'm taking a big risk here. What if the market is at fifty cents by then?"

"And what if it's at two and a quarter? You going to suddenly up my contract, just to be a fair-minded kind of a guy?"

"There ain't ever going to be two dollar wheat again, Joe. That was only in the war, when the government was underwriting it."

"Okay, then, tell you what: you give me a contract for one-seventy-five, with half in cash up front, and I'll store the stuff for you all winter if you want."

"A dollar even, and that's being generous."

"A buck and a half and that's just being fair."

"Somehow I get the feeling there's a number somewhere between those two that we're both headed for, you know?"

"A buck and a quarter?" said Joe. Half a cup of burnt coffee earlier, he had really been hoping he could get one-fifteen.

"Hey, there's an interesting number! How about it?"

"Maybe. But I got to have at least five thousand cash money now."

"The banker again?"

Joe nodded. "Him, plus paying off the crew."

"Mr. Wick, you just sold a crop. Throw out the rest of that bad coffee, and let's have a real drink."

"What about the five thousand?"

"I don't keep that kind of cash here. I have to give you a check, for a bank in Ithaca."

"Son of a bitch."

"Does your wife know you talk like that?"

"Are you plumb tetched? I'm still alive, ain't I?"

◇◇◇

Charlie woke a second time, well after dawn. A cold, gray light was seeping through the cracks in the barn siding, and outside, it was still raining. He had a hangover that would stop a horse dead in its tracks, but he had no regrets. He sat up and looked at Emily, lying by his side. She had partially thrown off her blanket in her sleep, and her scar was totally visible. He wondered how he could have once thought it was ugly. He bent down to kiss her gently on the breast. She smiled but did not open her eyes. He got up and pulled on his clothes as quietly as he could and left.

On the threshing floor below, some people were already up, stitching sacks of wheat closed while they sipped coffee from thick mugs. One was sitting on a pile of filled bags and playing a harmonica softly. Charlie found a big pot of coffee that some-body, probably Annie, had placed on top of a milking stool. He poured himself a cup and strolled with it over to Avery's machine shop, which was at one end of the floor. He found himself hum-ming along with the harmonica.

In the machine shop, he opened a drawer in the workbench and looked at the broken Pittman-arm gear. Then he looked at the stocks of metals and welding rods and bronzes they had on hand, and he felt an idea begin to emerge.

The problem was that the gear was cast iron. The factory called it "crucible steel," but everybody knew it was really just cast iron with a little extra carbon thrown in. Weld metal would not fuse to cast iron. And that was too bad, since weld metal was as hard and strong as most steels. Braising alloy would fuse to cast iron, but it was soft and malleable, like brass. If you tried to make gears out of it, they would wear out right away. The question was, would braise alloy fuse to a welding rod? If it would, then maybe Charlie could braise a welding rod, or a bundle of them, to the stump of a broken gear tooth. Then he could file the whole composite mess down to get it back to the correct shape of a new tooth. The welding rods would reinforce the mix, and with any kind of luck, they would also wind up being the wearing surface of the tooth. If braise metal would stick to weld metal, that was. He put some of each material on the workbench, made up a little test bundle, and lit the gas torch.

Three and a half hours later, he had a gleaming, solid, whole gear. He couldn't wait to show it to Jim Avery. Where the hell was Avery, anyway? He should have been back by now.

◇◇◇

Emil Puckett left his LaSalle Deluxe Touring Car at the garage in Ithaca and strolled down Main Street through the continuing drizzle. He told himself he was looking for a good place to eat, and at some level, he was always doing so, but what he was also looking for was somebody who would be impressed with his custom-tailored three-piece suit and his gold watch fob with the real Harris timepiece on the end of it. And of course, his splendid umbrella with the carved silver handle. He had had quite enough, lately, of people who failed to show him proper respect.

It was an epidemic. Hell, it was a *pan*demic. Probably all due to the war, he thought. People went over to France, picked up its loose morals, and brought them back home. Pretty soon the whole country was full of upstarts and Bohemians. There was a rumor just that month that a professional baseball team had taken some gamblers' money to deliberately lose the upcoming

World Series, if you could believe such a shocking thing. If you paid a certain amount of money to a certain person in Minot, the story went, he would tell you which team to bet on, as long as you didn't bet with him. Puckett believed it. He had heard other stories about things that went on in Minot. And in the larger world, a formerly sensible President of the United States was advocating giving up the nation's sovereignty to that wobbly-commie League of Nations. Worst of all, it looked as though women were about to get the vote. No, the world was definitely not what it was supposed to be anymore.

He sighed, thinking of the decline of the western world and Joe Wick. Should he really call the note, at the twenty percent discount? It was a game of liar's poker, of course. If Wick could actually come up with the cash, then Puckett would take a real beating on the transaction. But if Wick hadn't managed to cash out his crop yet, then Puckett could wind up owning a twelve hundred acre farm for a song. It wouldn't be the first one, of course, but it would still be satisfying. If he had his car back, he could be out making the rounds of the elevators, bribing operators not to buy Wick's crop. But that impudent mechanic wouldn't even promise him a time exact. It just never stopped, did it? It was becoming a whole nation of backsliders.

He looked down the street and saw a crowd of migrant work-ers in front of the County Courthouse. They, at least, would be impressed by the watch. They would also steal it if they could. Across the street from them was the sheriff's office, and on a sudden burst of inspiration, he headed there.

The bell on the door announced his entrance. Sheriff Drood was at his desk, looking as if he had his usual chip on his shoulder. Standing next to him was another man with a sheriff's badge, whom Puckett did not recognize.

"...saw him in the alley behind the bakery, but he got away. He was riding a motorcycle with some kind of advertising painted on the gas tank."

Drood's face got darker, and he formed a steeple out of his hands and stared off into space. Puckett ignored the conversation, strode up to the big desk and put his well-groomed knuckles on its polished top.

"Good morning, Sheriff. I just stopped in to inquire as to whether you have any reports of a stolen Peerless steam engine?"

"Look, Mr. Puckett, I've got a fugitive to catch this morning, and I don't have time to—"

"Peerless?" said his deputy, seated at a desk toward the rear. "Did you say Peerless? The stiff who was in here last night said the Krueger guy was with an outfit that had a Peerless."

"What else did he say?"

"Nothing. I threw him out."

"Nice work, Otis. Remind me to kick your ass when I get some free time."

One minute later, they were all outside, looking for Stringbean Moe in the city park. They jerked people rudely out of pup tents and rolled over drunks who were sleeping on park benches.

"How long ago did he leave?" asked Drood.

"Half an hour at least, maybe three quarts. He could be most anywhere by now. No, wait a minute! I think that's him over there, sleeping under that big bush. Hey, you! Hey, 'bo!" He began to run.

They grabbed the pair of worn shoes that were at the edge of the bush and dragged the man out. It was, indeed, Stringbean Moe. The bad news was that he had a bullet hole in the center of his forehead. Puckett, two sheriffs, and a deputy looked at the body without being able to grasp what it might portend. Then the sheriff whom Puckett didn't recognize spoke,

"Well, it looks like our boy Krueger has got himself a gun."

"I'll buy it for now," said Drood. "So exactly where was it, Mr. Puckett, that you saw this Peerless steam engine?"

"I didn't get a serial number, mind you."

"Oh, I don't think we have to worry about that. We're not going to bother to get a warrant, either."

◇◇◇

They drove out to the Wick farm in Drood's four-door Dodge sedan, the sheriff and a deputy in the front seat and the Windmill

Man and the banker in back. The Windmill Man controlled his anticipation with a force of pure will. Was he finally about to be forgiven for the time he had missed his quarry by delaying a day? Would he be able to make up for letting the silly bakery girl live? He believed it, but he didn't yet let himself get excited about it.

The farmyard had a single set of tracks in the mud from Wick's Model T, going out but not coming back. There were no people or vehicles out in the yard. In the mowed wheat field behind the barn were two huge piles of straw. Drood told the deputy to drive in a wide circle around the farm buildings, then around the stacks.

"Hah!" said Puckett. "You see that? They didn't get those last two headers threshed, at that. Wick is not going to be able to pay his note!" He rubbed his hands together in the classic gesture of greedy people the world over.

"We didn't come here so you could gloat about some of your goddamn money, Puckett," said Drood. "Where is this steam engine you say you saw?"

"Well, the guy who was running it, the young guy, must have cleared out and took it with him."

"Why would he have done that, if they aren't done threshing yet?"

"Because I bribed him to."

"*What?*"

"Sure. I gave him two hundred bucks not to finish the job, and he must have—"

"Are you seriously telling me that you brought us all the way out here, on muddy roads that could have thrown us in the ditch in a thousand bad places, all to look at a *possibly* stolen steam engine that isn't here because you paid somebody to make it go away? Is that really what you are saying, *you stupid shit?*"

"I'll thank you to watch your tone, sir. You are, after all, a public servant. And *I* am—"

"A goddamn blithering idiot."

"Could we please drive up to the house now? I'm going to call in Wick's note."

"I don't work for idiots, Puckett. And if we stop in this mud, we might never get going again. Let's get out of here, deputy."

◇◇◇

They drove a little more than half way back to Ithaca in silence. Then they stopped at about the place where Puckett had first driven in the ditch, though they had no way of knowing that. And once again, Emil Puckett, under-respected titan and land-owning mogul in no less than seven counties, found himself walking at the side of a muddy road in a misty drizzle, muttering invectives to himself.

"Why did you dump him there, exactly?" said the Windmill Man.

"I didn't want to do him the favor of a ride back to Ithaca. Absolutely, damn never. But I didn't want to leave him close enough to the Wick place to walk back and maybe stay the night, either."

"What difference would that make?"

"If the harvest really isn't done, there will be a bunch of bindles-tiffs and threshers at that place somewhere, probably hiding right now, and at least one of them knows where Krueger is. When we come back, I don't want any *important* people around as witnesses. And Puckett thinks he is just so goddamned important."

"When will that be, that we go back?"

"Tonight, if the rain lets up. Late. You drag people out of their beds and push them outside with no clothes, it takes the fight right out of them."

But the rain went back to being a serious downpour. Drood's deputy had to squint hard to see past the feeble vacuum-powered windshield wiper, and nobody talked for the rest of the trip.

In the back seat, the Windmill Man silently wondered where he could get a cartridge belt. When they came back in the morn-ing, he wanted to be sure he had enough bullets to kill both Krueger and the sheriff. He didn't trust the sheriff. Maybe he should do the deputy, too. Maybe a lot of people. He hadn't decided yet. The City of Ithaca did not have a newspaper, but he pictured a headline, all the same: BLOOD BATH AT LOCAL FARM. Wouldn't that just be something, though? Just what he needed.

Chapter Twenty-seven
In the Belly of the Rooster

Joe Wick didn't make it back to the farm until late evening. His Model T was almost completely coated with brown mud, and so was his face. He had obviously given up on trying to keep the windshield clear and had folded it up to full horizontal and looked under it instead.

He went out to the barn first, to talk to the crew of the Ark. Annie Wick came out of the front door of the house and joined them. Some of them were working on sewing up the tops of wheat bags, but most were just sitting around aimlessly. They all looked up eagerly.

"You missed supper," said Annie.

"I'll get over it," said Joe. "I saw the tracks in the yard. Did Puckett come back?"

"We couldn't tell," said Jude. "There was a blue Dodge with a white star on the front door. But nobody got out. They just circled around the yard once and then left. We all stayed out of sight."

"That would be Sheriff Drood's rig," said Joe. "But if he had Puckett with him, I can't figure why they didn't get out."

Neither could Charlie. But if some lawmen had come to the farm, and they weren't there about the banker's money, he was very much afraid he knew what they were looking for.

"Maybe they got confused when they didn't see the Peerless," he said. "If so, they won't stay that way for long. We should figure on them coming back." And what the hell would he do then?

"Maybe so," said Joe, "but not anymore today. The roads are terrible slick. I barely made it back from Ithaca."

"What were you doing in Ithaca?" said Annie.

"Getting money from the bank, Mama. We sold the crop, but we got to bag it and store it for three months."

"Well, we know how to do that, all right."

"A nickel a bag to anybody wants to help with it," he said to the group.

"Who keeps track of the count?" said one of the crew.

"I trust you."

"Wow, a fair man!" said another. "That's good enough for me."

Some of them drifted away from the group to start work that night. Some just went to bed.

"I don't suppose you ran into Jim Avery in your travels?" said Charlie.

"No, but I wouldn't worry much. Nobody's traveling tonight without a powerful reason."

Like running from the law, ran through his mind, but he said nothing. It seemed to him that Avery had been gone far too long for him not to worry, but he could see nothing he could do about it.

Then he remembered the Hungry Rooster. He had resolved to clean and grease and oil it one last time before it got put away for the winter, and it had completely slipped his mind. He went to the machine shop and collected some tools in a canvas bag, put on his leather jacket, lit a kerosene lantern, and headed out to the corncribs. Emily gave him a kiss on his way out.

Two hours later, he was fast asleep. Inside the concaves of the big machine once again, he had greased, oiled, tuned and adjusted everything in sight. Afterwards, the pace and tension of the past few days and the lack of sleep finally caught up with him. He fell into an exhausted heap on a cushion of straw that was left in the separator. Sometime between then and dawn,

Emily found him there, put a blanket over him, and put out his lantern.

◇◇◇

The lawmen returned to the Wick farm just before dawn. They came in two vehicles this time. Drood led the way in his Dodge, with his two deputies, Otis and the big former farm kid, whose name was Clete. The banker, Puckett was not with them.

The Windmill Man followed in his official Mercer County pickup. He hadn't bothered to explain his reasons for that to Drood. The truth was that he didn't trust the three goons not to make a mess of the whole operation, and if that happened, he wanted his own way of getting clear. And of course, he didn't ever like somebody else having control of his actions, even in a small way. It did not worry him that he did not have a plan yet. He had always been lucky at improvising. Part of his luck came from being opportunistic without being emotional. And part of it, of course, was just pure Providence. He trusted Providence. But even so, there were definitely too many wild cards in this game.

The roads were still treacherously soft and slippery, but the rain had finally stopped, so the drivers could at last see where they were going. That was enough. Both vehicles had high undercarriages and good tires, and their progress was steady, if not fast. Drood pulled into the Wick place and came to a sliding stop in the middle of the main farmyard. He motioned to the Windmill Man to pull up alongside him.

"Put your pickup around on the back side of the barn," he said. "Keep anybody from running off into that corn field out back, while my deputies and I search the outbuildings. Anybody we find, we'll herd them toward you. You see the Krueger guy, you sing out."

"What about the house?"

"Most likely nobody there but the Wicks. I know them. They're old, and she's a Jesus freak. We'll let them sleep for now. They won't come and interfere. If we need them later, we'll go back and slap them up."

That seemed far too careless to the Windmill Man. But he went along with it for the moment, giving Drood no expression that he could decipher. He drove the pickup around behind the barn, near the staged water tanks by the windmill. He put the driver's side away from the buildings, so he had the bulk of the vehicle between himself and anybody who might come out of the barn, shooting. He shut off the engine but then put the magneto switch back to "on," so if he had to start it in a hurry, one quick crank would do it. One nice thing about the T, he thought, was that the crank was always right there, in the ready position. It didn't detach, as on some of the newer models, just to get lost somewhere. He got out of the rig, turned up his collar against the morning chill, laid his hands on the warm hood, and waited.

◇◇◇

Charlie woke to the sound of voices in the corncrib bay. He was about to stick his head out of the Rooster to see who was there, when he caught a glimpse of khaki trousers, polished boots, and shotgun barrels. He pulled his blanket over his face and waited.

"See anybody?"

"No. The place is empty."

"Should we look in the corn?"

"The cribs are full. Nobody can get in there."

"How about inside the threshing machine?"

"Judas Priest, Clete, you are dumber than a sack of hammers. Who the hell would be *inside* a threshing machine?"

"Hey, come on; it's possible."

"It's also dumb. I looked under it, okay? Let's get over to the barn. That's where they're all going to be. You mark my words."

"It wasn't so dumb."

"Just move it."

The footsteps receded, and after a minute of silence, Charlie risked a peek out of the Rooster. Then he climbed out as quietly as he could, went to the end of the machine bay, and peered around the corner into the yard behind the barn. Thirty yards away, by the windmill and water tanks, the brown Model T pickup from Mercer County was parked pointed away from him. But the man in the uniform, leaning on the hood, was definitely not the man he had seen in Minot. There was something dimly familiar about him, but he couldn't place it. He moved back into the shadows and then hunkered down behind one of the wheels of the Rooster and continued to watch.

Soon the blue Dodge with the white star stopped by the far corner of the barn, and another uniformed man got out. Then the crew of the Ark came shambling out into the yard in their nightclothes, followed by the two men who had been in the shed by the Rooster, with their shotguns up. So it had happened. The law had come for him, and somehow or other, they had known where to look.

Jim Avery, of course, would tell him to stay where he was. The people of the Ark had gone to a lot of trouble to hide him, and it would be an insult to them to throw all that away. But Avery wasn't there, and Charlie had to do something.

He needed a weapon. His bayonet was back in his pack, in the barn loft, and he saw nothing in the machine bay that would be a substitute. There wasn't even a corn knife or a sickle. He picked up the biggest wrench he could find and moved to the other end of the enclosure, the one facing the farmhouse. Looking out, he saw nobody in that part of the yard, and he ran as fast as he could from the corncrib to the front of the barn. If somebody saw him dash between the two buildings, he was done for. He flattened himself against the barn and held his breath for half a minute. When nobody called out, he continued on his way.

He entered through the small door of the horse stable and quickly climbed the ladder to the hayloft above the main barn. At the place where he and Emily had slept, he found his pack, with the bayonet in it. He put the sheath on his belt, buckled it up, and descended to the old threshing floor. He put the wrench in his boot.

Partway down the ladder, he saw a door open and shut at the front of the barn. He dropped to the floor, drew his blade, and moved that way, ducking behind stacks of grain bags as he went, his heart throbbing in his ears.

Most of the barn was in deep shadows, and he concentrated in vain on trying to see into the corners. The hair on the tops of his hands and arms stood up as if he were in an electrical storm, and he was dimly aware that he was sweating. He tried to breathe quietly. Was he doing that? His heart was beating too loudly for him to tell. Finally, the intruder stepped into a patch of light from an upper window, and he saw her clearly. He put the bayonet back in its sheath and stepped out into the open space.

Annie Wick was carrying the biggest double-barreled shotgun he had ever seen, quite probably an eight gauge. When she saw him, she made a sign to be quiet and moved quickly over to whispering distance.

"You're a sight for sore eyes, Annie. How did you avoid the party out back?"

"Me and Joe been watching from the upstairs window of the house. They didn't bother to roust us, and a lucky thing for them, too. Joe's got his rifle, but he can't get a clear shot at anybody. I saw you run out of the crib shed and come here, so I came, too. What are you fixing to do, Charlie?"

"I don't know yet, but I've got to do something. This whole mess is my fault."

"You don't know yet if it is a mess. Let's watch some."

They went over to the big doors in the back of the barn and each picked a knothole to look through. The crew of the Ark was standing around in a loose cluster behind the barn, women in long flannel nightgowns, barefooted in the cold mud, and men in wool long johns, some with work boots hastily pulled on but not laced. Now and then they were pushed or prodded by the two deputies with shotguns, and they folded their arms against the cold and squinted into the light. They looked confused, sleepy, and frightened. A few, including Maggie Mae, looked boiling over with rage. She had her arms folded across her chest in a defiant posture, and her eyes spoke of murder.

The sheriff from the blue Dodge paced arrogantly in front of the group, hands on hips. Soon the sheriff from the Mercer

County pickup came over to join him, limping slightly, and suddenly Charlie remembered were he had seen him before.

The two sheriffs spoke to each other, too quietly for Charlie to hear. The one with the limp was shaking his head.

"Who is it that wants you, anyway," whispered Annie, "that lawman from Mercer?"

"Probably. Only he isn't a lawman." Charlie kept his voice to a whisper, as well.

"*What*? What is he, then?"

"Good question. The night I left home, I saw him dressed like an ordinary stiff. He was in a harvested field, pitching straw in the moonlight."

"Why on earth?"

"I don't know, I just—oh my God, yes I do know. He was trying to hide something. Something he couldn't let anybody see. That son of a bitch!"

"I don't understand."

"He was hiding a grave, Annie. The grave of the woman everybody thinks I killed. That bastard killed her. And he doesn't know if I saw the grave or not."

"Oh, dear. If that's true, then he wants to kill you, too."

"He surely does."

"I think he's evil, Charlie. You should get away from here. You can't kill evil."

"We'll see about that. I don't know anything about the other guys in uniform, though."

"They're from Ithaca. We know them. The sheriff's name is Drood. He's meaner than a dog that's been bit by a skunk. He'd as soon shoot you as look at you. His deputies aren't quite as bad by themselves, but they try to show off for him, act like tough guys. But they won't chase you past the county line. None of them. That's about ten miles east. I think you ought to go that way, real quick."

"I'm not leaving the others to be beat up or killed."

"What else can you do?"

"I'll know when I do it, won't I?"

"Bad plan."

Out in the yard, the sheriff named Drood raised his voice and addressed the group.

"Well, well, well. What do we have here? Looks like a threshing crew to me." To one of his deputies, he said, "You sure you got all of them?"

"Unless there's somebody in the house, boss, that's it. We looked in every building, even in the lofts."

"How about the steam engine?"

"Didn't find one. Threshing machine is in one of the corncrib bays, but no engine, no how."

"That's not good. And no Krueger, either? Hollander?"

"He's not any of these people," said the Windmill Man.

"Not good at all. All right, people, what's the story here? Where's the boy and his little toy steam engine? Where's Charles Krueger?"

"I'll tell you what the story is, Sheriff," said Emily. Charlie held his breath. "The story is, you produce a warrant or get the bloody hell out of here. This is private property, and the owners have rights and so do we."

He wanted to hug her. That might not have been the smartest thing to say, but damned if she didn't have guts.

The sheriff walked up to her slowly, fixing her with a hard stare that she returned without flinching. When he got within a foot of her, she uncrossed her arms and put her fists defiantly on her hips. He looked her up and down, then grabbed a handful of gown at the top and ripped down. As she reached down to grab her garment and cover herself again, he backhanded her in the face with his other hand. She staggered to her knees, dripping blood on the wet ground.

Charlie yanked the bayonet out of its sheath and lunged for the door, but Annie Wick managed to grab him before he got to it. "No!" she whispered.

"But I've—"

"You can't!"

"God *damn* it, Annie!"

"They'll just kill you."

He knew she was right, and he replaced his weapon in its sheath. It might have been the hardest thing he had ever done.

Outside, the lawman continued to shout at the group.

"Your rights are what I say they are, folks, and not one damn thing more. Now let's try this again. Charles Krueger is nothing but a common murderer. You don't owe him a thing, least of all a beating and a trip to jail. Now who wants to tell me where he is?"

"He went to shit, and the hogs ate him," said Jude the Mystic.

"Who are you talking about?" said one of the others.

"He fell off a cliff and drowned."

"Fuck you," said yet another.

"And the bucket of bolts you rode in on."

Emily was still kneeling in the mud, her head down, crying softly and bleeding from her mouth. Drood looked around at the rest of the group, and his gaze stopped at Maggie Mae. "What do you think?" he said to the other sheriff.

"Perfect. She's the most defiant-looking one here. Break her down and the others will fold in a hurry."

"You!" he said, pointing.

"She can't talk," said Jude.

"She'll talk to me, by the twisty. Or somebody will talk for her." He grabbed her by the hair at the side of her head and pulled. He was obviously unprepared for the knife that she had hidden under her folded arms. She slashed out with it, stabbing him just below the left armpit. The blade didn't penetrate very far, probably hitting a rib. He screamed in shock and rage and doubled partway over. With his good side, he pulled out his big Colt revolver and jammed it up against the bottom of her jaw.

"Clete!" he screamed, and the deputy came up behind her and grabbed her knife hand, twisting viciously and pulling her arm up behind her back. The knife fell into the mud. Drood holstered his gun, doubled over with pain, and pulled a kerchief out of a back pocket and pressed it against his wound, which was bleeding profusely.

"Son of a *bitch*, that hurts! You're going to be very, very sorry you did that, missy. Clete, run her over to one of those stock tanks. Let's see if she can breathe underwater."

The big deputy handed Drood his shotgun while he continued to hold one arm pinned behind her. Then he grabbed her hair with his free hand, frog marched her over to the biggest tank, and pushed her head under the water.

"Can I fuck her, too?"

Drood looked over the rest of the group. "Anybody ready to tell me what I need to hear? No? Sure, Clete, give her a stiff one up the ass."

The deputy named Clete released the woman's hand so he could undo his trousers. Then he pulled her nightgown up around her waist, still holding her head underwater.

"Give me your shotgun, Annie," whispered Charlie.

"You can't just—"

"I've got to."

Annie handed over the big gun, but before he could get to the door, the deputy's chest exploded. A heartbeat later came the sharp, echoing report of a high-powered rifle.

All heads turned to the east, the source of the sound. A quarter mile away, by the corner of the unharvested cornfield, a green flatbed truck drove toward the group, picking up speed quickly.

"Jim Avery is back," said Charlie.

"Praise God."

The phony Mercer sheriff sprinted to his pickup and dropped to the ground, taking cover behind the rear wheel. Drood took cover behind the dead body of his deputy, which was now slumped down over Maggie Mae. Her face was still pushed down into the tank. Her arms were too short to reach the rim of the tank on the far side, and she didn't have any leverage on the near rim, so she couldn't push herself back up. Her hands flailed uselessly in the water.

Drood pulled her body and head up and let her gasp some air. He did not pull the deputy's body off her. Even from their hiding place in the barn, Charlie and Annie could hear him shout. "That's all you get, bitch! I'm going to make that asshole buddy of yours with the long rifle come over here, nice and close, where we can have a friendly chat."

From the far corner of the cornfield, Avery proceeded to do just that. He drove the Chevrolet truck across the stubbly field with reckless speed, straight at Maggie Mae and her tormentor. When he got to within fifty yards, the sheriff and his remaining deputy opened up on him with their pistols. Most of the shots missed wildly, but a few hit the windshield, shattering it, and the radiator, which immediately began to gush live steam in a cloud that almost completely hid the driver. Charlie had a better angle and could see that Avery had the driver's door open now and was crouched with one foot on the running board, returning fire with his own pistol.

At ten yards, Avery had still not slowed down or swerved. He managed to shoot Drood in the arm, and as he drew a bead on the man's head, the lawman abandoned his position. As he ran away, the truck came to a skidding stop alongside the tank. The motorcycle that had been lying on the truck bed went spinning off it and fell on the ground. Avery jumped out of the cab and ran to Maggie Mae, wildly spraying bullets in the general direction of Drood, who was still running away.

He threw the dead deputy off Maggie Mae's back and pulled her up to him. Then he pulled her back to the truck, getting her partly onto his lap, her feet on the running board. Charlie couldn't tell if she was helping. He thought he should join the fight, but the deputy nearest him was intermingled with the Ark's people and too far away to rush, and the other lawmen were too far away for an effective hit with Annie's shotgun. He felt a frustration that was close to panic, and the whole scene went into slow motion. Simultaneous actions seemed oddly separated, each with its own narrow focus.

Back by the Mercer County pickup, the man calling himself Hollander stepped out from behind the vehicle and took a two-handed shooting stance with his revolver. The Chevrolet jerked left and headed straight for him. He fired blindly into the steam cloud, as Avery continued to accelerate. The bumper and radiator of the truck hit him full front, throwing him backwards, head over heels, twenty feet or more. He landed in an awkward heap and did not move.

Drood and the remaining deputy now had a line of fire from behind the cloud of steam, and they resumed shooting at the truck. To no effect. Miraculously, wonderfully, Jim Avery's bullets had eyes on them and a sense of purpose, while theirs were crippled and blind. He was bulletproof, while they were mortal. He was right and they were evil. He was going to win.

He slewed the truck around broadside to them and fired his rifle, using the windowsill of the truck for a brace, and the deputy dove for cover in a rut in the mud. Avery dropped the rifle and jerked the wheel again, heading for the main gate. He was blind speed and focus, and he was going to make it out of the yard. He was almost there.

And then he wasn't.

Even as Charlie was about to grab Annie Wick and give her a celebratory hug, he saw the back of Avery's head erupt with red spray. The truck coasted for another twenty yards or so and then bounced to a stop. Maggie Mae fell off Avery's lap and did not move. She had probably been dead for some time.

Charlie wanted to scream. He had hesitated about joining the fight for the stupidest of all possible reasons, the lack of a plan, and now Maggie Mae and Avery were both dead. Avery. What in God's name would they do without him?

"I'm sorry, Charlie."

"You're not half as sorry as I am."

◇◇◇

Time shifted back to normal, and Charlie sized up the situation. Somehow or other, he had to get the people of the Ark out of harm's way, as he should have in the first place. He could see the Indian motorcycle on its side in the mud, fifty yards away from him. Would it start? Another fifty yards to his right, the Dodge sedan sat facing away from them, with nobody in it.

He turned to Annie.

"You know where the gas tank is, on a Dodge?"

"Why would I know a fool thing like that?"

"Because you're going to shoot it."

"I am?"

"You are. It's right ahead of the back bumper. I want you to go out the front door of the barn and around the corner and shoot it with your shotgun. If it doesn't blow up, count to ten and shoot it again. Then, whatever happens, run back in the house with Joe. Can you do that?"

"Praise God, I can. And then you'll get away?"

"And then I'll get away, Annie. And with any luck, they'll see me get away and follow me."

"What if it doesn't work?"

"Then there will be no more praise for God today."

"When should I do it?"

"Now."

Chapter Twenty-eight
Fight and Flight

The barnyard went quiet as all eyes stared at the still bodies of Avery and Maggie Mae. Charlie could hear the last of the steam escaping from the radiator of the riddled Chevrolet. Apart from that, everything was silent. He risked cracking open the barn door, ready to dash out of it as soon as Annie had made her diversion. What would happen after that, he dared not imagine. He would or wouldn't make it to the Indian without getting shot and the Indian would or wouldn't start, letting him get away, leading the lawmen behind him. In any case, the Wicks and the people of the Ark would be clear of his troubles. He thought of a bit of advice his maternal grandfather had once given him about playing the game of whist: "If you've got a weak hand, play it as if the other cards are lying just the way they have to for you to win. What's the point of playing any other way?" Too true. He took a deep breath and pushed the door open a bit farther.

Out in the yard, Emily turned away from the sight of the wrecked truck. She had one hand clamped tightly over her mouth, probably stifling a sob. As she turned, she glanced over at the barn, and her eyes locked with Charlie's. The hand went down and her jaw dropped. She made some kind of frantic shooing gesture that was probably meant to tell him to get out from the other end of the barn, while the getting was good. He held up a hand in a gesture that said, "Wait."

Nothing happened for several achingly long minutes. Then there was a loud bang by the far end of the barn, and the blue Dodge sedan squatted down in the rear, its tires blown. Gasoline streamed from several holes in its tank. A few seconds later, there was another bang, and the back end of the car exploded in a huge orange fireball, lifting it off the ground and tossing it end over end.

The sheriff ran toward the burning wreck, and when he got clear of the end of the barn, he started shooting at something or somebody. But the deputy stayed where he was, with the others from the Ark, nervously fingering his shotgun. Behind him, Emily pointed at him with great exaggeration, as if Charlie might have somehow failed to notice him. He eased partway out of the barn door, his bayonet drawn. If the deputy looked even slightly over to his right, he would spot Charlie in plenty of time to shoot him dead. He would have to chance it.

Emily obviously had a different idea.

"What's the matter, there, fizzle-wick? Haven't you got the bollocks to get into a real gunfight?"

"Are you talking to me, you little bitch?" He turned toward her, away from the barn.

"Is there another gutless twit around here? Why don't you show us what you're made of?"

"Oh, I'll show you, all right. But you ain't gonna like it." He turned and strode over to her, grabbing her by the throat and shoving his shotgun in her belly. He was now completely turned away from Charlie.

Suddenly the plan was different. Charlie exploded out of the barn door and ran the ten yards to the deputy, bayonet in front of him. He stabbed the man in the back, just below the rib cage, so hard that the blade went in all the way to the hilt. He hoped that it hadn't erupted out of the man's belly and accidentally stabbed Emily. He pulled it out and prepared to stab again, but it wasn't necessary.

The deputy's eyes turned to saucers, and his mouth fell open in a silent "oh." His hand on Emily's neck went slack, and he dropped his shotgun. Charlie grabbed it before it hit the ground, and he also took the pistol out of the man's holster.

A torrent of blood gushed out of the deputy's mouth and back and belly, and he sagged to the ground.

"What the—"

Emily spat on him as he fell.

"Run, Charlie! Get far away from here."

"But you're—"

"Just go! Please, please go!"

He tossed her the shotgun, stuck the pistol in his belt, and sprinted to the Indian. He stood it up and kicked the starter pedal. It took him four kicks to get it on the right cycle.

"Hurry!"

He switched on the ignition and kicked it a fifth and sixth time. It did not start. He tried a different timing setting. It still didn't start.

Over by the burning Dodge, Drood was reloading his revolver, apparently much recovered from his stab wound. His face was a mask of pure rage.

In another part of the yard, slowly, inexplicably, the sheriff with the brown pickup, the one who had been hit by Avery's speeding truck, began to stand up. It wasn't possible, but it was happening. He got to his feet and began walking toward the motorcycle, haltingly at first, then with more assurance.

"To your right, Charlie! There are two of them now."

After four more kicks, the Indian still had not started. Charlie jiggled the sparkplug wires, found one of them loose, and tried to push it more solidly onto the plug. The man who should have been dead was forty yards away from him now. Drood had reloaded his gun and was also walking toward him.

"Charleee!" Emily put the shotgun to her shoulder and pointed it at Drood. But before she got off a shot, the modern-day Lazarus spoke.

"Leave him alone, Drood."

"You go straight to Hell. Why would I do a damn fool thing like that?"

"Because he's mine."

"He's whatever I—"

The resurrected man shot him three times, twice in the torso and once in the head. "I appreciate all your help, Drood. I truly do. But I don't need you anymore."

As the sound of the last shot was echoing away, it was replaced by the sound of the Indian. Charlie gunned it a few times and then kicked it in gear and disappeared into the cornfield.

Emily moved her aiming point over to the last shooter, but he was already too far away for the shotgun to be either accurate or effective. He turned his back on her, went over to the brown Model T, and turned its crank once. It started immediately. He put his gun back in its holster, got in the pickup, and drove off, rounding the corner of the cornfield and heading in the same compass direction Charlie had taken.

From what already seemed far behind him, Charlie could hear Emily shouting to him. "You keep running, Charlie Bacon. You get away from that crazy bastard."

Or kill him, he thought. *Killing him would definitely be good.*

Chapter Twenty-nine
Fox and Hound

Keeping the Indian upright on the greasy, soft ground was a major balancing act, but he managed it, with great concentration. He had a few near spills, but he kept going. And the mud, he reminded himself, was his friend. If the ground had been hard and dry, his pursuer could have just crashed into the field of corn after him, mowing down the stalks as he went. If he tried that now, he would get stuck in a hopeless tangle of muck and brittle foliage.

He. His pursuer. Who the hell was this guy, anyway? And how could he not only be alive, but up and driving a Model T? Maybe he wasn't even human; maybe he was just pure evil. It made no sense, but it fit. And somewhere in the back of his mind, he vaguely remembered somebody telling him that you can't ever kill the bogeyman.

Annie Wick had said the others were real lawmen. But whoever they were, they had all acted together to hurt Emily and kill Jim and Maggie Mae. And God help him, it was all on account of him. Even Stump's death was on account of him. And all he could do about it was run away. He wanted to scream.

The bike slewed especially violently, and the wheels flew out from under him. They hit the bases of a few corn stalks and jolted him back upright, his body knocking off a few ripe ears along the way. *A little slap in the face there, to tell me to pay attention.* He let his speed bleed off a little.

Going straight through the cornfield while the pickup went around would give him a lead of about half a mile, tops. After that? He wasn't sure how fast the motorcycle could go on muddy roads. He knew that a Model T was reliable and sure-footed and rugged, but nobody had ever accused it of being fast. It would do forty, period. But it could do it almost anywhere. How much could he do in the mud? Enough to have an edge?

He looked down the cross-rows as he traveled, trying to see the pursuing vehicle, alternately checking right and left. After a while, he spotted it, paralleling him and a little behind, driving on some kind of field road or machinery trail. West of him, headed south, a quarter of a mile off. Not far enough.

He let the bike coast to a near stop, kicked it down into the lower of its two gears, and turned left, running down an east-west row. God bless Joe Wick for a good and careful farmer, who always lined up his corn plants on both axes, making a true grid. He wound the throttle out, advanced the timing, and shifted up. Now when he broke out of the field, he would be a mile or more ahead of the pickup. Not a huge bit of cleverness, but a start. That was, of course, unless the field ended at a fence.

Oh shit, could that be? As the jumble of brown stalks ahead of him began to thin, he slowed down a bit. If he hit a barbed wire fence, he would have to go back. There was simply no time to take it down, and he had no tools to do it with in any case. He came to the last ten yards of cornrow and slowed even more.

And sure enough, straight ahead, amid the jumbled maze of leaves and stalks, he spotted three strands of barbed wire. The adjacent field was cow pasture, most likely. He skidded to a stop at the end of the cornrow. A quick look to the right and left showed him nothing to base a choice on, so he headed left, away from the end of the field that the pickup would be traversing. Fifty yards farther along the fence, he came to a crudely fashioned gate, and he opened it and walked the bike through. It was cow pasture, sure enough. Green grass, even this late in the year, and a dozen spotted Holsteins milling about, waiting to be called for morning milking. He headed straight, to the far side of the green, dodging cow pies, occasionally having to just plow through them. On the far side, he found another gate, leading to a short gravelly apron and a raised road. It was a real County road, an east-west artery with a packed gravel surface. It was salvation.

He headed east, as Annie had advised. With all the lawmen from Ithaca dead, the county line wouldn't matter, of course. The crazy man who was still chasing him certainly wouldn't care about it. But it was still the direction where he had a bit of an initial lead, and he pushed it. Less than a mile later, he turned his head around and saw the Model T pull out onto the same road. So now it was a straightforward horse race.

It was also a question of endurance. He knew that the Model T had a cruising range of about a hundred and fifty miles. When people took them on long trips, they carried extra gas along in cans or Mason jars. But the phony lawman wouldn't have known that he was going on a long trip that day, so he probably had no extra gas with him. And he wouldn't have started at the Wicks with a full tank, either. So somewhere, some time soon, he would have to stop for gas. That most likely meant at some farm, since gas stations or general stores were not all that common out on the prairie. But sooner or later, Charlie would have to stop, too. He didn't know what the Indian had for a cruising radius, and he definitely didn't want to find out by exhausting it.

He coasted to a stop in the middle of the road, opened the gas cap, and stuck his finger in the tank. Almost full. Too bad Avery wasn't alive, for Charlie to thank him.

Before he started out again, he had another look at the road behind him. In the short time he had been running at road speed, his pursuer had fallen noticeably farther behind. This was good. Charlie figured that on a dry road, for every hour he rode, he could gain a half hour on the pickup. Unfortunately, he didn't have dry roads, and the mud would slow him down more than it did the Model T. So his edge would be less, but he couldn't tell how much. He decided he would run another sixty miles and then start looking for a place to get some gas.

Five miles later, the motor sputtered and almost died. Since it didn't quit completely, he figured it must be the bad spark-plug wire. Just what he needed. He had figured a wire was loose when he was first starting the bike up, back at the Wick place. Now he thought it might actually have a break in it, under the insulation. He looked at the road behind him. The pickup was still out of sight, but it wouldn't be for long.

He couldn't fix anything if he didn't know which wire had the problem. He reached down and pulled the wire off the front plug, and the motor died completely. So it was the rear one. He put the bike up on its stand and began frantically searching through a saddlebag. Was it still there?

In the road behind him, a tiny dot came into view.

He rummaged some more. Please, please, please. And suddenly there it was: the magneto wire he had pulled off the Model T in Minot. He looked again at the road behind him. If he didn't get the Indian working in another five minutes, he would just have to take his chances in a straightforward gunfight. And he had no illusions about how good a shot he was. But if he died fighting, at least the people at the Ark should be safe.

He cleaned up the wire ends with his bayonet, put the spark-plug clip from the old wire onto the end of the new one, and replaced the wire. Then he put the plug end of the front wire back where it had been before he had pulled it off, and he kicked over the motor. The pickup was a quarter of a mile away now, and he could see the driver pointing a revolver around the windshield. He kicked the Indian over again. The pickup driver was shooting now. On the third try, the Indian fired, settling into as smooth an idle as he had ever heard. He threw it in gear and opened it up. The evil chugged along behind him, again falling behind.

The evil? *Give it a name.* He didn't know the name of the bindlestiff pretending to be a lawman. He had heard the other sheriff call him Hollander, but he knew that to be completely phony. He decided to call him The Hound, as in the game, "foxes and hounds" that he and his brother had once played in the snow. And that, of course, made him the fox. And indeed, he would need all the sly cunning he could muster, if he was going to survive, since, as his brother had told him so long ago, he did not have the instincts of a fighter.

Or did he? He had spent so much time being mad at himself for not defending Emily from Stringbean, that it had never occurred to him that he might have changed since then. And when she was being threatened again, this time by a deputy, Charlie had run the man through with his bayonet without a second thought. It had all happened so fast, he hadn't even had time to digest it yet. When his woman was threatened, he had been able to swallow all his fears and do the necessary deed. Did it also mean the fox could turn the hound into the quarry? It at least seemed possible.

Fifty miles later, the land turned rocky and barren again, and the farms were few and far between. Ahead of him, on the left, he saw a lone man with a pack on a bindle stick. He was about Charlie's age and build, and he walked with a bad limp. Would he know a place to get gas? It couldn't hurt to ask. And if he left him on the road, the Hound could well shoot him by mistake. He slowed to a stop.

"Where you headed?" said Charlie.

"Home."

"Is that far?"

"Only about five more miles. I'll make it before dark, all right."

"Why don't you hop on, and you'll make it for sure."

"I would surely appreciate that, mister."

"Charlie."

"Lee," said the other man. His handshake was firm without overdoing it. He climbed on behind Charlie, and they were off.

"What's wrong with your leg, Lee?"

"Ahh, I got stabbed with a pitchfork."

"Nasty. Threshing?"

"Yeah. I do it every year after our own crop is in. Brings in a little extra cash. The guy who stuck me didn't mean anything by it; he was just careless."

"Bad place to be careless, on a threshing crew."

"Ain't it, though?"

Ten minutes later, they were pulling into the yard of a farm with a small, run-down house and a barn with a shed addition on only one side. Charlie stopped in front of the house.

"I don't suppose your folks would have some gasoline they would sell me?"

"Hell, if Pa knows you brung me home, he'll give it to you, sure as anything."

"I'm in kind of a hurry."

"I'll tell him so." He disappeared into the house. The forty-something man who came back out with him introduced himself as Oscar Loman, and together they went to a machine shed on the side of a corn crib, where they filled Charlie's tank out of a fifty-five gallon drum that was up on a steel frame. They also filled the oil tank.

"I surely do appreciate you bringing my boy home, mister."

"It seemed like the right thing to do."

"It's too bad he had to quit the harvest early, of course, but he's a fine lad and I'm just happy he made it back. Every time he does, it's a celebration. Will you stay to lunch?"

"I wish I could. But I've got a long ways to go and a short time to get gone."

"Well, just take a bag of food with you, then. I'd be insulted if you didn't."

"I really can't take the time."

"You got somebody after you?"

Charlie nodded.

"Then, we'll be really quick." He called into the house. "Mother, fetch this fine young man a bag of food, toot sweet. I think he's got some mighty hard traveling to do."

Inside the house, Mrs. Loman made sandwiches while Charlie met three of Lee's sisters of various ages and a brother who was much younger. They were all seated around a kitchen table that was already set with some kind of coiled sausage on a platter and a bowl full of boiled potatoes. It didn't look like enough food for three people, let alone seven, but nobody looked disappointed. There were candles on the table. "We don't really need the extra light," she said as she stuffed food into a small burlap bag, "but I like the candles on special occasions. Don't you, Mr...?"

"Bacon. Charlie Bacon."

"Is your family from around here, Mr. Bacon?"

"My family? No. My family travels. We're sort of like Gypsies."

"Then you must hurry and catch up to them. Will you say grace for us, before you go?"

"Huh?"

"Anything at all."

"Oh. Okay." They had never said grace at Charlie's home, and he was amazed at how easily the words came out of his mouth. He continued to stand, but he took off his snap-brim hat and lowered his head.

"Lord, for the bounty of the earth and the joys of family and friends, may we always be truly grateful."

Oscar Loman added, "And may those alone on the road find guidance and comfort."

By the time people had finished saying "amen," Charlie was already out the door and running for the Indian.

◇◇◇

As he pulled back onto the main road, he could see the Model T, maybe a mile and a half away. This was good. Because even though he was well into another county by now, he definitely wanted to be followed. He watched the distant vehicle for a moment, waiting to be sure it was close enough to get a look at him. As he watched, it started to snow, first light, dust-like flakes and then puffy, thick ones. This was even better. He wanted to leave a track that the Hound couldn't miss. He had told Mrs. Loman the truth about his family. His true family, the one that mattered, traveled. And it was up to him to do whatever it took to make sure the Hound never followed them again.

Chapter Thirty
Way Station

Charlie risked a look over his shoulder, always a chancy maneuver, as it threatened to upset his already precarious balance. The single line of his own tire track stretched back through the new snow as far as he could see, a wavy black line on pristine white. Better and better. With no chance of Hound missing the track, he didn't have to hold back on his speed to keep the Model T from losing him. He held the throttle open as far as it would go, keeping alert for every tiniest change in traction and balance, and he didn't look back for the next two hours. When the sky began to change from merely dark gray to genuine black, he again started looking for a place to get gasoline.

Just as he was easing down on the throttle to conserve the last of his tank, he saw a light ahead, maybe two or three miles off. He cruised smoothly up to it, saw that it was a store of some kind, and pulled off the road.

The sign said Hale's Corners Store, and it was, appropriately enough, at a crossroads corner. If there had ever been a Hale's Corners town, it was nowhere to be seen. Much more likely, somebody named Hale thought there *ought* to be a town there and had built a store to get in on the ground floor market.

A smaller sign said, "If we don't have it, you don't need it." *Are you sure?* he thought. *I need just one hell of a lot.*

He pulled the bike up on its bipod stand near a gas pump, climbed off, and took stock. His body was not happy about the long ride. Or maybe it was still complaining about the night in the Hungry Rooster. Whatever the reason, it didn't move all that well. In another time, he might have paid attention to it. Now, he just moved a little awkwardly. He opened the pack that was strapped to the top of the rear fender of the bike and took inventory.

The first thing that he found was the Luger. He pulled out the magazine and worked the action a few times. Avery had not only retrieved it, he had cleaned and oiled it, too. The magazine had six rounds left. That fit. It would have started with nine, with no extra in the chamber. Then two were used to kill Stump, and—

He was suddenly racked with deep, retching sobs. He gave himself over to them for a moment, then found himself, hands on his knees, bent over, looking again at the road he had just traveled and his telltale track. When he thought about the enormity of what he still had to do, it seemed certain that it would kill him.

What would your brother say? Shape up, soldier. You chose the road; now see it to the end.

And suddenly he knew he could do exactly that. His brother was gone and would never be back, and that would always be a sad thing. But it was also okay. He was his own father now, and his own brother, too. And with what he had learned from Rob and George Ravenwing and Jim Avery, and even from himself, he could do what had to be done. And for the first time since he had left the Wick farm, maybe even for the first time since he had left the home of his childhood, he knew exactly where he was going. He must have known as soon as he had turned south. He was going back to the sacred grove. And if Wakan Tanka wouldn't help him, then the strange god would just have to accept Charlie's blood as a sacrifice, because he was going to kill the Hound or die trying.

He went back to taking inventory, and he noted that his hands had stopped shaking. So he had a Luger with six bullets, a revolver with—well, how many? None, he found. All empties. Not much of an arsenal.

"You look to me like a highway robber."

Charlie turned to see a big bear of a man with a full black beard, wearing an oddly incongruous red vest over a white shirt with teller's sleeve garters. He didn't seem to care about the snow or the cold. He was holding a lever action rifle at waist height, pointed straight at Charlie, but his manner seemed more curious than menacing, almost jovial. Maybe he was happy to see a customer at long last.

"You must be Mr. Hale, if the sign is right."

"That's me. Jacob Hale. Direct descendant of Nathan, for what it's worth. Are you impressed? You better be. And who the hell are you?"

"Charlie Bacon." He put the Luger back in the pack and tried for a sincere look with just a touch of a smile. "And I'm not a highway robber, or a robber of country stores, either."

"Then what's all the hardware for?"

Charlie couldn't see any percentage in telling the man the strange truth. He settled for something simple and plausible.

"I'm carrying the cash from a whole season of running a separator, and I don't want some stiff shanking me for it."

"You got a big knife, I see. Not good enough for you?"

"Some men are a lot better than me with a knife. But nobody with a knife is better than somebody with a gun."

Jacob Hale looked at him for a long moment, staring into his eyes, which did not look away. Then he broke into a grin, and he lowered the rifle and extended his hand. Charlie shook it.

"I wouldn't mind relieving you of some of that crop cash, but only if you need some of my fine merchandise."

"You got any camping gear at your store?"

"Camping gear, hunting gear, farming gear, trapping gear, you name it. We ain't got a lake within fifty miles of here, but believe it or not, I sell a fair bit of fishing gear, too. Come on in."

"I need some gas in my Indian, too."

"Sure, sure. We'll get to that."

"And some bullets for my revolver."

"I don't know what size it takes, but I've got them, too."

"I figure I need to be out of here in fifteen minutes, tops." The grin faded a bit. "It's like that, is it?"

"No, it's not 'like that,' but it's not good, either."

"And?"

"Fifteen minutes, or else I'm gone right now."

"Got it. Come back someday and tell me the whole story, hey? Now, what do you need?"

Charlie told him.

◇◇◇

Eleven minutes later, he was back on the bike, with a full tank of gas, a new, bigger pack on the back fender, and a cup of hastily gulped coffee and a doughnut in his belly. The two hundred dollars he had gotten from the banker was still back in his pack at the Wick place, but he had his share of the threshing fees in his pocket. It turned out to be more than enough for all his wants. He paid Jacob Hale and shook his hand again. "If I take the road north from here, where will it get me?"

"It peters out to damn near nothing in thirty miles or so. Just a trail after that, really, up into the Turtle Mountains. It's not the Indian Nations, but it's their territory, all the same. It's sacred to them. Lakota Sioux. Nasty critters, I hear, if there's any of them still there."

"Sounds like the place I've been looking for."

"I can't imagine why."

"If somebody comes here looking for me, feel free to tell him I went that way."

"If you say so." He offered his hand again, and his grip was firm and reassuring. "You take care out there among those injuns, you hear?"

"Count on it." He kicked the bike back into life, skidded around in a tight two-seventy to the left, and headed north.

Chapter Thirty-one
The Night of the Fox

The Windmill Man cruised at an easy thirty-five, not taking any chances on skidding out of control. The Krueger kid had led him on a hell of a chase, he had to give him that. And he was a hell of a motorcycle rider. But he had left a trail that a myopic clerk with cataracts could follow, and now that it was dark, the kid wouldn't be able to go as fast. His fate was sealed. This time, there would be no missed departure or empty campsite. The shopkeeper had said he was headed into the foothills of some little mountains. What an idiot. He was running into a dead end.

The road blended into the rest of the countryside now, and if it hadn't been for the track of the motorcycle, he wouldn't have been able to tell where it was anymore. The new snow told him that Providence was back on his side again. It had to be. He slowed down to thirty, then twenty-five. The track wandered back and forth for a while, as if the rider had been looking for something. Then it straightened out again, and in the distance, maybe two miles ahead and a hundred feet above him, he saw a fire. So the kid had finally stopped for a rest. And the pathetic fool had built a campfire! Well, why not? He must be damned cold and tired by now. Might as well die in comfort.

The Windmill Man killed his headlights, drove perhaps another mile, and then stopped. He would sneak up to the camp on foot, and Krueger would be dead before he knew what hit him. No bleeding for this one. He might survive a mere bleeding. This one would be fast and sure. He felt his temples throb.

◇◇◇

The fire was in a stone ring in the center of a small grove of mature hardwoods. There was a pup tent pitched there, too, with its end open to the warmth. Ten yards behind the tent, the motorcycle lay on its side in a small ditch. It had a tarp over it, which had already accumulated a heavy coating of snow. Had the idiot seriously thought he could hide it there? Even with the new snow over them, the tracks between it and the fire ring were easy to read.

The kid must be really tired, he decided. He must have been hoping the snow would hide both the motorcycle and the white pup tent, and he had probably promised himself he would only have the fire for a short time. And then, of course, he had fallen asleep. That was exactly how it would have happened. He was sure of it. He began to feel hot, and he opened his coat.

He circled the outer perimeter of the entire grove, shotgun at his shoulder, looking in all directions, careful to make no sound. Finally, satisfied there was nobody else up and about, he approached the pup tent from the end that was away from the fire and toward the dumped motorcycle. Inside, he saw a sleeping bag with a body in it. Without the slightest hesitation, he emptied both barrels into it. Then he reloaded, went up much closer, and did it again. He hated denying himself the pleasure of the full fugue, but he was taking no chances. He was about to draw his pistol, to deliver a final *coup de grace*, when he heard an odd hissing sound behind him, followed by a voice.

"I figured that was about how you would do it."

"Krueger?" He whirled around. The kid was maybe twenty feet away, and he had a pistol aimed squarely at him. The Windmill Man realized with some chagrin that he must have been under the tarp, with the motorcycle. He had underestimated him, badly. But a face-off would still go to the one who could kill without hesitation or remorse, and he certainly knew who that was.

"Bacon, to you. But that's not important. You should have looked in the sleeping bag. Don't draw that pistol, by the way, or you won't live long enough to see what a mistake it was."

"Your hair is different, Krueger."

"It's Bacon. And a lot of things are different."

"Not the ones that matter." His hand moved toward his holster. "I'm going to—"

There was a deafening roar behind him, and he felt as if he had been hit by a locomotive. It knocked him to his knees and made his eyes bulge. He felt something odd at the side of his head, and when he touched it, he found that his ear was gone. His back and legs felt prickly all over, and he felt weak. He dropped his arms at his sides, letting the empty shotgun fall to the ground.

"Mr. Hale has a lot of stuff back in his store, including dynamite. He was the one who told me it works better for killing if you use some rocks for projectiles. That's why the sleeping bag looked so full. He also told me it wouldn't matter if I buried the fuse in the snow."

"This can't...possible. I've never..." He suddenly found it hard to speak. He could form the words well enough, but they didn't seem to want to make complete sentences. What the hell was happening to him?

"I just want to know one thing. Why?" The kid's voice was blurry, somehow, as if it came from under water.

"Why? Why what?"

"Mabel Boysen. Me. Any of it."

"My work." He tried to make a broad gesture at the prairie behind him but found it horribly painful. "Holy calling. I'm purifying the land." His legs failed him, and he slumped backward on his haunches. "Keeps the earth from taking its own revenge. If I let you stop me, let you turn me in, then... Well, then, a storm like nothing in history, nothing in the Bible, even. Storm, yes. Sweep across the plains, wipe out everything. Any fool can see that."

"Well, I guess I must be a special fool, then."

"I don't—"

"Not just any fool. Fool enough to believe that evil can be killed."

The Krueger kid walked up to him, put the muzzle of his revolver against his forehead, and pulled the trigger. The Windmill Man had a split-second vision of a black storm cloud the size of a mountain range, rolling across the prairie, overwhelming him. It was the last thing he ever saw or thought.

Chapter Thirty-two
The Place of the Five Trees

Charlie woke before dawn. He threw off his blankets and the scorched remnants of his tent and poked at the embers of his dying campfire with a stick. There were enough coals to rekindle a fire, and he quickly added fresh tinder and fuel. Then he sat on a rock in front of the fire and looked inside his burlap sack to see what was left of the food Mrs. Logan had given him. One apple, three oatmeal cookies, and a ham sandwich. He munched on a cookie while the fire gathered strength.

"You need some coffee with that."

"Yes I do. But I figured if I waited a while, maybe somebody would bring some. Hello, George."

"Hello, Charlie Bacon. It took you a long time to get back."

"It felt like long, that's for sure." He stood and embraced the big Lakota, who, as expected, had a coffee pot and two cups in his hands.

"Did you bring tobacco this time?"

"As a matter of fact, I did. Got it at a place called Hale's Corners."

He reached in a jacket pocket and produced a pouch of Bull Durham and a pack of Zig Zag cigarette papers. George Ravenwing solemnly threw a pinch of the tobacco in each of the four compass directions and a fifth one into the fire. Then he rolled a cigarette, took a long drag, and passed it to Charlie.

"I don't smoke."

"This is not smoking, this is ceremony."

"Well, that's different, I guess." He took what he hoped was a respectable size puff and worked hard at not coughing. They passed it back and forth several more times without talking, and then George set about brewing coffee.

"Who's the dead guy back in the ditch?"

"I called him Hound. I've never known his real name. A lady I know says he's evil."

"Not anymore. I won't ask if you killed him, but if you did, that's good."

"He didn't give me a whole lot of choice."

"Then maybe he was part of what you needed to do. Maybe you killed some evil in yourself, too."

"I know better than to argue with you, George."

"Then you know more than the last time you were here. Have you found the god of steam, too?"

"There is no god of steam. There are a lot of things to know about it, and it feels good knowing them, but there's no god. I found a lot of fine people, though."

"Did Wakan Tanka speak to you?"

"I honestly don't know. I couldn't remember his name, for a while."

They poured coffee, and Charlie shared the last of his cookies. For a long time, they munched and drank in silence. It was George Ravenwing who finally broke it.

"So now you will go back to the real world?"

He nodded. "Not the one where I started, though. And never as Charlie Krueger. First off, I have to help a bunch of other people on their journey. They're counting on me."

"And a woman?"

"And a fine woman, yes." He smiled as he remembered what George Ravenwing had told him about women. "A woman who doesn't care about owning land."

"Ah. I think Wakan Tanka did speak to you, whether you remembered his name or not."

"Maybe so. The dead guy had a Model T pickup, by the way. Any chance you might want it? It's got a star painted on the door that you would have to do something about."

"Sure, I can use it. Maybe I'll paint it brown and white, like a pinto horse."

"You'd look good in that, George."

"I'd look better on a horse, but sometimes you have to take what you get. Will you be coming back to this place again?"

"Yes. Not any more this year, but I will come back. Maybe every fall."

"Then you will always prosper. Goodbye, Charlie Bacon."

"Goodbye, George. Thanks." He stood up to shake the man's hand, but the Lakota was already walking away. That seemed right, somehow.

Suddenly Charlie found that he was tired, right down to his bones, and he put some more wood on the fire and had a long nap before setting out on the road again. He didn't know how long he slept. When he woke, the snow had stopped, but the sky was uniform gray, and he couldn't tell how high the sun was.

He packed up and headed back on the Indian. On the way, he noticed that the body of the man he had called Hound was gone, along with his Model T. Were they ever real in the first place? He didn't let himself think about it.

◇◇◇

The snow amounted to about eight inches, but now it was on the verge of melting, turning into heavy slush. Oddly enough, it was easier to navigate than the mud or rain had been. The thick cover seemed to help the motorcycle stay upright. Charlie could still see the traces of the two sets of tracks, from the Indian and the Model T. That made him smile, for some reason.

Back at Hales Corners, he again bought gasoline, including a couple of extra one-gallon jugs of it to put in the saddlebags.

"Everything turn out all right?" said Jason Hale.

"Pretty much. Thanks for asking."

"That guy who was following you, um…"

"I don't know his name, either."

"Yeah. Anyway, was he a little off in the head?"

"Definitely. But what makes you ask?"

"Well he was wearing a sheriff's uniform, but he told me he was a weatherman."

"Yeah, I think he told me something like that, too."

"He's crazier than a clock going backwards."

"That he is. But he's gone back to Mercer County now. They can worry about him there."

"Good riddance. Can you stay for some lunch?"

"Thanks. For a change, I have time."

◇◇◇

It took him until the following morning to get back to the Wick farm. He pulled the Indian up on its stand and took off the snap-brim hat and goggles just in time to see Emily burst out of the front door of the house. She ran to him and wrapped herself around him, and he thought of that first day he had seen Maggie Mae greet Jim Avery.

"I told them you'd come back."

"Not even God could keep me from it."

"Nor evil?"

"No. Annie was wrong about that. Sometimes you can kill evil."

Annie herself appeared at the door then, squinted a bit, and put her fists on her hips. "You look to me like a man who needs a big plate of ham and eggs."

"Annie, as usual, you are absolutely, dead-on right."

"Well, get in here, then. Praise God!"

They went inside, and Charlie sat at the kitchen table while Emily poured coffee and Annie threw a bunch of extra corncobs into the stove.

"Are you still on the run, Charlie?"

"Not unless somebody is after me for stabbing that deputy."

"That sorry piece of work? Joe and I took care of that. We took all the bodies into town and told another deputy that the man from Mercer County did all the killing and then took off."

"I'm shocked, Annie. You actually lied?"

"Certainly not. Joe did it for me." She threw a slab of ham onto the griddle top and cracked eggs into a bowl. "So you're all clear now? No more phony lawman, either?"

"No more."

"You know, Joe and I have lost all our children now. I don't suppose you and Miss Emily would like to stay with us, maybe take over the farm someday?"

"Oh, Annie. There was a time when I'd have died to hear you ask that. But now there are other people who need me, and I can't just abandon them."

"I respect you for that. I surely do. Maybe it's for the best. Joe's been wanting to sell out here, maybe go to California and buy an orange orchard."

"I hear it's nice in California."

"Nicer than the high prairie, anyway. Do you know they don't even have tornados out there? How do you like your eggs?"

"I like them any way you want to do them."

"I'm proud to have known you, Charlie."

"Likewise."

◇◇◇

Back outside, the Peerless had been cleared of all its straw cover, and Charlie shoveled coal in the firebox and lit it off. As soon as he had steam up, he blew a long blast on the whistle and then climbed to the platform atop the boiler. Soon the crew of the Ark was gathered around in a loose circle.

"Listen to me, people! The harvest is a hundred miles north of us now. We need to get up by Winnipeg and work our way west."

"Are you taking over for Jim?" said Jude the Mystic.

"Any problem with that?"

"Not from me."

"Not from anybody," said somebody else.

"All right, then. You folks know the routine. Let's get packed up, cleaned up, and hooked up."

Emily climbed up onto the platform with him, wearing Maggie Mae's old striped train engineer cap. She stood up on tiptoes and said something in Charlie's ear.

"Oh yes," said Charlie, quietly. To the group, he said, "Time to part the Red Sea, people!"

◇◇◇

They rolled across the prairie, Emily and Charlie riding the engine and Jude the Mystic acting as fireman, keeping the firebox stoked.

"Did you ever find out who that horrible man really was?" said Emily.

"Not really. He was a crazy man, that's for sure. Said he was saving the world."

"From what?"

"From a storm. The biggest, most god-awful storm in all of history, he said. He said it will happen soon now."

"You know what, Charlie?"

"What?"

"We can weather it."